Phyllis slowed her jog to a walk, but the burn would not leave. It had gone past her hips into her torso now. Phyllis tore off her sweatband and threw it across the room, then felt her pulse again. It was supposed to go down now, but something was wrong.

She felt her brow again, which was wet with new sweat, and felt the burn reaching her shoulders. She stopped the workout entirely now, working at her breathing to slow down that pulse. Her hands shook, and now real fear filled her thoughts. But that, too, had to be controlled. She had pushed herself too much. If she could just get home . . .

Phyllis rushed to get her bag and almost passed the window on the way, then stopped and looked out. The moonlight was bright as the sun to her, and she held up her arm to shield her eyes, then cried out in pain. The burning doubled in intensity, and she fell to the floor, holding her gut as if afraid it would burst open.

She began to convulse, but she was in too much pain to scream as her body began doing things that it wasn't supposed to do. She tried to roll onto her belly to crawl across the floor, but saw her arm throbbing and pulsing, then stretching. Other things happened to her body, but Phyllis could do nothing about any of it, especially not while her mind itself was being assaulted. A flood of old thoughts and new, strange ones, smashed through her defenses.

In the end, Phyllis's scream of physical and mental pain gradually became a howl.

THE WEREWOLF CHRONICLES

TRACI BRIERY

ZEBRA BOOKS
KENSINGTON PUBLISHING CORP.

*For Julie, Julie, Mike, Tami, and
my mother, for the usual reasons.*

ZEBRA BOOKS are published by

Kensington Publishing Corp.
850 Third Avenue
New York, NY 10022

Zebra and the Z logo Reg. U.S. Pat. & TM Off.

First Printing: February, 1995

Printed in the United States of America

One

Roxanne used to make jokes about how she and her roommate, Phyllis, were an "odd couple" because she liked ballet, and Phyllis liked jazz dancing. She only stopped making that joke because it grew old real fast. Still, they made an "odd couple" in other ways. Phyllis did tend to be neurotic, and Roxanne was more in control. Phyllis also preferred men, but Roxanne did not. At least, not romantically. As friends they could be acceptable. Phyllis's boyfriend Michael was acceptable, for instance, even if Phyllis wouldn't admit to herself that she was probably better off without him. It wasn't that he was an arrogant twit or a jerk, but he tended to take his time making certain important decisions. Phyllis was probably too patient for her own good.

She had first met Michael after a dancercize class one night, when she had stopped into the cafe where he waited for his big break while waiting on tables. In between acting auditions, of course. Performing artists require understanding bosses when it comes to time off for auditions.

An advantage to the performing arts is its extraordinary variety. A disadvantage is its extraordinary diversity in salaries. One can either live in several mansions, or barely pay rent, if at all. The roommates and Michael fell into the latter category, and Phyllis was the worst off of them all.

Roxanne's claim to fame was that she had once been the understudy for Jennyanydots in *Cats,* but lately she was able to find enough small dancing jobs to just make ends meet. She could also sing and had that advantage whenever musical auditions came up. Phyllis could only dance, and she was only making rent because she taught "dancercize" part-time at a health club, not to mention her other part-time job waiting tables.

Their latest audition was for a music video. Both of the roommates were going. They were in competition, but not really, for they never wanted a job at the expense of the other losing it. So far they had worked only once on the same job. Occasionally one would get it, but the other would not, but usually neither of them did.

"How's this?" Phyllis asked, pursing her lips. Roxanne looked up from tying her shoelaces to glance at Phyllis's lipstick.

"Too dark," she said.

"No, it isn't; I wear this all the time," Phyllis said.

"I know," her roommate said. "But I've never liked it. You're not supposed to wear a lot of makeup to these, anyway."

"I'm meeting Mikey like right after it, though," Phyllis said, working on the mascara now. "I don't wanna mess around with this afterwards."

"It'll be running all over the place."

"Uh-uh," Phyllis said. "This is the stuff that stays on during a shower. I don't think it's too much. You've seen some of the other girls there. Swear to God, you'd think the mannequins were out dancing."

"Yup," Roxanne said. "You never see them at call-backs, either, do you?"

"Hmmmm," Phyllis said, frowning at her reflection. Finally she grabbed a Kleenex and wiped off the lipstick, then replaced it with a lighter color.

"Okay, so I'll keep it light," she said. "But I'm not going naked. This isn't so bad. Just the eyes and lips."

"You look beautiful; we're going to be late," Roxanne said, and grabbed her roommate's arm to drag her kicking and screaming from the room.

Nobody walks in Los Angeles, even if their cars are screeching junk heaps like Phyllis's old Datsun. It had worked its way past three tries to get it started, and was threatening to get to six soon enough. The finest mechanics in the county had looked at it long ago and had advised her to shoot "Old Yeller," but she refused to part with an old friend.

When they got to the audition the director wanted "Angry" from all of his hopefuls. It was all part of his statement, of course. Phyllis knew she was angrier than Roxanne, and gave him all her pent-up rage and frustration at the world. She was good, dammit; why wasn't anyone opening their eyes for once and seeing this? She showed him "Anger," and threw in a little sex for an extra wallop.

"Thank you," the director said in that same, unfathomable tone she seemed to be hearing a lot of lately. Phyllis hated the kind who never let their decision show in their voices. "We'll call you," he said, but they never did. Not as often as they should, that is.

Phyllis wanted to stick around and watch Roxanne, but she really did have to take off to meet Michael. She was a stickler for punctuality, even if he was not. That was another sore point she had with him.

"Well? Did you split his pants open?" Michael asked after he'd greeted her appropriately.

"What?" Phyllis asked. "Did I what?"

"Sorry, just a joke," Michael said. "How'd you do?"

"I dunno," she muttered. " 'We'll call you.' He said it the same way for everyone."

"I know what kind you mean," Michael sighed. " 'Don't call us,' etc. That's why you need to get away right away once you're done."

"You'd think they'd just tell you right away if you're hot or if you suck," Phyllis said.

"Not when they have so many people to see."

"I know," she said. "I'm just bitching."

"I love it when you bitch," Michael said, pressing his face into hers. Phyllis laughed, but turned away. He nuzzled at her neck while she giggled, until he kissed it and leaned back again. Their cocktail waitress brought their drinks. Phyllis always had her diet Coke; Michael ordered a beer, as usual. He had one of those metabolisms where he could eat anything and just barely make his ideal weight. This, too, was another sore point with Phyllis, but then, this would be a sore point with almost any woman.

Their waitress took their orders, and Michael settled back, happy to be served instead of serving others. Roxanne had been trying to convert Phyllis to the ways of vegetarianism, but she had yet to resist the turkey slices of the chef's salad. But no beef or pork anymore, so off went the ham slices.

Michael watched her eat for a while, then touched her

hand. Phyllis glanced up and smiled, but quickly resumed her eating. She looked up again when she felt him staring at her.

"You okay?" she asked warily.

"Am I okay?" Michael asked. "Yeah, sure, I'm okay. I was just . . . I have good vibes about you."

"You do, huh?" she said. He patted her hand, then held it and squeezed it once.

"I think good things will happen to you," he said. "That's all."

"Since when are you a psychic?"

"I didn't say I was a psychic. I just think you're gonna make it someday. Maybe it'll be in this latest job. You'll get picked, then get discovered by the star. Janet Jackson, right?"

"I wish," Phyllis said. "Come to think of it, I'm not even sure *who* it's for. I didn't even pay attention to that. Usually I only know where the auditions are, not who they're for."

"Same with me sometimes," he said. "Maybe you'll get all the closeups."

"I wish," she said.

"Just trying to make you think good thoughts," he said.

"I know," she said, pulling her hand away to hold her bowl steady. "I'm sorry, Mikey. I'm in my 'pity me, pity me' mood. I *could* use a break. Hell, we all could."

"We'll all get it somewhere," he said. "So when I get my starring role, you'll have to be the costar."

"Not until I get acting lessons," she said.

"Ahh, you don't need lessons," he said, waving her off. "We're all just bullshit artists."

That made Phyllis laugh while she had a mouthful of food. Michael grabbed his napkin to catch what came out, but most of it ended up on her chest. Fortunately the waitress came by in time to fetch a wet towel to wipe off the stain and Phyllis resumed eating in a much better frame of mind.

Phyllis tried to be happy for her roommate, but she was never good at lying. She wanted to strangle Roxanne for getting yet another job when Phyllis had nothing. She had showed the man "Anger." What did he want? Uncontrollable rage?

"Look, I don't know what was so great about my stuff," Roxanne said. "Maybe he just likes redheads or something."

"I'm not mad at you," Phyllis said. "It's me. I don't know what the hell's wrong with me. I haven't gotten anything in three months! If I didn't have the classes, I'd be out in the streets tap-dancing for quarters!"

"You're just in a slump," her roommate said. "Everyone's had 'em."

"You haven't," Phyllis pointed out.

Roxanne held out her arms. "Do you see *me* on Broadway?" she asked.

"Broadway's in New York."

"Okay, have you seen me in anything bigger than as an extra in a Pepsi commercial?" she asked.

"At least I was in that, too."

"Anyway, my point is that we're both just barely hanging on," Roxanne said. "And don't think I haven't been dead flat broke before, either. You should have seen me just before I did *Cats*. I was flopping around from friend to friend, with no money *at all*. You'll get over it, darlin'. You gonna use the phone?"

"No," Phyllis grumbled. Roxanne smiled and patted her cheek, then dialed up her girlfriend Linda to relay the good news. She hung up on the machine that answered. Roxanne never talked to them, even if everyone on earth seemed to have one, except for her and her roommate. They couldn't afford one.

Phyllis reconsidered, then called up Michael to talk to his machine.

" 'Well, Michael's not here, but I am. I'm his machine; tell me everything, and I just *might* let him know you called, Hoo hoo ha haaaa! Beeeeeeep.' "

"Michael it's me call me back," Phyllis rattled off, then hung up.

"You know what I hate about these jobs?" Roxanne asked while poking around in the refrigerator's veggie drawer.

"What?"

Roxanne found a carrot, and worked at cleaning it off.

"They always work your butt off all day long, and you get something like fifty bucks for it," she said. "If I didn't love dancing, I'd hate it."

"That's why they can get away with fifty bucks," Phyllis said. "I still hate you for getting picked."

"You know," Roxanne said, pointing at her with her carrot, "I've been thinking. I wanted to talk to you after your number, but you had to take off."

"What about?"

"Maybe I'm wrong about it," Roxanne continued, "but it's kind of like—well, you know how Ted—oh, that's the director?—you know how he wanted everyone to be 'angry?' "

"Yeah?"

"You get angry at people," she said. "It's kind of—ohh, it's hard to explain."

"I gave him as much anger as I could," Phyllis said. "I don't know what else he wanted."

"If you ask me," Roxanne said, "and I know you won't, so I'll tell you anyway: you seemed like you were more pissed off at *him* than . . . 'at the world,' or whatever he wanted."

"I didn't think so."

"Like I said, I could be wrong about it," Roxanne said, shrugging. "It's just what it seemed like to me. It's all attitude, you know."

"Well, that's what I gave him," Phyllis said. "So what're you—?"

The phone interrupted her question. Phyllis was closer and reached for it.

"I'm not here unless it's Linda," Roxanne said. "Oh, or Ted. The director."

"I know," Phyllis grumbled, bringing the phone to her ear. "What?" she said.

"What," a voice mocked.

"Michael, knock it off," Phyllis said. "Where are you?"

"At home."

"What? I just called you!"

"Well, I was screening my calls."

"I hate it when you do that," Phyllis said. "Why do you do that?"

"Because somebody's making his living by selling my

phone number to salespeople," he quipped. "Don't they ever bug you?"

"You're the only one who ever calls me."

"Ooooo, I've got exclusive rights to you, then. What did you want, my little Phylly?"

"Why did it take you so long to call back, anyway?"

"Well, sor-ry," he said. "I didn't mean to have such a weak bladder that needs emptying sometimes."

"Ohhhhh," she said. "I wanna go out tonight, that's all."

"Ooo, can't it be tomorrow night?"

"Well, I'd kinda like it to be tonight," she said. "I didn't get the job."

"Which one?"

"The video, you butt!"

"Jeez, come on, you've had other auditions since then, you know," Michael said.

"Oh, yeah," Phyllis said. "Sorry. It's just—well, obviously I'm a little depressed about it. It's hard to keep your attitude up if you haven't had a gig in three months."

"You'll get one of the other ones, then," he said. "Trust me.

"Sure you can't tonight?"

"Believe me, I'd like nothing better than to hold you in my arms and tear off the buttons from your blouse with my teeth," he said, "but I've got something tomorrow, and there's a whole goddamn speech to memorize."

"You got a play?" Phyllis asked excitedly.

"No, just an audition," he said. "A soap."

"What? God, not a soap!"

"Why not?"

"If you get on one of those, you'll be working fifteen-hour days every day, and never have time for anything else, least of all me."

"Come on, I'd trade in my penis for something that steady!"

"What??"

"Uh . . . well, not *that,*" he said. "My big toe."

"You're damn right," Phyllis said. "But soaps are hell; trust me."

"How would *you* know?"

"I just do," she said. "I don't watch them, but I've read about them here and there. The actors are exhausted all the time."

"No, they aren't," he said. "I know someone who worked on one before his character got killed off, and—"

"Yeah, that's another thing," she interrupted. "One day you go in and find out that your character's dead or something. That's a screwed way to get fired."

Michael was silent for a moment, then was somber when he next spoke.

"Phyllis?" he said. "Do you think you can try to wish me luck for tomorrow? Even if you don't mean it?"

"God, I'm doing it again, aren't I?" Phyllis said meekly. "I'm sorry, Mikey. Yeah, good luck and break a leg and all that. Hope you get the lead."

"Well, there are no 'leads' really on soaps, but I guess it'll be a fairly prominent character," he said, and there were sounds of paper shuffling. "Um . . ." Michael said, "oh, yeah, he's 'Louis, a drifter with a shady, but mysterious, past.' "

"Everyone on soaps has a shady but mysterious past," Phyllis said. "But hey: let me know what happens, okay?"

"Sure," he said. "Um . . . sorry about tonight, though. I'll make it up to you tomorrow night, right?"

"I'll see how I'm feeling then," she said.

Michael then proceeded to outline in detail how he was going to "make it up" to Phyllis. The more obscene he got, the more she laughed, and the less she believed him, too. He meant well, though.

"I don't think either of us has the stamina for half the stuff you're talking about," she giggled.

"If I get the job, we'll see how much energy I can dredge up," he said. "Listen, I gotta go, babe. Hey: you'll get something. You're too hot to ignore for long."

"Thank you," she whispered. "Same to you. Bye, Mikey."

"Bye, Phylly," he said, then made kissing noises. Phyllis hung up, then slumped into her sofa and shut her eyes. "Maybe you're right," she said to her roommate. "Maybe it's the wrong kind of anger that I project. Maybe it's just pity or whininess, instead."

"Could be," Roxanne said, sitting next to her. "You only need to watch it if it starts making you thoughtless."

Anyone else would have had her head bitten off—even Michael. But for some reason Phyllis had never had a problem taking Roxanne's blunt honesty. That was part of why they made such good roommates.

"I was being thoughtless to him, wasn't I?" Phyllis asked, rubbing her eyes before opening them again. "Usually it's the other way around. I've been getting too stressed out, I guess."

"How about a vacation, then?"

"Oh, yeah, like I can really afford one," Phyllis said.

"Just a suggestion," Roxanne said. "Doesn't the club ever give you a vacation?"

"It's not a full-time thing. They don't have to give me anything."

"Oh, b.s., they have to give you some perks somewhere," her roommate protested.

"Well, yeah, I could say 'I'm taking a vacation,' but they'd never pay for it," Phyllis said. "They don't have to."

"Still," Roxanne said, putting her arm around her, "I haven't seen you go anywhere or do anything for a long time."

"Well, neither have you."

"I could use something, too," Roxanne agreed. "Hmmm, I wonder if Linda's up to it? But then, I could use something steady, too, before running off to Jamaica or someplace."

"We'll see," Phyllis said, and patted her roommate's hand before rising from the sofa. Roxanne turned on the television and clicked through the channels until she reached one of those "dating" shows.

"Hey, think they'll have a gay couple on this time?" she called to Phyllis, who was in the bathroom now.

"What?" Phyllis called, poking her head out.

"Never mind," she called back, and sipped at her cabbage juice. Just then the phone rang. Roxanne leapt up from the couch excitedly.

"I'll get it!" she said, as if Phyllis had even made a move toward it, which she hadn't. Roxanne answered it, and she beamed; it was Linda. Phyllis listened to her excited cooing for a little bit, then turned back to the mirror that showed a tired, frustrated, twenty-five-year-old wash-up. She checked the reflection for blemishes, of which there were none, but frowned at herself, anyway.

Don't know where Mikey gets his "good vibes" about me, she thought to herself. Maybe I can borrow some of them.

Phyllis brushed her teeth for no reason as her roommate lowered her voice to begin the "private" part of her phone conversation.

TWO

The apartment door opened, and Roxanne's body partially blocked the space it made. Phyllis tried not to listen to the smooching sounds that Roxanne and her girlfriend made. It wasn't that two women kissing bothered her, but she tried not to be the nosy kind when it came to couples.

Eventually the kissing stopped, and Roxanne made her goodbyes. Linda poked her head inside and waved at Phyllis.

"Hi, Phyllis," she said. "Bye, Phyllis."

"Oh, hi," Phyllis said, smiling and waving back. "Aren't you staying? Don't mind me."

"I would, but *she* needs her rest," Linda said, pinching Roxanne's bottom on "she." Roxanne yelped and swatted her on the shoulder.

"I'm getting up at five, you know," she said. "Or would you rather be my alarm clock?"

"No, thanks," Linda said. "But good luck tomorrow."

"You, too," Roxanne said, and gave Linda a quick goodbye smooch. She closed the door a little bit to whisper sweet nothings to her girlfriend, then shut the door and sighed.

"She is such a sweetie," Roxanne said, and smelled

the red and white roses Linda had given her. "Look, she gave me these," she said. "Her garden is in bloom."

"I didn't know she had a garden," Phyllis said.

"Just some rose bushes," Roxanne said, and pulled out one of the white ones and presented it to her roommate. "White, for friendship."

"Oooo, thank you," Phyllis said, taking it and smelling it.

"She took off the thorns, too," Roxanne said while heading for the kitchen. She set down the roses and started looking through cupboards. Phyllis turned off the television and let her head lean back.

"We don't have any vases, do we?" Roxanne called from behind a counter.

"I doubt it," Phyllis said. "Just use a really tall glass. Oh, and could you find one for my flower, too?"

"Yeah," her roommate said. "So, how was your night?"

"I didn't have one," Phyllis said. "I just sat here. Oh, actually, I finished my book, then vegged out."

"Oh," Roxanne said, examining a potential vase substitute, then shrugged and tried to cram her flowers into it. "Well," she continued, now looking for some scissors, "Linda talked a little about her new piece, but wouldn't show me any of it. She hates showing things that aren't finished. God, performing artists are so fickle, aren't they?" she said, then laughed.

"I'm glad *you're* in a good mood," Phyllis said. "You know," she said, rising from the couch, "I think I'll get in a workout before bed."

"Where?"

"The club, of course."

"What; they gave you a key?"

"Ahhh, I explained things to the owner," Phyllis said. "She's been pretty cool about it. I guess she 'understands' us performing artists."

"Go for it, then," Roxanne said, snipping off the bottoms of her flowers. "Just keep it down when you get back. I'll definitely be asleep."

"I know," Phyllis said, grabbing her sweatshirt from the closet. "Ooh, just thought of something."

"What?"

"I think some of my problem may not be how 'angry' I am at the world," Phyllis said. "I'll bet I've just been channeling it badly. I think I'll start up my karate again. God, why didn't I think of it before?"

"When did you study karate?" Roxanne asked, a hint of disgust in her voice.

"Oh, it was back in high school," Phyllis said. "But hey, I made it to orange belt."

"Is that good?"

"It's a pretty low rank. I think somebody's gonna be starting a self-defense class at the club. If that's true, I can take it for like half off or something, since I work there."

"Kind of a violent sport, isn't it? So unbecoming of you."

"It's not 'violent,' " Phyllis said. "They teach you self-defense, not how to beat up on everyone. You should take it, too. We *are* women, you know."

"I know; believe me, I've memorized the rape statistics for about every major city," Roxanne said. "I know it's a good idea, but—I can outrun just about anybody, in the meantime."

"What if you can't? What then?"

"I also carry mace.

"You? Since when?"

"Since . . . a long time now," Roxanne said. "Pretty soon after I got here, actually. Not because something happened to me, thank God, but . . . something bad happened to one of my friends, so . . . I don't believe in violence, and certainly not guns, but I'd like to be ready."

Phyllis nodded thoughtfully.

"Maybe I should, too," she said. "But you know me; I'd want to kick the guy's ass first, *then* mace him."

"G'night, sweetie," Roxanne said.

"I thought Linda was your sweetie," Phyllis said.

"You both are. Well, okay; g'night, darlin'."

"That's better," Phyllis said, smiling.

Phyllis used to be afraid of being alone in her old house in New York. It was not a big place, but had plenty of dark corners and things that made strange shadows. To get rid of the shadows, Phyllis usually turned on every light in the house until someone returned home, only to get a lecture for wasting electricity. She was not an only child, but was what some call a "miracle baby," or a child born to an "older" mother. Her two sisters and one brother may as well have been two aunts and an uncle, for all that they had in common with Phyllis. Needless to say, Phyllis had been made to feel more like an "unwanted" baby than a "miracle." Which is why she left home as soon as she was able, and skipped college to flee to Los Angeles, home of the stars and the never-will-be-stars. To her dismay she quickly discovered the huge ratio between the number of stars and the never-stars.

This frustration fueled her anger, as well as the anger of the thousands like her. But she was going to make it, just like all the thousands would, too. It wouldn't be long before *she* could say "Thank you; we'll call you" to the jerks begging to direct *her* movies and videos. This thought, and the loud music, fueled her workout tonight.

She no longer feared the dark or being alone, but thrived on them in times like this. No one knew she was there, nor could anyone see her in the darkened studio. She liked it that way, for then there was no concern about her appearance, and she could just let her body move to its own inner choreography. She didn't have to look in the mirrors to know that she could get any gig, as long as they didn't scrutinize her every movement the way they did. *Oh, right, like they cast them with their eyes shut,* but even Phyllis could have a fantasy here and there, right?

The music was done, and no one had discovered her there, so Phyllis switched it off and gathered her things to head for the showers. This time she left the light on in deference to "that movie's" shower scene. *That* she would probably never recover from.

She did not wake up Roxanne after returning, but did watch a little bit of the news while preparing for bed. More of the same: fatal car accidents, fatal shootings, fatal whatever. Unemployment the highest in California, which was no news to her. Phyllis shut it off after a few minutes and fell into bed. She had a dream about being naked in public, but grew bored of this and forced herself to dream about some strange picnic where Michael brought raw frogs' legs.

Michael had no news about the soap yet, but he did try to "make it up" to Phyllis. She was still tense that night and had to fake her climax. Michael had performed well enough; she was the one having trouble enjoying herself. Usually he had a smoke immediately afterward, but that night he seemed content to just hold her. That was fine with her. Maybe he was really trying to quit this time.

"Hey, guess what?" Michael murmured. "I get tomorrow night off, too."

"Do you?" she murmured, snuggling close. "I don't, though. It's a class night."

"Well, come by afterward, then."

"It gets out at like 9:30," Phyllis said. "I can come by, but I'll be too tired for sex."

"Maybe we'll rent a movie or something," he said. "What do you like?"

"God, it's been so long since I've seen anything," she said. "You pick something. Nothing bloody, though. I like funny stuff."

"Ahh, we'll both look," he said. "We'll be real 'together' about it."

Phyllis chuckled, then sighed and shut her eyes. After sex she always lay on top of him and let him rub her belly from behind. That almost always relaxed her, and when she was relaxed, he usually was, too.

"Mikey?" she said after a time.

"Mmmmm," he said.

"I was kinda wondering," she said, playing with his hands. "Do you think we should live together?"

Michael let out a half-sigh and half-groan.

"Mmmmm, you think it'd be safe?" he asked.

"What do you mean, 'safe?' "

"I don't know," he said. "You know, I've sometimes kinda thought about it, too, but—I don't know. What about your roommate?"

"What about her?"

"Well . . . she'd be okay, wouldn't she? I mean, if you just suddenly left?" he asked.

"Roxanne can take of herself," Phyllis said. "I'm talking about us, not her."

"I've got a 'single,' though."

"I assume we'd be getting a one or two-bedroom first, wouldn't you?" she asked. "Just give me a straight yes or no. Do you think it's a good idea?"

"A straight yes or no? No maybes?"

"Never mind," she grumbled. "You don't need to say, in that case."

"If you insist," he said.

"No, actually, I do need to hear," she said. "Do you think we should live together?"

"If you don't want any maybes, then I'll have to say no," he said.

"But why?"

"Because . . . I don't think we're ready for it yet."

"We've been together almost two years," she said. "That's more than enough time to decide if you love someone."

"I never said I didn't love you," he protested. "It's just that . . . it's a big step, you know?"

"It's not like we'd be married or something," she snapped. "It's just living together. You're an actor; you were supposed to marry me after two months."

"Yeah, but then we'd have to be divorced by now," he said.

"Seriously, though," she said. "I figure Roxanne is gonna commit to Linda pretty soon, so she'll move out, and then what about me?"

"I thought she had nothing to do with this," he reminded.

"Roxanne can take care of herself, but I can't," Phyllis said.

"Yeah you can," Michael said. "Or are you saying you just want somebody to take care of you?"

"Nooo, I'm not saying that," she said. " 'Course I can take care of myself. It's just that Roxanne has a better shot at a big break than I do."

"What makes you think that?"

"She's just more talented, that's all. She can sing and I can't."

"I can't sing *or* dance," he said.

"I can't believe you don't want to live together," she grumbled. "It's like I've got a curse on me or something."

"You don't have a 'curse' on you," he said.

"Seems that way," she said. "Nothing decent has ever happened to me."

"Oh, thanks."

"Well, how can I even say you are if you won't make any commitment?"

"Hey, come on, woman," he said. "You're just not asking me at the right time."

"What will be the right time, then, huh?" she asked.

"I-I don't know! Look, why don't you let me think about it a while, okay? I mean, you were pretty sudden about it. Let me think about it."

"You should have been thinking about it as long as I have," she said.

"So I'm a typical guy, okay?" he said, holding out his hands in exasperation. Phyllis rolled off of him and lay on her side. "Typical guys are afraid of commitment and drag their butts about it. So just let me think about it, okay?"

"And drag your butt for a while," she said.

"I promise not to drag my butt, though," he said. "Seriously, I'll give it some thought."

" 'Some' thought?"

"A *lot* of thought," he corrected himself. "Every waking moment will be consumed by it."

"You're such a liar," she said. He kissed her quickly and smiled.

"Not when I say I'll think about it," he said. "The other stuff was a bit exaggerated."

Phyllis seemed unamused, but allowed him his kiss. She was contemplative a moment, then rolled out of bed and onto her feet to fetch her clothes. Michael sat up on one elbow.

"Oh, come on, you're still mad at me?" he asked.

"Not really," she said unconvincingly. "I just feel like sleeping at home tonight."

"Come on," he said, patting the bed. "I promise not to snore."

"You don't anyway."

"See? It's a promise I can keep," he said. Phyllis

smiled quickly, but continued putting on her clothes. Michael watched her a moment before climbing out of bed. He went to her and held her shoulders.

"I'm not mad at you," she insisted. "I just . . . feel like being at home tonight."

"You sure? Do you want a ride home?" he asked.

"No, I've got my car," she said. "I'll be okay; it's not that late."

"Sure?"

"Yeah."

"Sure sure?"

"Now you're starting to bug me," she said. Michael pouted, then pulled her closer into a kiss. Phyllis wrapped her arms around him and kissed him back for several minutes. When they finished, she leaned into him briefly before parting from him to finish reclothing herself.

"Actually, one of the reasons is that I do have another audition tomorrow," she said.

"Why didn't you just say so, then?" he said. "Let me know how it goes."

"I will," she said, and pecked him on the cheek after finishing with her blouse. Michael returned to bed while she slipped her tennis shoes on.

Three

This director wanted "sexy and aloof." Most directors wanted this, except for the occasional "angry" video. Phyllis had once been in a video requiring ballroom dancing, but that was a long time ago. Roxanne was not there with her, for she had her previous job to attend. This director actually showed some fluctuation in his "thank you's," leaving Phyllis somewhat hopeful. She knew she had been exceptionally sexy and aloof, as had all the other hopefuls.

The rest of the day was spent at the club, topped off with the overweight housewives in the beginning jazzercize class. Phyllis had long ago learned to ignore how ridiculous they looked in their baggy sweats and/or too-tight leotards; now this was her favorite class, for these women seemed to have more fun. Still, few of them actually made much progress, especially since this class was about the only exercise most of them got all week. That, and cutting down on their food was somewhat important, except that they rarely did. But Phyllis understood these women's plight; she may have been in great shape, but she had to work her butt off to stay that way. Some of the women in her advanced class made her want to puke, as they obviously had no need whatsoever for exercise or cutting down or anything else to keep their fabulous bodies. She sometimes wondered if they took the class just to torment her.

Rent was due in a few days, so once again Phyllis had to ask for an early paycheck from the club. The owner, Chris, was pretty much used to it by then and was usually ready with a check for Phyllis. Chris was very understanding of her various quirks and difficulties, but she never became much friendlier than that. Phyllis used to take it personally before learning that the owner was deliberately that way with all of her employees, most likely to avoid the turmoil of having to fire a "friend," if it ever came to that.

Roxanne was still gone when Phyllis returned to the apartment, and was likely to stay at Linda's for the night. Roxanne almost always went there after jobs. Phyllis called Michael and told him she was too tired to see anyone. Afterward she took a long bath in lieu of a shower. She was very tired, but she also wasn't feeling up to seeing Michael after last night.

The next morning Phyllis called up her agent and chastised him for not getting her more theater auditions. Again, he explained how difficult it was to do so because Phyllis didn't sing. Not that she had never taken lessons, but all she had learned then was that a singing career was beyond her. He did have yet another video cattle call, which she accepted. No phone calls came about the other auditions; back to the jazzercize for survival pay.

Fortunately there was a self-defense class being offered. There was no karate or otherwise to speak of, but

Phyllis had not the money to find such a class outside of the club. So she learned all about gouging out eyes with car keys, but this was no way to work out her aggressions. Roxanne may have hated the violence of it, but Phyllis needed to hit things. Some of her old training came back while learning about throws and holds and whatnot. After two lessons she realized why the pure martial arts had appealed to her before she devoted all her time to dance. The martial arts, when properly practiced, could be just as beautiful as any dance performance. This "Women's Defense" class wasn't satisfying that at all.

This need to work out her aggressions was, of course, growing. She got one shot at a video over the next few weeks, but as a non-dancing extra. Definitely not her next big break.

Michael's good news was his new steady job. He had made it to the soap's callbacks, and was not "Louis," but had been hired as "Derek," the hot-shot lawyer for some character's rape case. Or maybe it was a murder or custody battle. Phyllis was going to have to start watching the soap, of course. Michael's fifteen-hour days began almost immediately, so he couldn't see much of Phyllis for a while. Nor did he have an answer for her about the "c" word.

As a purist, Roxanne tried to refrain from such pollutants as cigarettes, drugs, booze, meat, and swearing. Nevertheless Phyllis was gradually becoming what even her roommate would call a real bitch. Normally Phyllis would be taking out her anger on Michael, but he was never home, so she had to let Roxanne have it for various stupid reasons. As a result Roxanne spent more and more of her time at Linda's, leaving Phyllis a little bit more alone than before.

By the time she hadn't had a real gig in some five months, even Phyllis could tell why. Some directors wanted "angry," but they didn't want bitches, either. Phyllis needed time off whether she could afford a trip or not, so now where to? New York was out of the question. She had had almost no verbal and/or written contact with her parents, so home would never be home again. Besides, New York wasn't her idea of a very relaxing place. The point was to get away from the chaos of the city for a while.

She knew of no friends offhand who didn't live in a big city. Her family was a lost cause, too, except . . . yes, one of her sisters was supposedly in the suburbs in Massachusetts (or was it Maryland?). But she had a bunch of kids, meaning little relaxation. After some thought, Phyllis gave up and flipped on one of the day-time talk shows.

She felt her will being sucked away by the Women Who Love Their Kids Too Much, when a possibility came to her. She hadn't written him in a long time, but she had an uncle named Bill who lived in Wyoming (or was it Wisconsin?). Phyllis flipped off *Geraldo* and dug through her old letters.

It took her an hour to sort through the mess, but she found her batch of letters from Bill and remembered that he had once given her his phone number. She hadn't seen him in six years, when he married his second wife Joanie. That was the last time she had really seen anyone in her family, for that matter.

Another half an hour gave her the courage to call him up, and Joanie answered. After some reintroductions, Joanie did indeed remember her step-niece, and was quite happy to hear from her. Phyllis fumbled through some excuses for not having written, then dropped her bomb: Could she and Uncle Bill maybe sort of put up with her visiting them for a week or two?

"I mean, I know you guys have like a ranch or something, so I'll even do chores if you want," Phyllis said. "I just . . . I need to get away for a few weeks. I mean, just two at most. I wouldn't stay longer, I swear."

"Now you don't worry about that," Joanie said in her acquired drawl. "We'd be glad to have you. It's been so long, hasn't it?"

"Since the wedding, I think," Phyllis said. "Your wedding."

"Has it really been that long? Well, you just come and see us, then. We've got plenty of room."

"Are you sure? I mean, I don't want to be like some sponging relative. Uncle Bill won't mind?"

"Oh, I'll tell him you called today," Joanie said, "but he'll be just as pleased to see you as I will. Let me take your number, though, dear. Are you still in Los Angeles?"

"Yeah," Phyllis said, and read off her number. "I don't have a machine, though, so you'll kind of have to get me when I'm here."

"Uh-huh," Joanie said. "But listen: I'll tell Bill you called and that you'd like to come up here, and he'll call you back to let you know when you can come. Sound good?"

"You sure it's okay?"

"Not unless it's a problem for you."

"No, God no," Phyllis said. "God, Joanie, you don't know how much I need to . . . just get away, you know?"

"I understand, honey," Joanie said. "Oh, this must be costing you a fortune. Next time it'll be on our bill. I promise we'll call you back right away."

"Thanks, Joanie. Give Uncle Bill a kiss for me."

"Well, once I've given him my kisses," Joanie said, and they both laughed and finished off their goodbyes.

Phyllis hung up with a sigh and let her head rest on her arms. A vacation would probably solve no problems, but it might make things easier to take once she got back, by her thinking. She remembered that Bill lived on a farm (or was it a ranch)? She decided that it would be a good idea to reread those old letters.

Four

Uncle Bill greeted Phyllis at the airport with much love and affection. He was her father's brother, but somehow she had always liked Bill just a bit more. Uncle Bill had two sons, or her cousins, and used to have a horse ranch, but had sold the horses off, except for a few, to take up llama breeding. Phyllis had reread his letters about that; the big "career change" had occurred about the time he married Joanie. According to him, it was possible to make good money on llamas as long as one had some good studs, as he did. Bill preferred to remain in semi-retirement with the llamas, as they were apparently easier to care for than horses. Needless to say, Phyllis had never seen one up close before.

Neither of the cousins worked at the ranch. Bill had Roger, his hired hand, but apparently Joanie, Roger, and himself were the only people that Bill needed. The cousins had moved off to the big city; one was in Chicago, and the other was in Minneapolis. Bill preferred the slower pace of southern Wisconsin.

Joanie greeted Phyllis back at the ranch with a hug and comments about "how she'd grown," even though she hadn't. Phyllis had already survived puberty when they'd first met, but she admittedly was in better shape now than before. Joanie began ushering her inside immediately and would not let her take her own bags in. The sun was already setting, and Phyllis could smell the home cooking from where they were. She inhaled deeply and caught some of the other prominent smells of the ranch. She saw the llama herd off in the distance, and almost ran into Joanie while staring at them.

"Oh!" Joanie said, steadying them both. "Watch it, dear."

"Sorry," Phyllis said, pointing off at the herd. "Are those them? The llamas?"

"They sure are," Joanie said.

"So, um . . ." Phyllis began, "What exactly do you do with them?"

"Ohhhh, wool-gathering, mostly," Joanie said with a smile. "A little joke," she added, though Phyllis hadn't caught it. "You can watch us work with them tomorrow," Joanie said. "Or would you like to see some up close right now?"

"Um . . . tomorrow, I guess," Phyllis said, glancing at the sunset. Uncle Bill waddled by with her bags.

"You better get inside to get it while it's hot," he said.

"Are you sure I can't help?" she asked.

"You just worry about the dinner Joanie'll be spoiling you with," he said. Phyllis laughed and let Joanie take her by the arm to lead her inside.

"God, you don't know how great this is gonna be for me," Phyllis said. "Things are real quiet and relaxing around here, right?"

"Oh, yes," Joanie said, and took her the rest of the way inside. She led Phyllis immediately to the kitchen table, and went to check her oven and various pots and pans. She lifted one of the lids and resumed her stirring.

"That smells so good," Phyllis said, inhaling deeply. "What is it?"

"Oh, just soup," Joanie said. "Do you like vegetables?"

"You mean like in vegetable soup? Yeah, I like that."

"I used a ham bone for the stock, and cheated with a can of chicken broth," Joanie said. "Got the real thing in there, though," she added, pointing at the oven with her foot.

"Couldn't I . . . help you with this or anything?"

"No, you sit," Joanie insisted. "The plane trip must have been exhausting."

"Um . . . no, not really," Phyllis said. Uncle Bill entered from one of the rooms and inhaled deeply himself. He clasped his hands together and smiled, then patted Phyllis on the shoulder in greeting.

"She won't let me help her," Phyllis said.

"No one helps her in here," Bill said.

"That's right," his wife echoed.

"That's okay," Phyllis said. "Nobody knows how to cook in L.A. We just microwave everything."

"So do I, when she's not around," Bill said, pointing at Joanie.

"Get the chicken out, would you?" she asked Bill, who fumbled around for some oven mitts. Joanie kicked at a drawer.

"In there," she said, and Bill fetched his hot pads. He pulled the chicken from the oven and set it on a cutting board, then took a spoon to the broth. Joanie nudged at him.

"Ah-ah, that's my job," she said. Bill threw up his hands and looked at Phyllis to smile and wink at her. She smiled back and nodded in comprehension.

"The woman's place is in the kitchen" was something that neither Phyllis nor her mother had ever believed in. Phyllis's memories of her mother's culinary talents involved a lot of cans and frozen things. Phyllis graduated to independence with the same habits. She owned no recipes and probably wouldn't know what to do with one, anyway.

She watched Joanie bustle about, seemingly tending to four different things at once, and almost immediately felt . . . at home. Here was a woman whose place would be in the kitchen whether she had been taught that or not, for she clearly loved to cook. She was about ten years younger than Uncle Bill, and kept herself in good condition. In others words, it was unlikely that she tasted her food all day long and never did any other work. Phyllis figured that Joanie helped out at the ranch, but had otherwise become quite content with filling the traditional "female roles."

Where did Uncle Bill find this woman, anyway? Phyllis wondered to herself. If only Dad had found her first, then she could have been *my* mom. No, that's terrible. I shouldn't think that way, but I can't help it. God, do I need this vacation.

Before she knew it, the table was being set, and Joanie was just finishing pouring Phyllis's milk, when Roger came in. He was an average-looking fellow in his thirties, and was also in good condition from the ranch work. He yanked off his gloves and stopped at the table to take in all the food.

"You haven't met him yet, have you?" Bill asked. "Roger's the third one of us. Roger, Phyllis, my niece."

Roger smiled and stuck out his hand, which Joanie swatted away.

"Hey, hey, we've got food out here," she said. "Go wash up first."

"Sorry, Missus," he said, sufficiently humbled. He nodded at Phyllis instead, who smiled and waved as he slinked off into the bathroom.

"Nice to meet you, Roger," she said. Joanie finished setting out everyone's food, including Roger's. Phyllis was uncertain whether to start first or let them do it. So far they seemed to be waiting for something.

The water in the bathroom stopped, and Roger reappeared, rubbing his hands together. He seated himself next to Phyllis and fixed up his napkin, then Uncle Bill and his wife bowed their heads. Phyllis stared at them a moment, then understood as soon as Bill started murmuring grace. She tried not to feel uncomfortable about it, but she had not been to church since the wedding, and of course, never gave thanks at mealtime. Soon enough they all said "Amen," and Phyllis dug in to the meal while trying to remember what denomination they were. She was baptized a Protestant, but remembered that Uncle Bill had changed to something else. Presbyterian? It would come up later.

Conversation began with Bill talking about a livestock show that was to be coming in about a week and a half. Joanie would be in charge of seeing to the "weanlings." Phyllis asked about those, then learned that they were the freshly weaned llamas. They were to be prepared for selling at the next show. The menfolk were going to be busy with the dam, or female, that someone was bringing in the next day. Eventually Joanie steered the conversation away from business and asked Phyllis "all about Los Angeles." Phyllis shrugged.

"I guess things aren't too good there," she said. "That's why I'm here, mostly. I just can't seem to get my act together, you know?"

"Let's see, last time you wrote you were talking about joining the ballet," Uncle Bill said. Phyllis laughed.

"God, was it that long ago?" she said. "Ummm . . . I can still appreciate ballet, but I like the modern moves a lot more. Jazz and hip-hop, for instance. It's hard to keep up practice on ballet, too. You have to keep working the muscles it uses or you're screwed. Er . . . You're in trouble," she added sheepishly.

"I thought that New York was supposed to be the place for dancers," Roger said. "You know, Broadway and all that."

"It depends," Phyllis said. "New York's the place for stage work and yes, ballet. I'm trying to make it in TV and videos. And there's . . . other reasons for not being in New York."

"Hey, you probably work with Paula Abdul and people like her, don'tcha?" Roger said.

Phyllis blushed. "Nah, I've never worked on any of her things," she said. "Haven't met her, either."

"What have you been working on lately?" Joanie asked. "Are there any movies we can see you in?"

Phyllis laughed and shook her head.

"I wish," she said. "I haven't had anything for so long, I've—I've lost confidence. That's what it is. You gotta have confidence, or you can't do a damn thing. 'Attitude' is one thing, but that's only part of it. I've just been losing my confidence because it's been so long since I've really had anything. If it weren't for the exercise classes—and, uh, waiting tables—I'd probably be homeless."

"Ah, can't be that bad, can it?" Uncle Bill said. "Bet you'll get your own musical someday."

"That'd be nice, except I don't sing," Phyllis explained. "Actually, for someone like me, a 'real' break would be to get picked for a singer's dance troupe. For instance, um, people like Madonna have their own dancers that do all their shows and videos with them. That's our version of a steady job. Hell of a good one, too. Too bad not all of the big-time performers have backup dancers. Usually we have to go for one or two day deals for music videos. The pay is never great, but it's experience and exposure, and that's what you *really* need. Either that, or an incredibly lucky break, which I've yet to have."

"You will someday," Bill said.

"Thanks," Phyllis said, almost blushing. "But right now my problem is that everyone else believes that more than I do. *I'm* the one who has to believe it."

"That's for damn sure," Roger said, buttering his bread. "No matter what you do, gotta believe that you can."

"Right!" Phyllis said, and laughed. "Will you be my agent instead of the one I have now?"

"Uhhh, well, I'm not much of a city person," Roger said. "Indianapolis was enough for me."

"Oh, you're from there?"

"Yeah," he said, taking a bite of bread. "Lived in Illinois a while, then came here to work at a couple of other ranches before coming here."

"Hired him because he'd worked with llamas just when people were starting to bring 'em in around here," Bill said.

"I used to work out of Lacrosse," Roger said. "The biggest llama ranch is out there."

"Ohhh," Phyllis said, nodding her head in genuine interest. "Um . . . could I see them tomorrow? Or will I be in the way?"

"No, no, Joanie can show you a few," Bill said. He turned to his wife. "Why don't you show her the weanlings?" he asked her. "They won't give her much trouble."

"That's what I had in mind," Joanie said.

"Llamas aren't wild, are they?" Phyllis asked, warily.

"Well, they're a little bit 'wild,' " Uncle Bill said. "Less skittish than horses, though. That's why I switched. There's more work when we harvest the wool, but at least they're not psychotic like some horses I've run across."

"You know, honey," Joanie said, touching Phyllis's hand, "I hope you don't think I'm a bother, but—I was wondering if, after a few days, you could show us what sort of dancing you do?"

"Now, she's not here to put on shows for us," Uncle Bill protested.

"Oh, no, I don't mind," Phyllis said. "If you like, I can do kind of an 'audition' for you in a few days. You know, like what I'd do for an audition. I wouldn't mind."

"Well, you better let me watch, too, then," Roger said, wiping his mouth and setting the napkin onto his plate.

All of them had finished at about the same time. Phyllis had more left over, but it wasn't until then that she realized just how much food she had eaten. This had been so much better than those microwave things, and in some ways, better than restaurant food. For one thing, it was clear that loving care and pride were two very important ingredients in Joanie's recipes.

Conversation evolved into chit-chat before Roger excused himself and left the table for home. Joanie had trained him long ago to buss his own dishes, which he did, but left them in the sink for her to clean everything at once. Bill left to visit the television, leaving Phyllis to insist on helping Joanie. Joanie made a fuss about refusing at first, then finally relented in mock exasperation.

"I just don't want to feel like I'm mooching off of you guys," Phyllis said. "I mean it when I say I'll do chores if I have to."

"Well, we'll see, then," Joanie said. "It really isn't necessary, but if you insist . . . but then, I thought this was your vacation?"

"Well, it is, and it isn't," Phyllis said. "Sure, I need to relax, but I don't want to turn to mush, either, if you know what I mean. Any work I do here won't be at all like what I do at home."

"You're probably right," Joanie said, and set to work filling the sink. Phyllis finished clearing off the rest of the table, and partially listened in on Uncle Bill's television shows.

"Do you guys watch soaps?" she asked Joanie. Joanie chuckled.

"Oh, no, honey, I don't watch those things," she said.

"You wondering if you're going to miss your favorite show?"

"Hunh? Oh! Oh, God, no," Phyllis said. "I hate those things. Except—well, see, my boyfriend just got a job on one, so I kind of had to start watching his show. You know, to see what his character is doing."

"Do you mean that your boyfriend is an actor on one of those soap operas?" Joanie asked. "Which one?"

"Um . . . 'As We Live,' I think. Yeah, that one."

"Well, how about that! Bill? Bill!" Joanie called to him until he "muted" the television. "Did you hear that?"

"What?"

"Well, her boyfriend is one of those soap opera stars! It's—! Which one again?"

" 'As We Live.' "

"It's called 'As We Live!' " Joanie went on. "What channel, honey?" she asked Phyllis.

"ABC," Phyllis said loudly enough for Uncle Bill to hear. "It wouldn't be on right now. But—"

"Welll, congratulations, kiddo!" Bill called back.

"No, really, it isn't a big deal," Phyllis said. "He's not one of the 'stars' of the show."

"Well, I don't know anything about those shows or who's the star and who isn't," Bill said. "But, maybe he'll go on to be a famous movie star. You could be married to the next Kevin Costner."

Phyllis blushed a deep red. *"Pleeease,"* she protested. "So far it hasn't been so wonderful, anyways. See, people on soaps work godawful hours for five days a week. It's even worse when they're major characters. Thank God his character has just started. Still, it's been rough. And as for being married to him . . ."

"Is that part of why you need to 'get away from it all?' " Joanie asked. Phyllis blushed and shrugged.

"Well, yeah, kind of," she said, then leaned closer to Joanie. "Um . . . there's a little more to it than that," she said, her voice lower. "See, before this started, I asked him for . . . well, for more commitment, but he's been flaking out about it. And I'm getting impatient with him."

"So you have been thinking about marriage," Joanie murmured.

"Whoa, not *that* much commitment," Phyllis said. "I just wanna try living together, but he's even afraid of that. And now he doesn't have any time because of this new job."

"Oh, I'm sorry about that, honey," Joanie said, and Phyllis could tell that she meant it. Phyllis started drying the dishes that Joanie handed to her, then laughed a little.

"God, it's funny that I've told you that," Phyllis said. "This is practically the second time we've ever met, and I'm telling you this 'best friend' stuff."

"I'm a good listener," Joanie said. "Could be because I stopped trying to give advice to people, so they don't mind telling me things. But that's why you're here, honey; to say 'go to hell!' to some of your problems. For a week or two, anyway. Places like this are good for that sort of thing."

"I know what you mean," Phyllis said. "I didn't really notice it the first time I was here, but Wisconsin is so . . . I'd say serene, but that's almost a cliche, isn't it?"

"It *can* be 'serene,' " Joanie said. "It should be obvious that I'm happier here than in San Francisco."

"Oh, you're from there?"

"Raised the family there," Joanie said. "Then my husband and I got divorced, and the kids were getting out on their own, so I ran off to the Midwest to start over. I met your uncle a year later, and you know the rest."

"You two are really happy together, aren't you?" Phyllis whispered.

"He's a good man," she said. "It was never mad and passionate to begin with, but from early on we've been very . . . comfortable together."

"It shows."

"Well, that's a relief," Joanie said, smiling slyly.

"I wish the rest of the family was as good as Uncle Bill," Phyllis said. "He must be the only one who isn't completely fucked up. Oh! I'm sorry."

Joanie shrugged.

"You should hear the boys when they're working the herds," she said. "Shameful words for a lady like me to hear." Phyllis laughed with her step-aunt. Joanie wisely declined to add to Phyllis's previous comment about her family. Phyllis had always felt like an "outsider" in her own family, but Joanie really was one, at least. For some reason the New York relatives seemed to barely tolerate Bill's "country ways," not to mention his "country wife." It didn't matter that she had already lived the city life just like them. She could indeed empathize with Phyllis, but was not the sort to do so out loud.

Five

The sun had been up for hours before Phyllis lumbered into the kitchen in her robe. Joanie was there, just wiping off the rest of the breakfast on the counter. Phyllis yawned and fingered the morning paper, but it was a very local edition.

"Do you get the *L.A. Times?*" Phyllis asked.

"No, honey, just our little paper," Joanie said.

"Uh! What am I thinking? Like you'd get an L.A. paper out here. Um, where's Uncle Bill? I didn't miss breakfast, did I?"

"I'm afraid you did, but I saved you your portion in the refrigerator," Joanie said.

"What time is it?"

"Oh, it's about 8:30 now."

"8:30? Jeez, I haven't overslept like that in . . . I always get up at about six, sometimes earlier. I'm a morning person."

"Well, you know, we're about two hours ahead of California," Joanie said. "Over there it's still 6:30, right?"

"Hunh? Oh, yeah, yeah," Phyllis said. "Even so, I didn't have much trouble falling asleep, even if I still had two hours to go. Well, let's hope that I haven't turned into a lazy toad in only one day."

"But then you'll get back to California and find yourself getting up two hours early," Joanie said.

"That's all I need," Joanie grumbled. "So, I guess Uncle Bill is out doing chores and things now, huh?"

"Yes, he got started at eight. They're just sending the animals out for grazing now."

"What do you need to do today?" Phyllis said.

"Oh, I'll be looking in on our weanlings. See which ones we can take to the show for sale. I'll let you get ready before I go, if you like. Are you hungry?"

"Um . . . actually, I think I'm still recovering from last night," Phyllis said, leaning back and patting her belly. "I gotta watch myself around your cooking. I'll have to roll home."

"What, you? You're just a little stick, don't you know," Joanie said.

"No, seriously. I have to work twice as hard to stay this way. All the girls in this family are like that. You remember how fat Mom was at your wedding, right?"

"Well, I don't remember those sorts of things," Joanie said. "You can never ask the bride to remember details. It all comes across as a dream after a time."

"Or a nightmare," Phyllis mumbled.

"Now I thought we had a lovely wedding. Didn't you enjoy yourself?"

"Oh . . . yeah," Phyllis said quickly. "I don't mean your wedding. I just mean how some weddings turn into disasters."

"I see," Joanie said. Phyllis insisted that she needed no breakfast and left to get ready for the day. She returned in some of her good workout sweats, confident that they were just right for hard work on a ranch.

The ranch itself was close to twenty acres. Uncle Bill had once considered expanding it to include another ranch, but he decided to keep his business manageable for two or three people at best. The land had obviously been cleared of the sparse woods that surrounded the area, and no doubt it would be expensive to clear away more. So Uncle Bill kept things as they were. He had eighteen animals in all: two stud males, one "gelding," or castrated male, and the rest were the females and their weanlings. Phyllis saw the two males from a distance, and noticed that they were kept separate from each other. She figured out why on her own, but let Joanie talk about the place at will.

Joanie brought her over to a female. This was certainly much closer than Phyllis had ever been to such an animal. The llama could be considered "unusual" by those who are easily impressed. Phyllis knew a llama when she saw one, but it was fun to see the goatlike, camel-like appearance of one up close.

The female allowed Joanie to approach, then touch her. She stroked at the neck a little and leaned toward the animal. The female leaned her own face over and blew lightly at Joanie's face. Phyllis tried to reach out, too, but the animal took a step back and made a different blowing sound.

"Hmmm, figures she wouldn't like me," Phyllis said.

"Oh, don't worry, they'll get used to you," Joanie said. "I'll show you some weanlings; they're not quite so suspicious."

They walked past the female to a separate area where some much smaller llamas milled around. The entire ranch was fenced off, plus the separate areas for the various sexes and ages. Each area was fairly large, as the animals did need to eat all day. Most of the young ones were content to try out the moss and lichens growing around, and largely ignored their visitors. Joanie went inside the area to walk among them, and Phyllis followed cautiously.

"Some of these will be sold at the show," Joanie said. "We're not going all out this year, though. Bill has some pretty good studs over there."

" 'Studs,' " Phyllis echoed. "So . . . like . . . people pay you guys to breed with them? Like a stud service?" Phyllis asked.

"Yes," Joanie said, and went to one placid weanling to feel at its wool. "Here's one that looks ready, for instance," she announced. "We'll have to comb out a lot of this wool first. Say, if you really mean you'd like to help, I could show you how to comb out the young ones."

"Um, really?" Phyllis asked, eyeing the animal warily.

"Combing can be a real pain and an awful mess, but it can be fun, too," Joanie said. "These young ones won't be much trouble for you. Now we wouldn't ask you to comb out an adult, so don't you worry about that."

"Well . . . I'd probably just mess up, wouldn't I?"

"Well, you can just watch me comb one out later, then let me know, okay?" Joanie said.

Phyllis shrugged, then laughed nervously.

"Sure," she said. "If I'm going to offer to help, I should back it up, right?"

"It's your choice, honey," Joanie said, then left the young female to her grazing. "Come on, I'll bet you'd like to see our looms."

"Looms? You mean like for weaving?"

"We have two," Joanie said, holding up her fingers. Phyllis followed her step-aunt to a building next to the barn. They went inside to see the two looms, and Phyllis was amused to find all the stray hairs stuck here and there between the strings. Joanie rattled out a quick lecture on how the wool was woven, but Phyllis probably would not have survived a pop quiz even if given only a few minutes later. Fortunately none of this information was necessary for her survival, but she was enjoying all of it.

"I think I've noticed the one big disadvantage to the country," Phyllis said after leaving the looms behind.

"Which is?"

"The dirt," she announced, and Joanie laughed.

"The dirt?" she said. "Heavens, I thought you were going to say the mosquitoes. They're the only thing I haven't gotten used to."

"God, yeah, they're terrible here," Phyllis agreed. "Are they always this bad?"

"No," Joanie said, then smiled. "During the summer they've been known to carry off people's pets."

Off in the distance somebody had parked his or her truck, and was talking to Uncle Bill and Roger. Phyllis and Joanie were already heading in their direction, so after a time Phyllis could see that a woman had arrived with one of her own llamas in tow. They reached the side of the house, where Joanie proceeded to fill a bucket with water from an outdoor faucet. The llamas tended to stand nearby the water trough, which was understandable. From the house Phyllis could see the other visitor better. She was a medium-sized woman with blond hair and more appropriate clothing for a ranch than workout sweats. Uncle Bill seemed to be examining her llama, until Roger led it away so the other two could speak further.

"Are they buying another one?" Phyllis asked. Joanie looked up.

"What's that?"

"That woman over there is selling her llama, right?"

"Hm? Oh, no, she's using one of the studs," Joanie said, now lugging her bucket over to the trough. Without asking, Phyllis helped her carry it over, even though it wasn't terribly heavy.

"She'll leave her dam here for a month or so, then come back, and hopefully the stud will have done his job," Joanie said. They reached the trough and emptied the bucket into it. Some of the animals began heading toward them at this sound. Behind them, Roger was leading the other woman's dam to wherever he took them to use the stud. Uncle Bill and the woman were now by the other male, looking him over. Phyllis caught herself smiling and shaking her head at the whole affair.

"God, this place is so bizarre, it's wonderful," she said.

"Bizarre?" Joanie said, heading back for the faucet.

"Well, I guess not really 'bizarre' so much as just . . . it's so different from L.A., you know."

"Oh, yes."

Phyllis caught a glimpse of a farm cat bolting away at the sight of them. Just a mouse-catcher, she thought. Not a pet.

"Of course, this may be nice and slow-paced, but there isn't much for the dance community," Phyllis went on. "I couldn't give that up."

"Too bad there isn't some happy medium for you,"

Joanie said. "But, it's true that all the show business is in the cities, or actually, where you are now. Los Angeles."

"And New York."

"That, too. No ballets here, though."

Later in the day Phyllis watched Joanie give the basics on combing out a weanling's wool. The problem wasn't in the combing so much as keeping the animal still for it. The combing was done where the looms were kept, and there were special pens for the animals to stand in while being groomed. Joanie had been right, though; the young ones were more docile than the adults. Phyllis was eventually willing to give it a try the next day.

She did give it a try, but only created an unholy mess of the wool. Joanie agreed to take the weanling off of Phyllis's hands, and reassured her that no harm had been done. Phyllis took a long walk around the boundaries of the ranch, and stopped at the edge of some of the thicker woods on the northern side. All sorts of things could live in there. Probably a lot of animals that liked to eat llamas. No doubt Uncle Bill had some interesting stories about renegade bears, or whatever wild beasts lived around them. She tugged at the chainlink as if testing its strength, then moved on, apparently satisfied.

Phyllis made it back to the ranch house just in time to see the second half of Michael's soap. The "stars" almost always had their segments first, so his character was still a commercial away, she discovered. It always amused her how wooden the makeup made him look, but it was a necessary evil for videotape work. So far his scene was pretty straightforward with "Karen," or "Kathy," or whoever she was, but Phyllis knew it wouldn't be long before "Derek" went to bed with her. The thought of this momentarily put butterflies into Phyllis's stomach, but of course, they would only be acting. He wouldn't *really* fall in love with her.

Another day they made a brief stop into town, where Phyllis picked up the latest bestseller in paperback. She tried to get into this book, but her mind turned to mush after only a half an hour. This was when she realized that boredom was setting in. Incompetent at ranching chores, Phyllis had little to do except walk, sleep, or watch television. There was not enough room to dance, but she did treat her hosts to one of her simple routines after a day's work, as promised. The ground was not very accommodating for fancy turns, twists, or leaps, but they all thought she was the next Baryshnikov, or at least his female counterpart.

It had been an exhausting day for all except Phyllis, but she slept more soundly than the others. Boring or not, her vacation had helped her start getting a good night's sleep for once. She dreamed of being on a float in a parade, where she danced to the delight of the crowd, until somebody in the audience screamed.

Phyllis's eyes popped open, her ears filled with one of the more awful shrieks she had ever heard. Something was happening outside, and she soon heard much scuffling and voices from inside. She sat upright and listened some more, and recognized Uncle Bill's voice, then Joanie's. And still those shrieks from outside assaulted her ears. What? The llamas? What was happening?

She ran outside of her room to see Uncle Bill cocking his rifle that he had yanked from above the mantel. Joanie was trying to help him with a robe, and still the llamas were sounding their alarms. Her hosts were ignoring Phyllis, until she tried to follow Uncle Bill outside. Joanie caught her and pulled her back gently.

"No, honey, you stay inside," she said. "Let Bill handle this. Something's just spooked them, that's all."

"What is it? Why are they making that horrible noise?"

"You're going to have to stay inside, honey," Joanie repeated. "If there really is something out there, you'll be safe in here."

"Don't worry, I'm not going out *there*," Phyllis said, backing up to lean against the sofa. She folded her arms and rubbed her shoulders.

"You might as well get back to bed," Joanie said. "Bill will take care of it. Do you need a robe?"

"I guess I do; it's freezing!" Phyllis said, rubbing her arms even harder. Joanie turned to fetch a robe for her, when Phyllis screamed at the sound of the rifle firing.

"Goddamn it!" Uncle Bill's voice called from far off in the darkness, followed immediately by a long string of more colorful obscenities. Phyllis got up from the sofa to back away even more.

"Oh, honey, don't you worry, Joanie said, obviously quite worried herself. "Bill is frightening something off, that's what."

"I thought we were all fenced in."

"Ummm . . ."

"Joanie!" Uncle Bill's voice called from far off. Only the light of his flashlight was visible. Joanie stepped out onto the porch.

"What's happened?" she shouted.

"Get the goddamned sheriff out here!" he called. Phyllis was almost too afraid to approach the doorway and peek outside.

"The . . . ? My God, Bill, what is it?"

"Whadda you think?" he yelled. "One of the males! Get somebody, quick!"

Joanie nodded and bustled past Phyllis to fumble with the phone. Phyllis stepped out onto the porch herself now and tried to peer into the darkness. She barely heard Uncle Bill yelling more obscenities to himself. His flashlight was pointed at something on the ground, and sometimes he stood up to scan the area with it. Sometimes a llama let out a stray shriek, and Uncle Bill would holler at it to shut it up, but in vain.

In the background Joanie had reached the sheriff, but could give no specifics other than that something had happened to the animals. She hung up and returned to the porch just as Uncle Bill was making his cautious way back to the house. He shined the flashlight into the darkness again, and seemed satisfied of its emptiness.

"I didn't know what to tell them," Joanie said. "Something hurt one of the males, you said?"

" 'Hurt' isn't the word," Uncle Bill said. "That thing's been . . . Goddamn it!" he said, scratching his head. "That was the one breeding with the female."

"Oh, no," Joanie said. "Oh, Bill, what hurt it? What happened?"

"Hurt it?" Bill said. "That thing's been chewed up and spit out again."

"What??"

"God*damn* it!" he said. "Come on, let's get the others

inside now. Goddamn, why didn't I just put them all in tonight?"

"It's not your fault," Joanie said. "What did it? What were you firing at? Surely not a bear?"

Uncle Bill had already turned away from them to go outside, and he waved away the question angrily, but not from anger at his wife. Joanie left to find warmer clothes and continued trying to reassure Phyllis that all was well. Instead, Phyllis stood on the porch and watched them usher the rest of the herd into the barn. Before this, she heard Joanie's horrified cry at the sight of the butchered male.

After a time her eyelids were growing heavy again. There was nothing she could do to help them, and once the sheriff's jeep pulled up, Phyllis yawned and stretched, then crawled back into bed to sleep uneasily.

Six

There was the equivalent of a circus the next morning, as far as ranches go. The sheriff's jeep was back, as well as another car that Phyllis learned had come from the Game Commission. Joanie greeted her with a hot breakfast, which she was too upset to eat. The llamas were out grazing again as if nothing had happened, but the butchered one had been removed. Joanie explained that Uncle Bill and the others were now scouring the grounds for clues.

"Bill did shoot at something last night," Joanie said, "but even he isn't sure what it was. He says it looked sort of like a bear."

"You have bears around here?"

"We don't. That's the trouble. You know, I wouldn't be surprised if it were something that escaped from a zoo or a circus. The game warden ought to know. I can't believe something like this could happen."

"Neither can I," Phyllis said. "Um . . . aren't there animals like mountain lions, or um, wolves or something? I thought this was all fenced off, anyways.

"The gate could have been left open," Joanie said, shrugging. "And no, honey, there aren't any mountain lions or wolves nearby. The wolves are up north, and folks pretty much keep them in line."

"Um . . . do you think Uncle Bill would mind if I kind of watched what they were doing?" Phyllis asked. "I just want to see what's going on."

"I suppose you could, but um . . . just make sure to keep out of their way," Joanie cautioned. "Especially your uncle. He's been having a couple of cows about this."

"I don't blame him."

"Neither do I," Joanie said, peering out the window.

Phyllis finished her breakfast in a few minutes, then excused herself to wander out to where the men were. Joanie returned to preparing the weanlings for sale. First, Phyllis scanned the dirt at about where the dead male seemed to be, then found the spot marked with blood. There was a very short trail of it that seemed to go off toward the north, away from the gate. Phyllis kicked at the dirt a while, then headed off north. The men were all the way over to the fence, so she quickened her step.

After a time Phyllis reached the north end of the ranch and stopped some fifteen feet from the men. Uncle Bill had no doubt been repeating his story over and over to the deputy and Game Commission person. At least he was not tired of it yet, but it only made him angrier with each retelling. The source of their concern lay before her eyes; one part of the fence had been torn wide open. Something had actually ripped its way through a chain-link fence just to slaughter a llama. It had either been something hungry and insane, or just so strong that it didn't care what was in its way. She then began picking up on their conversation.

"—that I know can do this," the deputy said.

"Well, Jesus Christ, man, haven't you called the zoo or something?" Uncle Bill snapped at the commissioner. "What's strong enough to rip through *this*? What killed my stud?"

"All we've got now is what you've told us yourself, plus what we're seeing here," the deputy said.

"And we'll get back to you pronto on that autopsy," the commissioner said.

"I want it *today* if you've got it," Uncle Bill said.

"We're doing the best we can," the commissioner said. "Now that I see this, it's obvious we've got something more than just some misplaced wolf or bear."

"I'm going to ask the sheriff to get a posse out there," the deputy said, pointing to the woods. "Could be anything out there. Could even be a man."

"Christ, you can't tell me a man did *this*," Uncle Bill said, indicating the torn fence. "These weren't wirecutters here. Something just—tore it open!" he added, mimicking the action. "That wasn't no man I shot at."

"It was nighttime, Bill," the deputy said. "It's hard to say."

"I had enough light to see it wasn't a man. Or . . . or anything else I've seen, either."

"I'd like to start along the lines of maybe a rabid dog," the commissioner said, scratching his chin. "Bill," he said, slapping his hand onto Bill's shoulder, "I'm real sorry about this. We'll call you with anything we've got."

"You know we will," the deputy said.

"Yeah," Uncle Bill said, scratching his head. He glanced at Phyllis, then looked away. "Goddamn if this didn't happen to *that* stud. That dam ain't letting an-

other near her. This has really fucked things up," he
said. This swear word above all sounded comical coming from him, but Phyllis would not let herself smile
about it. She decided that she had heard and seen
enough just as the men had reached the same decision.
Still, she let them walk far ahead of her before Uncle
Bill turned around to look at her, then let her catch up.
He took her arm firmly, but not roughly.

"Come on, honey," Uncle Bill said. "You keep close
to us, you hear?"

"I'm sorry, Uncle Bill," she said. "I just wanted to
see, that's all."

"Yeah, well, you just keep off where it's safe," he muttered, then said no more the rest of the way.

Dinner was hardly the lively meal that it usually was.
Roger and Uncle Bill had been working on the fence for
most of the day, leaving Joanie to watch the herds. She
had not had time to create any culinary miracles this
time, but even her "open the can" meals were a treat.

Again, Phyllis slept uneasily, but this was eased somewhat by the lack of any further incidents that night. But
the next day, Phyllis called up the airlines to arrange her
flight home. She could leave the next day, and although
her uncle and step-aunt claimed they would miss her
company greatly, Phyllis was not going to impose on
them any longer. This wild animal incident was more
important to deal with than entertaining some self-pitying
relative. Their problems were about equal now, in Phyllis's eyes.

A slight breeze had started up during the day that had

become a pretty good wind by nightfall. Phyllis could fall asleep by now to any number of crickets, but somebody had neglected to latch the barn door decently. No llamas would be escaping, but the door was going to bang Phyllis's ears and mind into oblivion if something wasn't done.

Uncle Bill and his wife were blessed with a room on the other side, so they probably never heard the door whenever it acted up. Phyllis was quite nervous about going out alone, but she was more reluctant to wake them up just to escort her outside. The stud's death had rudely reminded Phyllis of why she used to be afraid of the dark. Nothing had ever happened to her, which was why her fear had finally died out, but now she was reminded that there really *are* dangers lurking in the darkness.

Of course, that door would never let her sleep otherwise, so she fetched a flashlight and quietly made her way outside. The full moon gave her the advantage of extra light; she almost didn't need the flashlight. Still, she swept the immediate area with the light, then stepped gingerly onto the dirt. Even from there she could hear that door banging away.

Unfortunately, when she arrived at the barn, there didn't seem to be much for her to work with. There were no extra bits of wood lying around with which to jam into the crack, so she decided to start piling as many rocks and as much dirt as possible against the door. It was a dumb idea, but it was all she could think of in the middle of the night.

Shrieks from within the barn toppled Phyllis onto her behind, where she scrambled to her feet in a panic. She covered her ears and dropped the flashlight, so she fumbled for it while trying to shush the beasts.

"Hey, hey, it's me! Shut up! It's not that thing!" she whispered at them harshly, but the shrieks continued. She then decided that the barn door could bang out a solo if it wanted to; she was going back inside, and quickly.

She did not bother wasting time to check the grounds with the flashlight, but ran. Up ahead, some lights were appearing from inside the house. Dealing with Uncle Bill's wrath would be just fine if it meant getting away from that thing, if that was what had alarmed the llamas.

Something grabbed Phyllis and tossed her easily to fifteen feet away. The ground smashed into her ribs and wrist as she rolled along the ground; she felt her shoulder pop. There was no time to lick her wounds before she was flung onto her back and struck several times with what felt like a sharpened sledge hammer. Phyllis tried, but could not open her eyes for fear of seeing what the thing actually looked like. Her ears were filled with a growl and a roar and she felt a breath like a volcano burning her face. She tried to raise her arms to flail away at her attacker, but her wounded shoulder felt as though it had burst into flames. Before she could try kicking, she was pinned down even further by the full weight of the beast clamping down hard onto her remaining shoulder. She felt and heard a soft snap before a loud bang assaulted her ears, followed by many loud snarls, and ending with somebody screaming. Without knowing why, Phyllis felt laughter mix with her tears before the darkness swallowed her.

* * *

She found herself in a bed upon awakening. No one was with her at the time, but she had plenty of tubes and beeping machines to keep her company. The drawn curtains were thin and did little to keep out the sunlight, which served to cheer her somewhat.

Phyllis tried to sit up but was unprepared for the soreness and stinging that came of it. Her heart monitor sped up a little from the effort, until Phyllis gave up and fell back into bed with a groan. After a few moments a curious nurse peeked inside, then entered all the way.

"Goodness," the middle-aged woman said, bustling over to the bed. "It's so good to see you awake, dear. Can you speak? How do you feel?"

"Like shit," Phyllis mumbled. "What is this?"

"What is what?"

"Is this a hospital or something?"

"I'm afraid so, dear," the nurse said, fixing the sheets. "Do you know what day it is?"

Even if she knew, she didn't care.

"No," Phyllis said. The nurse nodded, but did not tell her the date.

"Do you know your name?" she asked.

"Yeah," Phyllis said. She looked away and felt the back of her head, then felt the nurse watching her. "It's Phyllis," she said, a little irritated.

"We have to check, that's all," the nurse said. "How do you feel, though? Are you hurting?"

Phyllis lifted up her arms, which were bandaged. Her face was stiff, so she felt the bandages there, and felt her chest, too.

"Yeah, everywhere," she said. "How did I get here?"

"Well, the ambulance brought you in just three days

ago," the nurse said. "You were badly hurt, dear. They say that something attacked you."

"Um . . . um, I don't know," Phyllis said, feeling the bump on her head. "Where are Joanie and Uncle Bill? My God, are they okay? I was at their ranch. Where are they?"

"Just let me get all your signs for you first, then I'll get the doctor, all right, hon?" the nurse said.

"I want to know if they're okay," Phyllis grumbled while the nurse set to work.

"The doctor will be here to talk to you real soon," was all the nurse said. Phyllis sighed and looked at the curtains. She hadn't been in a hospital in years, but remembered that it had been an awful, frightening place. This one was a little more inviting. It was not so cold as she remembered the first time to be, but that may have been because the windows here were bigger and faced the patients more. The room was obviously clean and scrubbed, but a new paint job wouldn't have hurt anything.

A doctor showed up just as the nurse was finishing the blood-pressure test; she had "buzzed" for him earlier when taking vital signs. He was an approaching-old-age sort of "country" doctor who smiled pleasantly as he went to the bed.

"Wellll," he said quietly, "Phyllis, is it?"

"Yeah."

"How long you been awake now?" he asked, whipping out an eyelight to check her pupils. Phyllis hated those things, but had had enough checkups to know what to do.

"Umm, not long, I guess," she said, letting him shine his toy at her.

"Just a few minutes now, doctor," the nurse said, now writing down the vitals. "She was able to speak right away."

"Good, good," he said, touching each side of Phyllis's face. "Feeling sore, are you?" he asked.

"It hurts to move much," she said. "How'd you know?"

"Well, you came in here needing a lot of patching up," he said. "I'm afraid you needed stitches."

"Oh, God, on my face, too?"

"Afraid so," he said. "Ten there, and on your chest," he said, pulling back the sheets and opening her gown to reveal the bandages. "You needed fifteen here, and twenty there. Then on the arm—"

"Forget it," Phyllis said, trying to close the gown. "I don't want to hear this."

"Sorry," the doctor said. He said a few things to the nurse, who handed the chart to him and left the room. "I'll tell you what, though—"

"Where's my uncle?" she asked. "And Joanie? Something attacked me at their ranch. Are they okay?"

The doctor looked up from the chart a moment, then set it back at the foot of the bed. He scratched his head, then put his hands in his pockets and sighed.

"Uh—" he began, "Miss Turner . . . you and your uncle were brought here a few days ago, and, um . . ."

"And Joanie?"

"His wife?"

"Yeah."

"No," he said. "She was here, but wasn't hurt. You

see, um . . . I think it's best that you get better rested before we talk about the others, but—"

"If you're trying to tell me that he's dead, then tell me now," she said. "The last thing I remember was somebody screaming. I guess it was him I heard, wasn't it?"

"Um . . . I'm afraid so," he said quietly, patting her hand gently. "Your uncle didn't actually make it to here. He was dead when the ambulance got there, and your aunt was—well, not physically hurt, thank God."

"What attacked us?"

"Um . . . I wish I could tell you," he said. "It was gone when we showed up, and your aunt wasn't up to giving a good description."

"Was it an ape dog?" she asked.

"A what?"

"Nothing," she murmured. "Never mind. I couldn't give a good description, either."

"Something attacked you, Miss Turner," he said. "I know it may be hard to think about it, but if you can give us something better, it'll make it easier for people to get the thing."

Phyllis had been trying not to think about it since that night. No matter how calm she seemed or normal her speech was, her mind had been filled with a broken record memory of that horrible growl, the boom of the gun, her uncle's death scream, that horrible crunch at her shoulder—

"A bear," she said.

"A bear? Are you sure?"

"A gorilla, then. I don't know what the hell it was," she said woodenly. "Uncle Bill's dead? It killed him? The same thing that killed his llamas killed him, too?"

"I don't know."

Phyllis tried to hold her face in exasperation, but her wounds prevented this. She pulled her hand away to reveal the beginnings of her tears.

"He was the only one in my whole family that I liked," she whispered. "My whole goddamned family. So why him? He was so—They let me stay with them because my own life is so fucked up back home and now . . ."

Her tears came freely now, making her whole body hurt from the effort. The doctor held her hand until Phyllis pulled it away.

"Where's Joanie?" she sobbed. "Is she here?"

"She's at home, I think," he said. "Getting ready for the services. I think other people in your family are here, too."

"Why?"

"Because of what happened," he said. "I'd think they'd come for the services, and for you."

"Better not be my parents here," she muttered.

"Er . . . actually, your mother and father visited here when you were still unconscious," he said.

"Fuck," she whispered.

"Um . . . I'll tell you what," the doctor said. "If you're not feeling up to it, you don't have to have visitors. I can tell people you need more rest."

"I can see Joanie," she said. "In fact, I *want* to see her. I want to apologize for all of this."

"Ohh, now, I don't think anyone can be blamed for what's happened," the doctor said. *"Especially* not you, no, not at all."

"Nice of you to say that," she said, "but I would like to see her. Can you call her?"

"The nurses should have called by now and let everyone know you're awake," he said. "And you can call them, too, if you want. You've got a phone right there."

"Thanks," she said, trying to wipe off her tears around the bandages. "I guess I should calm down first, then call her."

"Take your time. You need any of us for anything, then you push that button, you hear?" the doctor said, checking her tubes and bottles now. "We've got you on the sugar water and antibiotics, but if you keep up, we'll start you on regular food as soon as possible."

"Yeah. Thanks," she said distantly, and he turned to leave. "Um . . . doctor? Could you open the curtains a little?"

"Hm? Oh, certainly," he said with a smile. It would have been a perfect day if not for the fact that it was being spent in a hospital. Needless to say, Phyllis found it impossible to think pleasant thoughts. Her vacation was no vacation at all; now her favorite uncle was dead, his ranch could be ruined, and she had no insurance or money to pay for her treatment. And it was all her fault, of course.

Eventually Phyllis dried her tears and grabbed the phone. She wanted Joanie to know she was okay, and how sorry she was, but was afraid that the wrong person might answer. Her parents were there for her uncle's funeral, not for her. Phyllis's presence was just an unfortunate coincidence. She dialed the ranch.

A man's voice answered, and it had been so long since hearing it that Phyllis didn't recognize her brother, Richard. His tone betrayed relief, but no real excitement at the news of her recovering health. There was some confusion while he announced her to everyone, and Phyllis's fears were realized. Her mother grabbed the phone first.

"Phyllis?" a cigarette-ruined voice croaked. "Phyllis, are you okay? The hospital just called; we were about to call you back."

"Where's Joanie? Can I talk to her?"

"Well, she's here, but she's pretty busy right now. Did they tell you about Bill?"

"I know what happened to him," Phyllis said. "That's why I want to talk to Joanie. Doesn't she want to talk to me?"

"Can't I talk to you for a little bit?" her mother asked. "You haven't talked to me in so long. You haven't wanted to."

"Same with you, you know. Where's Joanie?"

"Now that isn't true," her mother said. "Do you think I haven't wanted to? No one knew your address, but then I found out you and Bill were writing to each other."

"So?"

"But you couldn't write to me? Phyllis . . ." her mother said, "I wish I knew what it was that I did to you to make you so . . . hateful. What did I do? What *can* I do?"

"I don't want to talk about this, Mother," Phyllis said. "I'm feeling like shit right now and I WANT TO TALK TO JOANIE!"

She heard her mother start something else, then heard the phone being set down and a voice calling out in the distance. A moment later it was picked up again.

"Phyllis?" her sister Jennifer's voice said. "Hi, little sister. How are you doing?"

"What's going on over there?"

"Everybody's here," Jennifer said. "Um . . . you see, Uncle Bill—"

"I know what happened to Uncle Bill. I just want—"

There was some shuffling sounds on the other end, and finally, Joanie spoke. Her voice wavered while speaking, letting Phyllis know that tears could come any time. She felt the same way.

"Hello, Phyllis," Joanie whispered. "We're all so glad that you're okay. Some of us would like to go see you now. Will they let you take visitors?"

"I'm so sorry, Joanie," she said. "I swear to God, I had no idea this would happen. It was the damned door; just a stupid, damned door."

"Easy, easy now, honey," Joanie said. "It wasn't your fault—"

"But I'm the one who went outside!"

"Nobody here blames you for what happened, hon. I don't blame you."

"What the hell did this to us, Joanie?" Phyllis said, her tears coming first. "What was it?"

"It was so hard to see," Joanie said distantly. "He shot at it, but . . ." Then her voice drifted away.

"You two were so wonderful together," Phyllis sobbed. "This shouldn't have happened. You two were the only ones I could even care about."

"Now that isn't true—"

"Yes, it is!"

"Almost the whole family is here right now, honey," Joanie said. "They've all been—very comforting. And not just for me—for you, too. They'd like to go see you, too. You know, both of your parents were there with you yesterday."

"I'm surprised they were together in the same room for any length of time."

"You're their daughter," Joanie said. "Why wouldn't they set aside their differences for you?"

"Joanie," Phyllis said, her tears drying a little, "please come and see me if you want, but I don't want—I don't want Mom or Dad here. Please don't let them come here."

"I—I think this is the best time for you to—"

"Just—! Don't let them come here," Phyllis said. "I'll heal better if I'm not upset all the time, and that's one way to make sure of it."

"I—I'll try, dear," Joanie said after a time. "But, things are pretty hectic around here. I'll do what I can. God bless you, child."

"Thanks."

"Is there anyone else you'd like to talk to?"

"No."

"Are you sure? Your sisters and your brother? Even your cousins, Bill's sons.

"Um . . . thanks, but I'm kinda tired right now," Phyllis said. "Really, I am tired, but I just—I wanted to see how you were doing."

"I'll be . . . okay, in time," Joanie said. "I'll survive. And I'll let you get your rest now. Goodbye, honey."

"Bye."

Seven

Phyllis demanded, and got, a hamburger for dinner that night, then had to send it back when eating it was too painful. The nurses eventually brought her various Jell-Os, soups, and puddings. She had tried walking earlier, but not without assistance. She was halfway through some chocolate pudding when her mother and oldest sister arrived. Phyllis looked up briefly, then resumed eating.

Her mother was not too old, but looked it because of the cigarettes. Phyllis was not surprised to see her dressed in one of her conservative outfits. The shoulder pads always made it look like two anvils were on her shoulders. Very Crawford-esque. Her sister Janice was only slightly less conservative; her shoulders looked like boards, not anvils. Her relatives smiled uneasily, then tiptoed into the room.

"Phyllis?" her mother said. "How are you feeling?"

"Better," she said, spooning another painful bite into her mouth. "They let me walk a little today."

"That's good," her mother said, nodding her head vaguely. "You know, just about everyone is here right now."

"I know," Phyllis said, taking the last spoonful. "Joanie told me."

"Oh, yes, Joanie," her mother said distantly. "She's been holding up very well. The service for Bill will be Saturday. Do you think you'll be out by then?"

"What's today, Thursday?" Phyllis asked. "Even if they won't let me leave, I'll go. I owe that to him."

"Well, you shouldn't go unless you're well enough," her mother said. "You don't want to end up back in here, do you?"

"Like I said, I owe it to him," Phyllis said. "And sick or not, afterward I'm going right home. I've caused them enough trouble."

"You're going back to California?"

"Yeah."

"You're in Los Angeles still, right?" Janice asked.

"Yeah."

"So you're going to leave us your address, right? So we can talk to you again?"

"I don't know," Phyllis murmured. "We'll have to see."

"Phyllis," her mother said, sitting in the visitors' chair, "I understand how upsetting all of this is to you, but—why us? Why do you hate us so much?"

Phyllis shrugged and drank up the rest of her soup.

"It's kinda pointless to tell you anything if you haven't figured it out by now," she said.

"So it's pointless," her mother said. "Tell me anyway. Tell me why you ran away from home, and—"

"I didn't 'run away.' I was eighteen, you know."

"Well, why—?"

"Mother," Phyllis said sternly, "I asked Joanie not to let you visit me. What happened?"

Her mother's mouth hung open a while, but no words came out. Eventually Janice stepped forward.

"What do you mean, you asked her not to let us visit?" she asked haughtily. "How can you say that?"

"Well, I guess I can't be mad at her," Phyllis said, wiping her mouth and hands carefully. "She has enough to worry about right now."

"Who?"

"Joanie, obviously," Phyllis said. "If you two don't mind, I'm pretty tired right now. I hate hospitals. You lie around in bed all day, but you're always tired."

"Why won't you talk to me, Phyllis?" her mother asked. "Talk to *us?*"

"Because I'm tired; I told you that," Phyllis said. "I need to get a nurse to help me get ready for bed, so I guess you two can't stick around."

"Well, we can help you do that," her sister offered. "You don't need a nurse.

"No thanks."

"Phyl, why are you doing this?" Janice snapped. "We're not just here because of Uncle Bill; we're here for you, too! Everyone is!"

"That's nice."

Janice made a noise in frustration, but her speech was not over yet.

"You haven't ever changed, have you?" she said. "You're still being the spoiled little brat who thinks everyone owes her."

Phyllis smirked and pulled her bed sheets up to her chest.

"Would it make you happier to know that I owe more people than owe me?" she asked.

"You know what I'm talking about," her sister said.

"Yeah, well, whatever," Phyllis mumbled, turning onto her side and pulling the bed sheets closer to herself. "Sorry to be such a disappointment to you all. I didn't really mean to be a dancer and not a banker or accountant or whatever the hell business people are."

"Hey, everyone supported your interests," Janice protested. "You make it seem like we were all laughing at you, and you *know* it was never like that."

"Uh huh," Phyllis said, yawning and shutting her eyes. "Not for one second. Anyway, thanks for coming to visit. Ask Joanie if she wants to come, too, when you get back, okay?"

"Phyllis, I'm not going to leave until you talk to me," her mother announced angrily. Phyllis contemplated staying just as she was and trying to fall asleep in front of them, then reconsidered. She turned slowly onto her back and opened her eyes.

"Mother," she said very calmly, "I've told you about ten times that I'm tired and want to go to bed, but I will say this, and then I want you to leave. Both of you. I don't have a steady job. I have barely any money, nobody knows who I am, and I can't even afford to pay for this hospital. Everything you were afraid would happen to me, has. Well, that's too bad. I'd die before working in some high-rise where everybody wears pantyhose and grey suits. I won't be some dickhead's slave who takes other people's phone calls all day. Dancing is what I want to do, and that's it. *You're* the ones who cut me off because you couldn't deal with that."

"Now wait a—"

"You're the ones who didn't want another kid, and god-

damn if you didn't let me know that. Did you think I was stupid because I was a little kid? I knew that I was a pain in the ass to take care of, but why you didn't just give me up for adoption, I'll never know."

"Phyllis!" her mother croaked. "I can't believe you'd— you'd even *think* something like that!"

"Visiting hours are over."

"Do you think I'm going to let you say those things to me without defending myself?"

"Yes," Phyllis said, pushing the nurse's call button.

"You don't mean any of that," her mother said. "You were never unwanted. You were *unexpected,* Phyllis—but *never* unwanted."

"Good night, Mother," Phyllis said, adjusting her bed to flatten out. "Let Joanie know I'm feeling a lot better, and I'll be there for her Saturday. I promise."

A nurse entered the room.

"Phyllis, you're just acting like a child!" her sister said. "You've been saying that all your life, and—"

"Flo," Phyllis said to the nurse, "I want to go to sleep now, but I can't get them to leave. Can you tell them visiting hours are over?"

"You're going to throw us out?" her mother said. "Phyllis! Listen to me for once in your life!"

"Um—um, ma'am?" the nurse said. "Uh—She says—"

"I *know* what she says!" her mother snapped, then shook her head in anger. "Oooo!" she said. "Nothing has changed for you, has it?" she asked her daughter. "Still the poor, suffering one who was never loved, hmm?"

"Ma'am? I'm going to have to—"

"She's been doing this all her life!" her mother said to the nurse. "Ignoring me! She has to have her way, and if not, then she—"

"I DON'T THINK I SHOULD HAVE TO REPEAT MYSELF, MA'AM," the nurse's voice boomed. "You're not helping her get better whether she's 'ignoring' you or not! Visiting hours are over!"

Phyllis had her eyes shut, but smiled and listened to her relatives make huffing and puffing noises before storming from the room. The nurse left with them, then returned to the door.

"I'm sorry about that, honey," she said. "No one else will be allowed to see you tonight; I promise. Would you like your door shut?"

"Yes, thank you," Phyllis said. "Good night."

"Good night."

The doctor did not want to release Phyllis, so she released herself. She was wheeled outside to her brother's waiting car, where she used the cane given to her to edge herself into the passenger seat. The pain was not due to leave until at least a few days, so she bore it out.

One of Joanie's children had made it to Wisconsin, and Uncle Bill's sons also sat beside Joanie in the front row. Phyllis had to settle for the second row. The minister delivered a most eloquent eulogy, helped by the fact that Uncle Bill and his wife were regular churchgoers, and were therefore known to him. Finally, the minister asked Joanie to rise and face the others. It had been her wish to stand up and thank everyone for being there. She asked everyone to bow their heads for a prayer. After this, she called attention to Phyllis and asked everyone to say a prayer for her speedy recovery. Phyllis had already given way to tears long before this, but they started anew as Joanie began to lead the prayer.

Phyllis's mother and sisters, Jennifer and Laura, wisely kept their distance, but her sister Janice did not. Phyllis could shut her out if necessary, and it became necessary after a short time. Her father went to her to offer comfort. For him, she probably had no feelings. No love, but no hatred, either. He had his new wife with him—Phyllis's stepmother—but this was the first time Phyllis had met her. After about a half hour of this, Phyllis rose painfully from her chair and hobbled over to Joanie. She put her hand on her shoulder, and Joanie turned around and made as if to hug her, then reconsidered in deference to Phyllis's wounds.

"Um . . . my plane leaves in three hours," Phyllis said. "I'd better get going."

"You're in no condition for this, dear," Joanie said. "Why don't you postpone the flight and get more rest? Why, your stitches aren't even out."

"I know," Phyllis said, trying to smile. "I . . . I just couldn't stay any longer. I *shouldn't* stay any longer. Look at all that's happened since I got here."

"These things would have happened if you hadn't come here," Joanie said. "Stay, Phyllis. You really should rest."

"Yeah, the doctor didn't want me to leave the hospital until after the funeral. But I wasn't going to miss it for anything. I had to be here."

Joanie kissed her on one of the few unbandaged spots on Phyllis's face.

"I can't force you to stay, dear," she said. "If you think you'd be happier going home now, then do so. Now that I think of it, with all the noise and fuss over here, Los Angeles will be your 'peaceful vacation.' "

Phyllis's smile hurt, but she didn't fight it.

"I'm gonna miss him," she said in a tone only Joanie could hear.

"I will, too," Bill's wife echoed. Then Phyllis kissed her this time and leaned into her ear.

"I love you, Auntie," she said. "And this time, I won't flake out on writing to you. Once a week, at least."

"God bless you, dear," Joanie said, and they parted. Phyllis glanced at the others in the house as she hobbled past them, but few of them approached her to offer her any comfort. Her mother watched her pass by, and took a step forward as if to speak to her, then stopped herself.

She had already called a cab, which arrived ten minutes later. Many were quite surprised an hour or so later to find that she had not gone to bed, but had gone to the airport. And again, only Joanie knew where she lived. Joanie believed in the absolute power of reconciliation, but would not divulge this secret, out of respect to Phyllis, to anyone else in the family. At least, not until she had asked permission from Phyllis first.

It was Roxanne who picked her up from the airport. She was quite surprised at Phyllis's condition, as no one in California had been informed of the incident. After enduring a barrage of questions, Phyllis finally made her point that she was not up to anything until after a good, long sleep. Roxanne was silent the rest of the way home.

Michael had left a message for Phyllis indicating his desire to get together with her after her return. Nobody's calls were returned that night, however, not even his. The next morning Phyllis was sufficiently braced to handle the onslaught of unanswered questions from her roommate. She held back few details and told the worst of it. Roxanne was understandably concerned about exactly what it was that had attacked her roommate. That was still to remain unanswered. However, she had had her rabies and other shots at the hospital, and even an AIDS test. Now Phyllis only needed time to heal her wounds.

"I know this is going to sound kind of—you know, premature—but did Gary ever tell you about Tamara Taylor?" Roxanne asked later that morning.

Phyllis looked up from a fashion magazine.

"Huh?" she said.

"I was wondering if your agent got you into Tamara Taylor's audition? But then, do you think you'll be up to it?"

"That depends," Phyllis said. "She's holding auditions? How come? And *when?"*

"Oh, man, you mean he hasn't called you?" Roxanne said. "Girl, you need a new agent, I'm serious."

"I know that, but what about Tamara?"

"She's going to go on tour, and she needs backup dancers. Could be part of a permanent troupe."

"No shit? When?"

"I'm not sure, but the audition . . ." Roxanne said, suddenly dejected. "It's in only two months. You're going to need that time to heal, not push yourself."

"I'll be the judge of that," Phyllis said, rising from the couch to grab their phone.

"I don't even know if you could get in now," Roxanne called to her. "It might be booked."

That was very likely. Although Phyllis did not own any of Taylor's records, she kept up with the entertainment scene as well as any performing artist would. Tamara Taylor's first album had gone gold in a few months, and the second was well on its way with two singles in the Top Ten. Somebody (Phyllis didn't remember) had once joked about Taylor at an MTV award show, calling her "The White Tornado" as much to describe her stage persona as how she had seemingly "dropped in from nowhere." She had already made the late-night rounds, but until now Phyllis had not heard of any tour. Every dancer in L.A. was probably going to be there.

Phyllis's agent rarely returned her calls when she left messages, but until now she had almost accepted this as normal. Now her patience was not what it used to be. By some miracle, he was in and available. Phyllis avoided any formalities and asked directly if he had been trying to get her in to see Taylor. When he answered "no," she fired him, on the spot. Phyllis hung up the phone very quietly in spite of her inner rage.

"What's the number of your agent?" she asked Roxanne.

Phyllis returned Michael's call that morning, but his answering machine took her message. She was still recuperating in front of the television when he called back at noon. He had wanted to meet her for lunch, but managed to convince her to have dinner with him. She was not up to going anywhere that day or night, but decided to brace herself for the inevitable onslaught of questions and agreed to meet him somewhere.

He pumped her with questions before she even had the chance to sit down. She gave him the basic story, including some of the problems with her relatives, but in time the conversation shifted to more pleasant topics, such as Michael's soap opera and what it was like to work on one. He had a few amusing anecdotes to share, but most of the time Phyllis only smiled or laughed to be polite. Finally she found the opportunity to become serious.

"Mikey," she said, "I know you're real happy about this job, and—I'm thrilled for you, too—but have you thought about my question at all?"

"Um . . . which one?"

"You know which one I mean," she said.

"Oh," he said, "that."

" 'Oh, that?' " she echoed. "Is that what you think about it?"

"No, it isn't that, it's just—okay, no. I haven't been able to think about it. I've been so busy with this, and—"

"I see," she whispered, sipping her water. He sighed loudly and tried to finish his meal. Phyllis caught herself staring at nothing, then set her glass down, and then . . . her growing anger was there, but it was becoming sharper, more focused. She had an outlet for it this time.

"I'll tell you this," she said very calmly. "I'm going to give you one week to make up your mind. So you've got a job that takes up a lot of time. So what. Guys in the military have girlfriends, too, and a lot of those girlfriends become wives."

"I thought you were just talking about living together!"

"I am," she said firmly. "I'm not asking for marriage. But I *am* asking for something more of a commitment after two years."

"So what happens at the end of the week?"

"You say 'yes' or 'no,' and one of them will lose you a girlfriend."

"Are you trying to say that if we don't live together *right now,* you'll just break up with me?"

"I am," she said. "But I'll give you a week to decide that. If that scares the shit out of you—if you think I'm just another broad who only wants to drag you into a marriage, well, feel free to think that. But keep in mind that you'd be crazy to want to lose me."

"I *don't* want to lose you."

"Good," she said. "At least we agree on that."

"What happened over there, Phylly?" he asked. "What did you do in Minnesota?"

"Wisconsin."

"I mean Wisconsin," he said. "Did you just think about this all the time?"

"Not to burst your bubble, but no," she said. "In fact, I only came up with this right now. I went there because nothing was stable in my life, Mikey. I've had it with that. Nothing good happened there, either, so I came back earlier than I expected. That doesn't mean I'm giving up, though. Hell, I'm gonna try even harder now! I'm gonna get these stupid stitches out, and work my ass off to get into *better* shape than before. You hear me?"

"Uh . . . uh, yeah, I do," he said as if waking from a sleep. "I'm . . . glad to hear all that. At least you didn't let this, um . . . attack pull you down. By the way, you sure you don't know what it was?"

"Nope," she said, poking at the remnants of her biscuit. "I don't even care anymore. They pumped me up with every kind of shot there is, anyway."

"But not AIDS," he said. "I-I mean, you really need to watch out for that."

"I don't know about anyone getting it from an animal bite," she said. "I've got a better chance getting it from *you* than from a dog."

"Hey!"

"Well, it's *true*," she said. "But yeah, of course I'm worried about what happened. It was too dark out to see; it all happened too fast . . ."

Phyllis began to drift off into her memories. For the first time she had a fleeting thought of the one instant when her eyes had opened. She remembered a flash of white against the darkness just before her shoulder was nearly crushed, but her face betrayed none of her inner turmoil. Michael watched her for a while, then patted her hand in an attempt to comfort her. She accepted it, but again betrayed no emotions.

Eight

A few days later Phyllis had her stitches out. The doctor told her she was healing quite well, but she was going to have scars. This was not promising for someone who relied on appearance almost as much as talent to find work. To help cheer her up, Phyllis got Roxanne to meet her for lunch during one of Roxanne's jobs. Phyllis had just enough for a steak and ordered one rare. Phyllis went to work at buttering her bread before she noticed that she was being watched.

"What's wrong?" she asked.

"Nothing, I guess," Roxanne said. "I thought you'd given up meat, that's all."

"Oh, that," Phyllis said. "Well, you know that I tried, but—I just gotta have this. I haven't had a steak in so long, and I need my protein."

Her roommate sighed, then threw up her hands in mock exasperation.

"Back to being in the minority," she said.

"I'll try not to eat it in front of you," Phyllis said. A silence followed while Roxanne rubbed the back of her neck and Phyllis ate her bread. She touched her wounds gingerly, which were going to be stiff and sore for a long time.

"Doctor says I'm going to have scars," Phyllis said.

"Oh, no," Roxanne said. "Really? On your face?"

"Everywhere that I had stitches," Phyllis said. "Sucks big time."

"But you'll be able to dance just like before, right?"

"I didn't ask," Phyllis said. "But then I'll have to be able to, right? God only knows."

"The mind is an important part of healing," Roxanne said. "You'd be surprised what miracles a positive outlook can perform."

"Yeah, I know," Phyllis agreed. She shoved the rest of her bread into her mouth, then shrugged. Time was passed with idle chit-chat before their lunches were brought. Phyllis poked at her steak a little before cutting into it. Roxanne glanced at her watch every now and then to make certain she wasn't running late.

"I only have an hour for lunch today," she said. Phyllis only nodded, her mouth full of half-chewed meat. "I'm starved," Roxanne continued. "Wish I could afford to eat a full meal."

Phyllis nodded again, fully understanding the need for easily digested, light meals when on a job. It wouldn't be long before she, too, would be eating light meals all the time. Phyllis's latest encounter with her family had renewed and strengthened her determination to make it on her own.

After the meal Phyllis grumbled that her lunch had been overcooked, even if her roommate could hardly stand to see the cooked blood and juice pouring out of every bite of meat. But it had been good enough for the price. Roxanne advised her roommate to go home and tend to her wounds, but Phyllis insisted upon working out at the club right away. Pain means that wounds are healing, after all; Phyllis must have been doing a lot of healing.

Phyllis had been spending at least an hour looking at herself in the mirror when Roxanne returned home. The doctor had to be lying when he said there would be scars. Not on her face, surely. Only perfect people can dance in close-ups; she *had* to be perfect. The only thing she could do for the time being was wait. And after that, maybe a plastic surgeon.

She had to call Michael herself at the end of the week. After much hesitation, his final answer was "no." Their conversation thereafter became somewhat heated.

"I don't understand why this has to be some ultimatum," he protested. "I'm not saying I want to break up; this just isn't the time!"

"But look how long we've been together already," Phyllis said. "How much longer do we have to be together before you stop being afraid of a commitment? Do you think I *want* to break up?"

"Then don't!"

"It's not that simple, Michael."

"Phyllis . . ." he said. "Honey . . . there's no reason for this. Look, why don't you meet me at the studio during lunch tomorrow, and we can talk about this some more, okay? I don't want to deal with this right now."

"What's there to talk about?" Phyllis asked, her voice threatening to break. Michael sighed from his end of the phone.

"Do you want to talk with me tomorrow or not?" he asked quietly. Phyllis thought for a while.

"I don't think so," she said finally. "I mean . . . no. No, I'm sticking with what I said."

"No compromise at all," he said. "That's it? I say no, so you just dump me?"

"Will you change *your* mind?"

"I wish I could," he said. "I swear to God, I wish I could, but—it's not the right time. Look, if it helps, everyone in my family who's married was—well, every one of them had long engagements. My parents dated for *four years* before getting engaged, and even then, they didn't get married for at least another year. And that was thirty-eight years ago! So you see? Two years is short compared to what I'm used to."

"Everyone in my family makes 'early' commitments, by your standards," Phyllis said. "And even if I don't like any of them, that's still what *I'm* used to. I guess this means your answer is still no."

"I guess it is."

"I'm going to miss you, then," she said. "A lot. Goodbye, Michael."

"Phyllis, why are you being so damned stubborn about this? Why does it have to be *right now* and not—?"

"Goodbye," she repeated, and hung up the phone quietly. She waited at the counter a while before slinking over to the couch and falling into it. A flick of a button brought the idiot box to life, but Phyllis had no idea what it was showing her. After a long time she came to some of her senses again.

"I'm off the phone!" she yelled back to Roxanne's room. Roxanne opened the door to peek out.

"What?" she said.

"I'm off the phone," Phyllis said in a dead tone.

"Oh, that's okay," her roommate said. "I've been cleaning up in here. Wanna see it when I'm done?"

Phyllis shrugged.

"If you want," she said. Roxanne waited at the door in case her roommate had more to say, then stepped out into the hallway.

"Not good news, huh?" she said.

"Not really," Phyllis said, flipping the channels around absent-mindedly. Roxanne stared at the television a few moments before walking to the side of the couch.

"Anything I can do?" she offered.

"Not really," Phyllis said. "I can't see him any more, that's all."

"Oh, no," Roxanne said. "Really? He really doesn't want to be with you anymore?"

"Oh, he said he did, but . . ." Phyllis began, but her voice trailed off. Roxanne glanced at the television, then stepped around the couch to sit beside her friend. Phyllis removed pillows and magazines to give her more room. Roxanne sat silently, waiting and watching.

"I'm okay," Phyllis said, then looked at her with a forced smile. "Really."

Roxanne smiled back and put a hand on her shoulder.

"I mean, I'm the one who broke up with *him*," Phyllis said. *"I'm* the one who has to commit now and not—not—"

Roxanne scooted closer to Phyllis to put her whole arm around her now.

"I know," she whispered. "I know. Everyone has their own schedule that's right for them. Unfortunately, it's usually that men's schedules are about three times longer than women's, so women end up waiting, and waiting . . ."

"You're probably lucky, then," Phyllis grumbled. "You and Linda probably agree on everything."

"Um . . . well, not everything," Roxanne said, rolling her eyes. "But . . . it really is over, huh?"

"Yeah."

For a long time the only sound in the room came from the television, until Roxanne leaned over to kiss her roommate on the cheek.

"What's that for?" Phyllis asked.

"Just friendship," Roxanne said. "Just to let you know that you can talk to me if you want to."

Phyllis looked at her for a long time, and tried to smile, but her lips became tight just before her eyes opened up into a flood of tears. She sank into Roxanne's arms and worked at staining her T-shirt, but this hardly bothered Roxanne.

"You can cry on me, too, if you want to," she whispered.

Nine

Phyllis kept her promise to Joanie, and wrote to her often. So far she had only gotten one response back, but this was understandable. According to Joanie, she had no plans to hire another hand for the ranch, so she and Roger did all the work themselves now. Phyllis had written to ask about her hospital bill, but Joanie insisted that she not worry about it. Phyllis did, anyway, but at the moment she was unable to pay back her aunt. The rest of the letter described how helpful everyone had been to her, even Phyllis's least-loved relatives. There was nothing left for anyone to do now but deal with their pain and losses as best they could.

No pain, no gain. Part of the pain came from Phyllis's rapidly dwindling bank account. Fortunately her bosses at the health club and the restaurant were willing to keep her jobs available while she healed. Roxanne indicated that she would have enough to cover the rent, but only for a month. Asking Michael for help was, of course, out of the question, but all of this would be defeating her purpose. Phyllis was going to make it alone, and make it big, injuries, scars, or otherwise. She could feel it, and *really* feel it this time, and not just tell herself that she could.

The healing process had allowed her to realize things like that about herself. Giving lip service to something often convinces one of its truth, which was what had happened to Phyllis. She had always been cocky, not confident, but things were going to be different now. They had to be.

Phyllis had never been one to wake up screaming from a bad dream. This was still the case, but her continual dreams of the attack left her feeling ill-at-ease, to say the least. Even the bad dreams were part of the healing process, she surmised. Even they would go away, in time. They had to.

After two weeks she forced herself to start teaching her beginning dancercize classes for little more than gas money, and continued her "therapy" at the club after hours. She started with a five minute workout at full effort, then ten minutes two days later, then fifteen, then twenty, and so on up to her usual one hour, full effort workout. Her wounds demanded much protein for the healing process, much to Roxanne's dismay, but to hell with her "veggie" ways. Phyllis had already broken her beefless diet back in Wisconsin.

Maybe pushing herself so hard was bad for the healing. Phyllis made her living with her body, so why endanger it? Still, the pain was going away, and pain meant that she was healing, so she must have been doing all right.

It was a month after the attack that Phyllis was working on a one-hour workout at full effort. The Tamara Taylor tryout would be a big break, not just for her, but for everyone. No one else had been almost ripped apart by a wild animal, but no one was supposed to know that she had almost been, either. No dancer ever got a job by making others feel sorry for her.

It would be a new record for her, even when she was at peak condition. She was already up to an hour and could have tried for another half hour. No, not even an hour and a half. Tonight, she felt good enough to make two.

She hit the first hour and felt "the burn" start in her legs. Good, she thought, and began to pace herself more. The burn leveled off at a point, and the music seemed to get louder, but it usually did that when her concentration increased. Phyllis jogged around the room and passed the open window to glance outside. As usual, the lights were off, but the night sky was bright tonight from the city lights and, she noted, from the moon.

Phyllis passed the window over and over during her jog, not stopping until her legs began to burn more. She jogged in place by the window, but this didn't seem to help the burn. She took in deeper breaths to help, but the pain only got worse. No pain, no gain, she thought to herself and kept on, trying to ignore the burn that worked its way up her legs and into her hips now. She wiped away the sweat from her brow and jogged briefly over to the thermostat, which registered a cool nighttime temperature. She pulled off her wrist warmers without stopping and felt her pulse, which was rising.

This can't be enough, she thought to herself, then felt her neck. She slowed her jog to a walk, but the burn would not leave. It had gone past her hips into her torso now. Phyllis tore off her sweatband and threw it across the room, then felt her pulse again. It was supposed to

go down now, but something was wrong. She felt he
brow again, which was wet with new sweat, and felt th
burn reaching her shoulders. She stopped the workou
entirely now, working at her breathing to slow down tha
pulse. Her hands shook, and now real fear filled he
thoughts, but that, too, had to be controlled. She ha
pushed herself too much. If she could just get home . .

Phyllis rushed to her bag, and almost passed the win
dow on the way, then stopped and looked out. There'
nothing there, she thought. Just the city, get moving! Th
moonlight was bright as the sun to her, and she held u
her arm to shield her eyes, then cried out in pain. Sh
grabbed her shirt and all but tore it straight off her body
then bent over to work on the leotards. The burning dou
bled in intensity, and she fell to the floor, holding he
gut as if afraid it would burst open.

"I'm healed!" she yelled to no one. "Don't do this t
me! I'm better! I'm better!" She began to convulse, bu
she was in too much pain to scream as her body bega
doing things that it wasn't supposed to do. She tried t
roll onto her belly to crawl across the floor, but saw he
arm throbbing and pulsing, then stretching. Other thing
happened to her body, but Phyllis could do nothing abou
any of it, especially not while her mind itself was bein
assaulted. A flood of old thoughts and new, strange one
smashed through her defenses.

Phyllis's scream of physical and mental pain graduall
became a howl.

After escaping from the stone caves, she leapt as fa
and as high as she could, and easily cleared one of th

many metal behemoths lying about. She landed and rolled through several somersaults, because it felt good to do so. She looked about, and listened, and smelled, and used every sense she had in ways she never dreamed they could be used. Everything was so sharp and clear now. She could hear the rushing of water beneath the ground where she had never heard it before, and smelled every last thing in the air. This she did not like as much. This air had too many things in it; how could anyone stand it? Perhaps hoping that the air was only bad where she was, she raced off toward more of those square, stone caves.

There were so many living things to choose from in this great, petrified forest that she decided not to take any of them down yet. This was a great, new, wonderful place for her. She could spend all night just exploring it and never eat anything. Besides, there were so many two-legged things around that there would be no challenge to any hunting. There would be no satisfaction unless she could find a place with many obstacles but hardly any two-legged animals.

None of the two-leggers could see her yet, or they pretended not to. She slipped in and out of shadows as she sought out more familiar territory. Everything around was already somehow familiar, but not in the way she wished. The two-legged beasts chattered loudly amongst themselves, which began to grate on her nerves. She could silence some, but not all of them, so she chose to seek higher ground, instead.

One good leap, followed by rapid climbing, brought her to the top of a tall cave. She sensed no other life, then ran to the edge of the cave and looked down. Tiny

two-leggers scurried by obliviously. Ignoring them now,
she scanned the area but was not high enough to see
everything. Far off, though, she spotted some real trees
and real bushes, so she leapt across this cave to land on
another. She leapt and climbed onto some others, but
grew weary of this. Stealth was unnecessary; she could
outrun any two-legged beast, so she scrambled down the
last cave to land on the ground. A lot of two-leggers saw
her now, but a good growl and snarl was enough to make
them give her a wide berth. A strange, powerful odor
came to her now, and she laughed inwardly after realizing
that it was fear.

She ran past them all and dodged moving metal behemoths that screamed and blared at her as she raced by.
Some of them hit each other in their efforts to leave her
be. Clumsy beasts, those round-legged things. None of
those could catch her, either. One of those might prove
to be a difficult kill, though, so she kept that in mind.
The other beasts scattered like deer around her. Some of
the beasts did not get out of her way; tonight, she shoved
them away as opposed to killing them.

The fun was wearing off quickly. There was too much
noise and too many clumsy beasts in this place. She concentrated her efforts on ripping through this mass of bodies and ignoring the chaos until she could reach the tiny
forest ahead. She rushed out in front of more of the metal
beasts, but one of them did not stop. She did not stop,
either, but tensed for a split-second, then leapt high and
far to clear the beast, which then smashed into another
one. More screams and cries. This was almost too much.
Was nothing quiet about this place? The consolation was
that the forest was here now, so she wasted no time in

losing herself in the bushes. The sounds of chaos continued as before, only a little fainter. Her pulse raced like a triphammer, but there was no time to rest before she had started up the steep hill.

There were not nearly enough trees, so she had to make do with the bushes. At one point she turned around to see some of the chaos below. Other metal things that howled and had colorful lights raced through the crowds. There was too much happening below to understand any of it, so she turned her back on it quickly and continued on. Sometimes the hill leveled off into that hard, black dirt that covered most of the ground, only to become a hill again when she kept going. Her goal was to reach the top and survey all the land around her before beginning any real hunting.

After a long time, she reached some huge, flat, white things that stuck straight up from the ground and almost vanished into the night sky. There was still a way to go before reaching the top, but she decided to climb these white things instead. They were held in place by many metal rods, so it was a simple matter to reach the top of one of the things and look at the tiny lights below her. It was a challenge to balance herself, but she managed to keep steady enough to look up at the moon. It was so round and shiny and bright that she heard it calling to her, so she called back again and again. As long as the moon called to her, she answered it, until it told her to find sustenance. She scrambled down her white perch and brought all her senses to bear. There was nothing warm nearby; the hunt had to go on elsewhere. The other side of the hill had to be better than this one, so she went on.

There were lights far off to one side. A closer inspection revealed another cave, but only one this time. Attempts had been made to hide it, which made it more fun to find. Two-leggers lived in the caves, she was certain. Now to see what kind lived in this one. There was a metal fence all around, and after running around it long enough, she grew impatient and grabbed part of it and pulled it open. It was easy to break, like thread. She took a step inside, then heard the loud barking of two approaching beasts. They were a four-legged kind that reminded her of herself, but they were a threat, so she tore out their throats the moment they got too close. They died quickly and with only a quiet whimper. This had not been much of a hunt, but she considered for a moment, then decided to feed on at least one of the beasts.

She had tasted blood before, but never this fresh. Then she heard chattering off toward the cave. It was still far and did not seem to get louder, so she finished with the one beast and left the other one intact. The meat was tough and stringy. Her ears pricked up at the sounds of approaching footsteps. She looked about quickly, then leapt into some bushes and waited. The footsteps grew louder, then stopped; the silence was broken by two two-leggers chattering to themselves. One of them screamed, then screamed again. After some silence, the footsteps came again, but grew fainter as the two-leggers wandered away. They didn't even reach the other beasts. They were not good hunters, then, but she wanted to test their mettle some more. She leapt from the bushes and raced after the two-leggers to leap up and over them just as they whirled around to see her. She spun around to face them and snarled and howled. They both screamed and froze in terror. Their smell of fear was strong enough to rival the earlier crowd's.

She snarled again and took a step forward in challenge. The two-leggers only screamed again, then ran. To her they were just barely hobbling, so she leapt up and over them again. The male yelled and fell over backward, and his mate fell to his side, where they both clung to each other and screamed. Now weary of this, she made a fist and brought it down over their heads to quiet them. They did, and fell over onto the ground silently. No challenge at all. She bent over to sniff at them. The spark of life remained in them yet, but she neither knew nor cared if it would remain long. The other beasts had been little sustenance, but perhaps these two-leggers would be better.

She set herself down to sniff at them more, and took one of the male's arms into her claws. Her mouth watered in anticipation of tasting fresher blood, and she brought the arm up to her mouth, then hesitated. She looked at the arm, then brought it to her mouth again, and paused. She looked at the beasts again. They lay side by side as though asleep, but they were not asleep. She sniffed at them again. They had distinctive scents, but there was something similar about them, too, as though they had been mates long enough to exchange their scents. These two-legged ones belonged to each other, somehow. If she tasted one, she would have to taste the other, too, for neither would be whole without the other. She could sense this; she knew this.

The moon was not calling to her, but she called to it in hopes that it would answer. The world around her made sounds, but the moon was silent. She looked at her claws and remembered very briefly—that they sometimes looked different. Or that they only sometimes looked like they did now. She was naked, but not naked. Not naked the way the hairless two-leggers would be if they took off their colorful skins. For some reason a brief image appeared of herself in a colorful skin, but that quickly disappeared from memory. She could never have been one of those two-legged things. She could walk on her hind legs, but she was not one of them, nor could she have ever been one of them. Yes?

The mated ones she could leave alive. But if any two-legger attacked her, she would not sit idly by and take it. This did not seem likely, as the two-leggers were so weak and cowardly. They were like little sheep or cows who couldn't protect themselves unless their four-legged beasts were nearby. She set off for the hills again. It was never very far for her to go before finding another lighted cave. It was becoming something of a bore; was there nothing else that lived here but two-legged screamers and yapping beasts? Perhaps, and perhaps not. This was a huge place that demanded much exploration.

Ten

Phyllis woke up feeling very cold. Her wild and violent dreams from that night left her feeling even more tired. She yawned and tried to stretch, but hit something hard behind her. After opening her eyes, she decided that she was still dreaming, and hit the white board behind her just to be certain. Now her knuckles hurt, and she wasn't any warmer.

It took a long time for any coherent questions to form in her mind, least of all the answers. Basic questions, such as Why am I naked? Where the hell am I? and How the hell did I get outside where all this grass is? No one and nothing offered any answers for her. Somehow, she was not in bed in her apartment, but had spent the night sleeping in the grass on a hill next to some big white board sticking out of the ground, and she was almost completely naked. There were still some shredded remains of her old sweatsuit and legwarmers, but nothing to cover her top.

Hoping to find at least a hint of an answer, Phyllis stepped out from behind the board to find herself near the top of a hill, overlooking what she could only guess to be Hollywood. If so, she must have been on one of the hills, but why? Phyllis sat down long enough to pull off the remains of her legwarmers to cover her top, then stepped slowly away from the board to go around it. There was a long line of huge, white boards standing high, high above her. She went past all of this to step timidly down the hill just far enough to see what she had been sleeping against. She looked up and up to see the giant "Y" that had served as her bedboard for the night. Beside this were two giant "L's and a "W" and a—

"What the *hell* am I doing here?" she said aloud to herself. She had wanted to see the "HOLLYWOOD" sign up close for years now, but not like this. She was supposed to get drunk with a bunch of friends and climb up here and maybe draw pictures on it or something, not wake up half-naked underneath it.

"My dream," she murmured, then remembered the rest in silence. She had climbed this thing during the dream and yelled in triumph or something. During the dream? Her whole body was filthy. She thought her hands were just dirty, too, until she looked at them more closely, and gasped. This was not dirt; it was dried blood. Phyllis wanted so much to believe that it was hers, but she felt no pain to indicate any wounds. There was something else to the dream—something about attacking an animal.

Phyllis was too cold and hungry to stay there. It was a long and treacherous way down that hill. Clutching her rags tight to her bosom, she climbed down and ran off toward her apartment building, now that she had a landmark to take directions from. Her one big hope was that it was still very early yet, and few people would be awake and outdoors. The sun appeared to be just above the horizon, so perhaps she would be lucky.

* * *

Every dog that she had the misfortune to pass sounded its vocal alarm. At one point she had half of a block barking at her, but there was nothing to do except run. Her apartment was in Hollywood, but it wasn't *that* close to the sign. The club was much closer, but it was also on a major street and was not likely to be devoid of onlookers. Phyllis had always been disgusted with the existence of weirdos such as flashers and streakers, and yet here she was doing her best imitation of them. She was hungry, cold, tired, and thirsty, but a growing terror kept her going at full speed for much longer than she had thought possible.

Tunnel vision had developed during her run. She had heard a police siren, but paid no attention to it and kept running. Then it sounded again, and made her all but jump out of her rags. She stopped long enough to glance over her shoulder to spot the black-and-white that had been following her. It was foolish to think that it was just passing by. Phyllis curled herself up tight and waited for the car to stop, and two officers emerged, trying in vain to conceal their amusement. Both of them adopted their habitual "towering" posture over her, which was not difficult, as Phyllis was not that tall.

"Hi," she said quickly, and smiled before bending over a little more.

"Kinda cold out this morning to be dressed like that, wouldn't you say?" one of the officers said.

"Yeah," Phyllis said quickly, her teeth chattering a little. She stepped from side to side to keep herself moving and thus, warmer. "Yeah, it is cold. Listen, um—"

"Mind telling us what's the occasion?" the other officer said.

"Um . . . um . . . I wish I knew," Phyllis said. "I'm—
I don't remember how I got this way. Uh—d-do you think
you guys could give me a ride home? I-I'm pretty close
by. I was on my way home, you see."

"Home from a party, huh?" the first one asked, pulling
out his pad and looking her up and down. "Must have
been something."

"I-I don't know what happened," Phyllis said, shivering. "Look, I know it's against the law to be naked and
all, but—I'm trying to cover myself up. Couldn't you
just take me home? Please? I just want to get home. I
don't know what happened . . . I don't know . . ."

The second officer seemed more sympathetic to her
situation than his partner. He leaned over to whisper
something to him, who nodded and went quickly to the
car. The second officer took Phyllis's shoulder firmly,
but gently.

"This way please, ma'am," he said. "We're going to
get you a blanket."

"Oh, thank you," she said. "Thank you, really. I-I
woke up on—I don't know what happened. I had these
weird dreams last night. Or maybe they weren't. Has that
ever happened to you? Where something seemed like a
dream, but turned out to be real?"

"Yes, ma'am," the officer said. "More than you might
think." He led her to his partner, who had produced a
thick blanket from the trunk. His partner shut the trunk,
then went to the front seat to grab the radio. He spoke
in code to headquarters while the second officer opened
the back door for Phyllis. She sat inside quickly, then
had the feeling that she might have made a mistake. It
was illegal to run around naked, so were they taking her

home or arresting her? She tried to comprehend the conversation on the radio, but again, it was mostly in code. Police had their own language, too, after all.

Neither officer said any more to her until they both sat in the front seats again. The second officer turned his head a little toward her.

"You say you had some bad dreams, huh?" he asked.

"Um . . . well, they were weird ones," she said.

"Do you remember what happened to your clothes?"

She looked at the rags that covered her, then shook her head.

"I think they were torn off of me," she said. "I don't remember what happened."

"Ma'am . . ." the second officer began, "we can take you home if it's what you want. But if something happened to you last night . . ."

"No," she said quickly. "That is . . . what you think happened, didn't. I mean, the thing that this looks like—with my clothes torn and all, I mean—it isn't what happened. I'm okay. Really, I'm okay. I want to go home."

"We're going to have to have directions, then," the first officer said.

"Oh. Oh, yeah," Phyllis said, and gave them her address.

Phyllis had some difficulty convincing them that she had not been drinking or shooting up, nor could she remember any violence having been committed against her. The ride back was thankfully short, and the officers escorted her to her apartment door, which was locked. Phyllis considered pounding on the door as opposed to simply tapping, but decided to avoid doing anything that might appear suspicious.

After some time Phyllis saw the peephole darken momentarily, then heard bolts being undone. Roxanne opened the door and stood there sleepily. She cocked an eyebrow at her disheveled roommate, who pushed past her immediately to head for her room, leaving Roxanne to stare at the two officers.

"Sorry to disturb you, ma'am. May we come in a moment?" the second one said. Roxanne seemed to wake up for the first time, and widened her eyes, then looked back at the door to Phyllis's room.

"Um . . ." she said, "um, yeah. Okay." She stepped aside to allow the officers inside.

"We're sorry to wake you, ma'am," the first one said. "Does this woman live here?"

"Who? Her?" Roxanne asked, nodding her head toward the room. "Phyllis! What—! Um, yeah, she lives here. We're roommates. What happened to you? Phyllis?"

Phyllis bustled from her room, now dressed in a robe. She went to her roommate and hugged her tightly.

"Thank God you're here," she whispered. "Um," she said to the officers, "thanks so much for taking me home. I'm okay now."

"Ma'am . . . did something happen to you?" the second officer asked. "Were you attacked by someone?"

"No," she said. "Um . . . I know it looks like . . . somebody did something to me, but—really, I'm okay. Thank you so much for taking me home."

"No problem."

"Are you sure about this, ma'am?"

"Yeah, I'm sure," Phyllis said. "Really, I'm okay."

The officers hovered about for a moment before begrudgingly accepting her word. They turned to leave, only the second officer stayed long enough to quietly ask her to call the station if she had anything to say. Phyllis thanked them both again and shut the door behind them.

"What is this?" Roxanne asked. "Were you arrested? Where were you last night?"

"It's okay now," Phyllis said. "Really, I'm okay."

"Why did cops have to take you home, then?"

"I didn't have any clothes on, that's why. Um . . . sorry about waking you, but—"

"What time is it?"

"I dunno," Phyllis said. "Five-thirty or something."

"Is it? God, I should have been up by now, anyway," Roxanne said. "You did me a favor. But . . . was I still sleeping, or did you show up without any clothes on?"

"That's what I just told you."

"Huh? Oh," Roxanne said, rubbing her face. "Oh, yeah. Will you tell me *why* you showed up with no clothes on, then?"

"You have to get ready, don't you? Um . . . jeez, come to think of it, I have to get ready, too."

"For what?"

"Work," Phyllis said. "I have breakfast and lunch shifts, remember?"

"Well—yeah, but—"

"I know how weird this all looks, but—I don't think I can talk about this right now. It's all too weird, even for me."

"But—"

"After work, okay?" Phyllis said, holding Roxanne by the shoulders and shaking her gently. "Okay?"

Roxanne's expression was blank all the while, and blank still when she spoke.

"Yeah," she said. "After work."

Roxanne was not up early to go to work, but to go jogging. In spite of the nigh-unbreathable air of Los Angeles, she still believed in exercising in it as often as possible. Phyllis stayed behind to get ready for work at the restaurant. She turned on the shower and shut the door, then let her robe fall to the floor. Out of habit she peered at her reflection to check for defects; thanks to the attack, she had had some to examine for some time. Until now. Phyllis blinked, then leaned closer to the mirror. She turned her face from side to side, then sucked her cheeks in.

Her doctor had told her that she would have scars. No matter how much they healed, they would be smaller, but would never disappear completely. Phyllis was hardly disappointed to find her doctor wrong, but was surprised, nevertheless. She checked again and again, but could find no trace of her scars anywhere. A smile of stunned, but genuine, joy crept across her face as she looked down enough to see that the rest of her was just as blemish-free. Or at least, it was as smooth as it had been before the attack. Phyllis caught herself giggling as she felt all over her body in disbelief, but now she couldn't be dreaming. Her scars were history.

Phyllis rushed from the bathroom before remembering that her roommate was gone, then went back inside to examine herself yet again. Still peeking occasionally at the mirror, she dragged herself into the shower. After the shower she resumed examining herself in happy disbelief, then put on her robe again and returned to her bedroom to find real clothes for the day. It was going to be a fantastic day now; that is, if the person now phoning her did not have bad news.

It was the health club's owner, and she was not her usual perky self.

"Were you at the club last night?" she asked.

"Um, yeah," Phyllis answered. "Oh . . . I left the door open when I left, didn't I? Oh, God, I'm—"

"Then that was your stuff we found?" Chris, the owner, asked.

"What stuff?"

"What happened here last night?" Chris asked. "Are you okay?"

"Am I okay?"

"Phyllis, somebody broke in last night," Chris said. "There was glass everywhere when we opened up, and a door was smashed to pieces. And you were here last night? Somebody's backpack was found, and I think this is your stuff. And your car is here. How did you get home?"

"My car?" Phyllis said. "Are you sure it's *my* car?"

"Believe me, I know your car," Chris said. "How did you get home?"

"Uh . . . uh, it's a long story."

"How soon can you get here?" Chris asked. "The police are here; they wanna talk to you."

"The cops? Why are cops there?"

"I called them about the break-in, why else?" Chris said.

"But why do they wanna talk to me?"

"Phyllis, please," Chris said. "Can you come to the club this morning? I told them that it looked like your stuff here, and that your car was here. No one's saying you did anything."

"But . . . um . . . I have to go to the restaurant this morning," Phyllis said. "To work, I mean. Is this going to take a long time?"

"I don't know," Chris said. "They just said they need to ask a few questions. How soon can you get here?"

"I dunno," Phyllis said. "Uhhhh, a half hour? Shit! No car. God, I don't know, Chris. Walking there might be faster than taking a bus, the way this place—"

"Just get here," Chris said, and hung up. Phyllis hung up much more slowly. Chris wasn't angry with her, specifically, but she wasn't in a pleasant mood, either. There was still a phone call to make to the restaurant. The manager was flexible this time, and allowed her to switch to the lunch-dinner shift for the day. Phyllis then threw on her shoes and gulped down a big chunk of meat before returning it to the fridge.

Phyllis had to take a bus for the first time in years and arrived an hour and a half after the phone call. Chris had been right; she found her car still parked at the club. Confused, Phyllis peeked inside and found nothing missing. She couldn't remember why it would still be here, but she had no memory of actually driving it home, either. The real challenge now was to find the keys to the thing.

Some clean-up people were just finishing sweeping the last of the shattered windows when Phyllis arrived at the front. She peeked inside before stepping all the way in. There were at least two things she noticed right away. One was that the police had departed, and two was that it was business as usual. If there had been a crowd of Peeping Toms, they had long ago dispersed and gone back to their usual workout regimens.

Chris soon appeared from a doorway, wringing her hands. It took her a moment to notice Phyllis approaching her. She smiled briefly in greeting and gestured towards an old duffel bag.

"That's your stuff, right?" she asked. Phyllis knelt down to open it and pull out a few things. She nodded her head.

"Um . . . yeah," she said, slinging the bag over her shoulder.

"Did you see the door?" Chris asked.

"No way I could've missed that," Phyllis said. "What happened to it?"

"That's one of the things the cops were having trouble trying to figure out," Chris said. "By the way, they want you to go to their station and make a statement."

"A statement? About what?"

"Anything that you saw or heard last night," Chris said. "As a witness. Like I said, no one's . . . Come on," she said, putting a hand on Phyllis's shoulder. "We'll go to my office."

Together they made their way past the glistening, sweaty bodies of patrons who were oblivious to anything else but themselves. Phyllis wondered if they would have come to their workouts even if the place had been completely destroyed. Some of them probably would have, but then, Phyllis understood this sort of dedication. She might have done the same thing herself. After a time they reached Chris's office and entered. Chris shut the door behind her and gestured for Phyllis to sit down. She waited for Phyllis to settle in before falling into her own swivel seat and letting out a long, loud sigh.

"Ahhhh, what a morning," Chris groaned. "And to think I woke up in a good mood for the first time in weeks."

"I'm sorry, Chris," Phyllis said. "Seriously, I didn't do . . . whatever happened here."

"I believe you," Chris said.

"Thank God," Phyllis sighed. "I mean, do the cops think I did? Do they think I smashed up the door?"

"I don't know what they think," Chris said. "Except, they did point out something weird before we started cleaning up."

"What?"

"They said that most of the glass was outside the building instead of inside," Chris said. "And it was."

"Which means?"

"Which means that they think that someone broke *out* of here, not in."

"And they think it's me."

"Phyl, no one's accusing you of anything," Chris said. "But you have to look at things their way a minute. And mine. You were here last night, right?"

"Well . . . yeah . . ."

"Working out?"

"Yeah . . ." Phyllis said cautiously. "But you know that I do that."

"Then, did you see anything? Hear anything?"

"Like . . . what?"

"You tell me," Chris said. "Anything. Footsteps, voices, anything like that."

Phyllis was silent in contemplation a moment before frowning and shaking her head.

"I don't know, Chris," she said. "I mean, I had the music on; I had the lights off. But that's the way I always work out."

"I didn't know you worked out with the lights off."

"It forces me to use my other senses besides seeing," Phyllis explained.

"Well, how do you keep from banging into the walls or tripping?"

"I know the room," Phyllis said. "Besides, it's not pitch black. Light comes from outside, usually. And last night was . . ." she said, but then drifted off. Chris was patient for only a moment.

"Was what?" Chris prompted.

"Hnh? Oh, um . . . last night was . . . wasn't real dark," Phyllis finished. "It was a full moon, wasn't it?"

"I don't know," Chris said. "Um, Phyl, I don't want to take too long with this. The cops were here, and there were crowds, and—"

"Just what is it you want from me, then?"

"I just want to know what you saw or heard last night, that's all," Chris said. "Anything. I don't care if it was the air conditioning; what happened here?"

Phyllis had had some time to work out what she was going to say. Telling the truth was ruled out immediately, because, in essence, there was no truth to tell. She couldn't tell her boss about some murky dream about running naked through the streets and climbing the hills of Hollywood. She could tell no one the truth until she had some idea herself of what it was.

"First of all, I didn't do it," Phyllis announced. "I know everything looks like I did, but I didn't."

"I believe you."

"Thank you," Phyllis said. "But the other thing is that I didn't hear anything. Or see anything, either. I—this was the first time since my accident that I've really been able to dance, and . . . and I tend to lose myself in my workouts. I made it to an hour, Chris! I wouldn't stop until I made it!"

"Are you sure you should be doing that?"

"I can't afford *not* to do this. Not anymore. My roommate can't pay for both our rent, and I gotta get work again."

"Well," Chris said, "well, good luck to you. And I mean that. But are you sure about this? About not seeing anything?"

"Seriously," Phyllis said. "I did my workout, and I was going to go straight home, but I kind of got . . . well, psyched up. I couldn't calm dawn, so I ended up taking a walk, and I guess I left my bag behind."

"Well, what's the deal? You never came back to get your car?"

"That's . . ." Phyllis said, shifting in her seat, "that's kind of embarrassing. You see, um . . . I ran into some old friends of mine while walking, and they asked me to go with them to this party, and . . . well, I kind of drank too much, and . . . either that, or someone spiked the stuff, because I was out. I woke up . . . woke up *somewhere,* so I ended up walking home. I completely forgot about my car. I know this makes me look like a complete idiot and a lush, but—"

"No, it's nothing like that," Chris said. "Whatever you do after work is whatever you do. I can believe your story, Phyl. But you better not be lying about something."

"But I'm not," she protested. "What do you think I'm lying about?"

Before speaking, Chris bent down to open a drawer in her desk.

" 'Lying' is probably the wrong word," she said, shutting the drawer and bringing up a handful of shredded rags. "I'm just wondering if you might be covering up something, that's all."

"What's all that?" Phyllis asked, picking at the rags.

"I found this by your bag," Chris said. "This is—well, *was*—a warm-up suit, right?"

Phyllis held up a piece to inspect it. She whistled once, then set it down and nodded her head. "I don't know, I guess so," she said. "This was by my stuff?"

"Yes."

Phyllis whistled again, then leaned back in her seat and shook her head. "I can't even tell what it was, let alone if it was mine," she said. "Maybe . . . maybe whoever broke out last night, tore this all up or something."

"Phyllis," Chris said, leaning back herself and locking her fingers together, "Please tell me, did somebody try to hurt you?"

Phyllis stared at her employer before looking away.

"Of course not," she muttered.

"You sure?"

"Of course I'm sure," she insisted. "Even a doctor could tell you that no one hurt me last night."

"What about tried to?"

"That didn't happen, either."

"Sorry. Um . . . insurance will deal with the damages, and we'll fix the door and . . . get better security, too, I suppose. I'll have to do something else, too."

"Hopefully not what I think," Phyllis said.

"I can't let you use the club after hours anymore," Chris said.

"So much for wishful thinking," Phyllis mumbled.

"You understand why, don't you?"

"Um, yeah," Phyllis said, reaching into her pocket to pull out her keys. She worked at removing the club key while speaking.

"I'm sorry, Phyllis," Chris said.

"No, it's okay," Phyllis said. "Really, it is. I know I was—well, that you were being especially nice to me. Um . . ." she said, removing the key now and handing it to Chris, "I . . . hope this doesn't mean something else, too."

"What's that?" Chris asked, dropping the key into an envelope.

"Well, that I'm . . . not allowed to teach anymore, either," Phyllis mumbled.

"You mean that you're fired?" Chris asked. "Of course not; there's no reason for that. You're a good teacher, Phyllis. We were all very worried about you when you were hurt, and we're even happier that you can work for us again."

"Thanks," Phyllis said, shifting uncomfortably. "By the way, thanks again for the great cards. And the flowers. You didn't have to, you know."

"That's all right," Chris said, holding up her hand.

"I'm just glad that you *can* still teach for us and . . . well, that nothing happened to you last night, either. That's part of why I took the key back. I started thinking, what if you *hadn't* left here in time last night? No, I *can't* think of that . . . I'm sorry, Phyllis."

"You're apologizing to *me?*"

"This whole business has about fried my brain," Chris said. "What time is it?" She glanced at her watch. "My God, is it only nine?" she said. "Maybe I should take a lunch, anyway. Ohhhhh . . ."

Chris shut her eyes and let herself sink into her chair. After some silence, Phyllis rose from her seat and went over to Chris. She put her hand on Chris's shoulder, and Chris opened her eyes as Phyllis dropped to one knee and made to wrap her arms around her. Chris accepted the hug but made certain that it was brief.

"Well," Chris said to Phyllis, "I guess this is as settled as it's going to be today. Oh, hell. There's still the insurance to call. Um, Phyllis? Thank you for coming."

"No problem."

"If the truth be told, I called you here to make sure that you really were okay," Chris said.

"Oh, that's sweet," Phyllis said.

"Yes, well," Chris said, turning pink, "thank you again for coming. I still have so much to do though, so, uh . . ."

Phyllis's eyes lit up.

"Oh!" she said. "Right. I thought you were going to lunch, though."

"I have too much to do, and now that my brain is working again . . ." Chris grumbled. She was still muttering to herself as Phyllis shut the door quietly. Phyllis leaned against the door and let out her breath quickly

before pushing through a crowd of employees. Most of
them tried to stop her for more interrogation, but she
deflected their questions with the near-skill of a celebrity.
Another saving grace was that her car keys were still
inside the duffel bag. She could escape on wheels instead
of by foot.

Phyllis contemplated going to the police station, but
she was in too much danger of being late to the restaurant. In fact, she made it there with one minute to spare,
and buried herself in work the rest of the day.

Eleven

It was late, and Roxanne was elsewhere, but she had left the morning paper on the breakfast table. As usual, only the front page and entertainment section had been touched. Phyllis read the entertainment and funnies sections religiously, and touched nothing else, but this time, she spotted a small article in the local news section. The headline read "PILEUP BLAMED ON BEAST." Phyllis snatched up the page and read with charged interest. According to the story, witnesses blamed a wild animal for plowing through a crowded section of Hollywood, scaring dozens of people half to death and causing a major car pile-up. Amazingly enough, no one said if the animal had directly attacked anyone, nor were there any fatalities from the accidents. One person described the animal as a "big ape-guy, like a Bigfoot or something." Another disagreed, insisting that it had been "the Big, Bad Wolf."

Phyllis stared at the article until its words became gibberish to her. She tossed the paper and overshot the counter, but she did not care to go over and retrieve the paper from the floor. She'd gotten away with an awful lot of lies throughout the entire morning, but what was she to do? As far as Phyllis was concerned, everything that had happened had been a marvelous dream until all those facts started popping up. She knew she couldn't have smashed a heavy wooden door, but she couldn't prove to herself that she hadn't, either.

Phyllis tried to piece together her soupy memories of last night, but made little progress. She couldn't get farther than working out at the club before waking up in the Hollywood Hills. Everything else in between was murky at best.

She caught herself staring into space, then snapped to attention and decided to get out of the apartment. She grabbed a coat from the closet and was almost out the door, then remembered to at least leave a note behind for Roxanne. Most likely Roxanne was with Linda, meaning that it was even money that she could be home that night or not at all.

Night had come, and the moon would reach its peak no more than an hour from then. Phyllis felt a wave of warmth come over her, but it passed as she climbed into her car and gunned the motor. Almost instinctively she twisted her rear-view mirror to inspect her face, but not necessarily to look for normal blemishes.

She used to walk along the beach a lot when she first arrived in Los Angeles, but that had been a long time ago, or so it seemed. Perhaps this was what had caused her to drive here now. A difference was that she used to come here to relax and escape her troubles, but now it was just to escape. Escape what? Even Phyllis could not explain the sense of panic that pushed her on. She knew that there was such a thing as a panic attack, where one is assaulted with an abrupt, intense feeling of terror for no reason, but until now, she had been immune to this phenomenon. The terror was not helped by the lack of parking spaces. She was ready to smash a few cars out of the way and make her own before a legitimate one was finally located.

She raced along the boardwalk for a little bit before heading for the pier. This would be anything but a crowded night, she hoped, and continued her rush for the pier. Everything in between was closed or closing, but shopping was not her concern. Other pedestrians minded their own business until, at the edge, there seemed to be no others about.

She almost ran over the edge of the pier entirely, but stopped herself in time. She gripped the rails and leaned over to watch the water lapping against the pylons. She caught herself hyperventilating, and shut her eyes before forcing herself to slow down and catch her breath. This so-called panic attack was meaningless. There was no reason to have something like this; why was it starting now?

After several long minutes Phyllis had succeeded in forcing herself to breathe slowly and deeply. She straightened herself up and zipped up her coat. There had been no reason for this; there had been no reason to be afraid. Afraid of what? The dark? Not anymore. It was probably unwise to be alone where she was, but this did not concern Phyllis for the moment.

Now that the "attack" was over, Phyllis stuck her hands in her pockets and kicked at some dirt while shuffling aimlessly. Perhaps it was good to be outside and alone for once in order to get in some good thinking. It wasn't easy keeping her thoughts focused on one subject for very long.

She tried to think about Michael, but those thoughts were interrupted when she glanced up at the full moon, and those thoughts flashed over to Aunt Joanie, followed by her "interview" at the club that morning, and the moon was full, and she remembered her workout from the night before—the moon had been full, then, too—and she remembered feeling "the burn" while working out. Phyllis had been pulling at her shirt a while before realizing that the heat was real. She wasn't working out now, but "the burn" was there.

Phyllis tried to make herself turn around, but she could only back away from the moon's light, and tripped over some unseen obstacle. She flipped over onto all fours and found herself unable to stand or even crawl away. The "burn" was getting worse. She was remembering more through the pain. There had been pain the night before. There had been heat, and the awful soul-wrenching nausea that was now making her collapse and curl into a tight ball.

Phyllis wanted to cry out, but could only whimper softly while her body began stretching and compressing itself simultaneously. So much of herself was changing so greatly and so rapidly that she gave up wondering what exactly was doing what. She ripped off her sweat-soaked shirt and was starting on her pants, when the real pain hit. Her shoes burst open from her feet stretching to at least twice their length. Now she was free to scream, but almost split her tongue with her unusually long and sharp teeth.

Phyllis howled in pain.

Twelve

This sand stuff was great fun to run upon. It was soft and cushioned well, and kicked up high into the air at each leap. Water licked endlessly at the shore and reflected the night sun so wonderfully bright. This was much better than the hills and trees from the night before, even if there were few places to hide here.

If she could have reached out and taken the moon's light from the water into her hand, she would have, but for now she would have to be content just following it along the water's edge. A few miles of this passed before she realized that catching the dancing light was impossible. She had always been aware of the two-leggers wandering about away from the water. They didn't seem to be aware of her, however, so she found great sport in sprinting into their small groups just as she had before.

Some saw her approach but appeared to be dumbfounded, and stayed rooted to the spot. Others saw and tried to run away, while still others suspected nothing until she was upon them. The ones who would not move were sent flying as she pushed past them. There were so few two-leggers in sight or smell in this place. She would eat, but not just yet. These two-leggers would never show her any good hunting, unless perhaps they were more of a challenge when alone. She would never find out if she stayed where there were so many. Still, if her hunger grew too great, she might take one down just for its flesh.

She stopped at one of the openings that showed her more of the two-leggers' abodes. There were more two-leggers who came near her, but not too near. There were more of those metal creatures from the night before, and plenty of concrete caves. Little seemed to have changed here, save for the water and sand behind her. Those would do for now. She turned quickly and went back to the sand, and ran. If it led to the green hills again, so much the better. If not, then it was sure to turn up equally interesting encounters.

A great roar and gentle shaking of the ground sent Phyllis sitting bolt upright. She almost cried out, then quieted down some at the sight of the receding waters. The ocean was still a good fifty feet away. Phyllis stayed where she was while taking in her surroundings. There was the ocean, of course, and the beach that she lay upon, but not one that she recognized right away. She couldn't remember if this was Santa Monica or Venice. It had been a long time for both.

A chill breeze attacked her body, and Phyllis shivered and tried to wrap her clothes tightly about herself, but there were no clothes. There were some remnants of her sweatpants and leg warmers, but nothing else. She had fallen asleep somewhere as equally strange as the Hollywood sign.

As soon as possible, Phyllis tore off her leg warmers and tried to cover her upper body with them. There were houses in sight here, but some distance away. Phyllis stood up slowly and heard a jangle from what remained of her pants pockets. A quick feel revealed that her car keys were still with her, and her wallet. She breathed a very great sigh of relief.

Hunched over, Phyllis trotted along the beach close to the road. The sun was about an hour past sunrise, so some people would be awake by now. If they weren't, they would be once she got to the door. She knew that people in cities didn't care; they refused to get involved and help people in trouble. They were going to help somebody now, she decided.

Phyllis ran up to the first house in sight. She wasn't familiar with these sorts of houses. These houses were more secluded: built on stilts and with fences or gates all over. In fact, there was a lot of climbing to be done before she could get anywhere near the house at all. She got as far as a locked gate but was in little condition to break through it or climb over it, so she rattled and shook it with all her might. This got the attention of two noisy Dobermans who were thankfully still inside. They woofed and barked and carried on until an angry figure appeared at a bay window.

Phyllis waved to the person to come outside, and he opened the glass door, but only enough to let the dogs out. They bolted for the gate, and Phyllis tensed, but they were safely cut off from her. She waved some more and jumped up and down and called out to the man. He ignored her and went back into the house. In frustration she grabbed the gate and shook it wildly. The dogs jumped up and almost caught one of her fingers. Phyllis flashed one of those fingers to the man inside, then stomped back down the stairs.

The next house did not seem so fortresslike, so she snuck along the side in order to get to the highway front. Houses on the beach had no "back" side; there was an ocean front, and a highway front, but never a back. This house also required some climbing, but she reached the highway and scampered toward the front door. The front gate, that is. There was a buzzer by the gate, so Phyllis pressed this. Again, her doubts rose about this place being Santa Monica or Venice. But that was where she had parked her car, so what—?

"Yes?" a voice squawked from the intercom. Phyllis had been caught unawares, and jumped and looked about frantically.

"Yes?" the voice said impatiently. Phyllis poked one of the buttons cautiously.

"Um . . ." she said, "um, hello? Um . . ."

"Who is this?" the voice said. A man's voice.

"I'm—I-I need help," Phyllis shouted, then cleared her throat. "Um—I-I need a phone. It's very important."

"A phone?" the man said. "Who is this?"

"Please . . ." Phyllis said. "I don't know where I am and—I need to get to a phone."

"Did your car break down?"

"No," she said. "Or . . . I don't think so. I've been—I've been attacked," she added finally.

"What?"

"I was attacked," she yelled. "Somebody attacked me last night. I don't know who it was. I woke up on the beach and—I don't have any clothes on and—"

"Did you say you don't have any clothes on?"

"Please, um, um, sir," Phyllis said. "All I need is to use your phone, and call my roommate. I swear to you that somebody attacked me last night. I swear."

There was a long silence from the intercom. Phyllis thought of ringing the bell again, but the silence was broken.

"Wait there a minute," the man said.

"Thank you," Phyllis shouted into the intercom, as people who are not used to such things often did. She shuffled back and forth in place and looked behind herself to see if anyone else was around. Like last morning, she was cold, hungry, alone, and somewhere very unfamiliar.

She was almost naked, just like last morning.

And she also had blood on her hands and arms, just like last morning.

The gate was unlocked, then opened a crack. A man's face peeked out. Phyllis stepped back and tried to cover herself more, and the gate was opened all the way now. The man widened his eyes at the sight of her.

"Oh my God," she heard him mumble. "You weren't kidding," he said.

"I'm not," she mumbled. "Do you think . . . do you think I can use your phone?"

"Hm? Oh, oh, yes, yes," he said, gesturing her inside. She followed his lead cautiously. The man looked familiar to her; in the back of her mind Phyllis suspected that he might be a movie actor, but she wasted no energy on trying to remember who.

He ushered her inside the gate quickly and shut it behind them. He had a nice front yard with many hanging plants and a little fish pond. She followed him through the front door and mumbled mostly unintelligible an-

swers to his questions about her condition. Eventually
they reached the kitchen, where he gestured to his wall
phone.

"Thank you," Phyllis mumbled as she grabbed the
handset. The man left the room momentarily. Phyllis began punching numbers, then stopped at the sight of the
dried blood on her hands and arms. She set the phone
down quickly and busied herself washing them off in the
sink. It took a bit of scrubbing, but she quickly got the
stuff off of her. It didn't matter whose or what's it was;
that stuff had to go.

Phyllis grabbed the phone again and redialed. Four
rings later the call was answered by a string of girlish
giggles.

"Roxanne!" Phyllis shouted over the din. "Rox—!
Come on, it's—!"

"(Giggle giggle) Hiiiii!" Roxanne's voice said. "(Giggle) we've got a—"

"Come on, this is serious! Stop—!"

"—machine, yayyy, yayyy!!" the voice continued. "So
please leave a mess—"

"Oh, Jesus," Phyllis mumbled to herself. They'd both
wanted—*needed*—an answering machine for months.
Now that they had one, it was already a pain in the ass.

"Roxanne, for Godssake, pick up the phone if you're
there!" Phyllis said once the beep had ended. "Roxanne,
it's me! Please pick up the phone! You have to be there!
Pick up the phone!"

After a few more words to that effect, Phyllis hung
up the phone in frustration just as her good Samaritan
was bringing in a big beach towel. She thanked him and
wrapped it around herself tightly.

"I can't believe she's not home," Phyllis said.

"Who?"

"My roommate. She gets up early, but wouldn't—ah, shit," she said. "I forgot that she's trying to jog in the mornings. Hmmm. Either that, or worried sick about me. Do you think she went to the police?"

"Uh . . . I . . ." the man said, shrugging. "But, if somebody attacked you, shouldn't *you* call the police?"

"I don't know if I do want to," Phyllis said. "I know that sounds weird, but—there's so much I don't remember. They'll want to talk to me for hours and hours, and I just want to get home."

"Where is home?"

"Hollywood. Just off—"

"Hollywood?" the man said. "Do you know where you are right now?"

"Um, no," she said. "It looks familiar, but I can't remember where—"

"Whoever attacked you took you all the way to Malibu."

"This is Malibu?"

"Malibu *Beach*," he clarified. "You're a ways from home, miss. I think you'd better call the police."

Phyllis was silent long enough to take in this new revelation, and to consider his words. After a moment, she nodded slowly and picked up the phone again. 911 got her a dispatcher who agreed to send someone right away.

"I wondered why it looked kinda familiar," Phyllis said to herself after hanging up. She looked up at her benefactor. "I'm really sorry for bothering you like this," she said. "It's just that—I don't know what's going on.

I swear I was at the pier last night. Santa Monica Pier, that is, and—and then—"

"Try not to think about it," the man said.

"I just want to go home."

"But the more you can tell the police, the better their chances of catching this—the bastard who did this to you," the man said. "Don't you want him to be caught?"

"Yeah," Phyllis whispered. "I'm sorry for bugging you like this."

"It's all right; really," he said. "Thank God I didn't have to work today, or I wouldn't even have been here."

"What do you do?"

"I'm an actor," he said.

"Ohh, I thought you looked familiar," she said, nodding her head but saying nothing more of this. Phyllis had learned long ago of the unwritten rule that "Los Angelinos" are not supposed to react wildly around celebrities. Not everyone followed this rule, but Phyllis always did her best. Nonetheless, the actor seemed somewhat fazed that she made no more of an issue about him.

By the time the police arrived, the actor had scrounged up some ill-fitting clothes for her. The police stayed long enough to get a brief statement from him, then tried to take Phyllis to the station. Once in the squad car, however, she refused to be taken anywhere but to her car in Santa Monica. Her escorts were hardly pleased by this turn of events, but they could not force her to press charges against someone. Normally Phyllis would be thrilled to help put some creep away, except that she could not shake the doubt that there was any "creep."

One of the officers tried to make conversation with her, but Phyllis needed this time for reflection. Her dream had been so similar to the one she had had before, yet once again, this could not be a dream. She vaguely remembered hitting something or someone, then ripping into it with her bare hands. Did she eat it/him/her? The taste of blood was there, but her mouth was clean.

By the time they reached her car, she was no closer to the truth than before. The car also had a ticket on the windshield. One of the officers assured her that she wouldn't have to pay the fine, and rattled off a list of instructions on how to successfully clear it. Phyllis nodded her head often, but would never have passed an instant quiz. She mumbled some thank yous to them and listened to their parting advice, most of which involved coming forward and describing her experience. Because she would not consent to be examined, either, there would be no medical evidence if a suspect were ever found. She was only making things harder for herself, she was told.

Again, Phyllis thanked them and watched them slowly drive away.

It was difficult for Phyllis to believe that two days could be so much trouble. She was already sick of reassuring Roxanne that she really was okay, and never mind why she was getting police escorts all of a sudden. She was also tired of Roxanne's continual apologies for not having been home; what was done, was done, and everyone was okay now. Unfortunately, Phyllis wasn't okay, but how to explain this when she didn't know where to begin?

The new answering machine (a gift from Linda) already yielded messages from Linda, a lot of hang-ups, Roxanne's (and now Phyllis's) agent, and a very agitated Phyllis. She had erased that message long ago. The agent "had something" for both of them the following week. Roxanne had already returned that call and gotten the details. After the morning's chaos, Phyllis announced her plan to sleep all day, until she remembered having another early shift at the restaurant. Roxanne begged her to call in sick, but Phyllis waved her off and grumbled her way through her morning preparations.

Few words were exchanged in spite of Roxanne's better attempts at prying information from her roommate. Again, Phyllis promised her a long talk after work, then opened the fridge to force down some leftover meat patties before rushing off to work.

Roxanne let out a loud sigh after the door shut behind her roommate. She looked down into the sink and stared blankly at the now-empty pan where the meat patties had been. She flipped on the faucet and watched the leftover juice and fat spill out and down the drain. So much for "converting" her friend to a more humanitarian diet. Lately she seemed to be eating more meat, and cooking it less. For all Roxanne knew, this latest batch may not have been cooked at all.

Upon catching herself at starting to think like her mother, Roxanne quickly shut off the water and stashed the pan away into the dishwasher. She had her own job to go to, so enough dawdling.

Thirteen

"I thought we were going to talk once you got home," Roxanne said.

"I never said 'once I got home,' I said 'after work,' " Phyllis replied. "There's a difference."

"Well, it's 'after work' for both of us," Roxanne said. "We don't get to be alone that often these days, and—" She stopped abruptly, then paced the room briefly.

"If you don't want to talk to me, fine," she finished. "I just thought you wanted to."

"You wanted me to," Phyllis said. "I know that I should say at least something, considering what's been happening, but—I don't even know what's been happening."

Roxanne sat down next to her friend. Her voice became soft and concerned.

"It's okay," she said. "Really, it is. I mean, if it's something that's been happening with you and Michael—"

"Him? Why do you think that?"

"I-I don't know, I'm just guessing," Roxanne said. "But—cops had to take you home one morning, and you were out all last night—Forgive me if I'm just a little bit concerned."

Phyllis stopped rubbing her forehead and straightened

up on the couch. She scratched the back of her head as if in thought, and in fact, tried to start speaking several times. Finally she slumped back again and folded her arms.

"Cops took me home this morning, too," she said.

"Whaaaat?"

"They took me to my car, actually," Phyllis clarified. "See, for the last few days—God, I don't even know where to start all this. Maybe I should start with the bizarre dreams."

"Okay, start there," Roxanne offered.

"I would, except—I'm not even sure if they *are* dreams. See—I've been 'dreaming' about—I don't know, like—Have you ever had dreams where it's like you're in a movie, but at the same time you're watching it, too?"

Roxanne shivered. "Rrrr, yeah, kind of, I guess."

"Like you're a different person, or a character, I mean, but you're still yourself? It's like that's been happening to me."

"Now, these are . . . these are the dreams you're talking about?" Roxanne asked, confused. Phyllis sat up and held Roxanne's arm gently. A light seemed to turn on in her eyes as she spoke further.

"Yeah, only I wonder just how real they might be," she said in an excited whisper. "I've been dreaming that I'm . . . that I'm bigger, and stronger than I am now. And I've been running. All night long I'll be running, and jumping, and climbing and running some more."

"Sounds exhausting!"

"But it isn't!" Phyllis insisted. "The whole time I'm doing this, it feels really good, you know? And I'm totally, totally free. I just run and do whatever I want, and people run away from me 'cause they're scared shitless."

"Why would they be scared?"

" 'Cause I'm so big!" Phyllis said, opening her arms as if to indicate. "In these weird dreams, I'm not me at all, but I am! Does that make any sense?"

"Yes, but—but how does this explain—?"

"But the reason I can't figure out if these are dreams or not is, is I keep waking up in bizarre places. The first night I woke up under the Hollywood sign with almost no clothes on, and then this morning I was at Malibu!"

"Malibu? Are you trying to say that you're sleepwalking all the way to Malibu? Noo, noo, I don't—"

"Sleeprunning is more like it," Phyllis said.

"I can't believe that. How did you get there? You drove, right?"

"I told you, cops had to drive me to my car this morning. I had to tell some guy that I'd been attacked before he let me into his house to use the phone. Oh—that's what that message was this morning. Why did Linda get us a machine? What do we owe her?"

"Don't change the subject," Roxanne warned. "You told someone that you were attacked? Is that what happened?"

"Nooo, nooo," Phyllis assured. "I just couldn't think of anything else to say. Everyone there lives in a goddamned castle, with moats and—what? Quit looking at me like that."

"Like what?"

"Like . . . look, I wasn't attacked," Phyllis said. "You're looking at me like you think I was lying about that."

"I don't know what to think," Roxanne said quietly.

Phyllis smiled awkwardly and rubbed the back of her neck.

"I know," she said. "None of this makes sense."

"Well, no, it's not that, it's just . . ."

"Nah, it doesn't make any sense," Phyllis said, waving it off. "I still need to figure this all out myself first. I should go somewhere quiet tonight. It's not such a big deal, really."

"Wait, you said you're leaving again?" Roxanne said. "Where? But every time you leave, you . . . you . . ."

"I'm just gonna go to a motel, Rox. It's going to be okay."

"Why won't you stay here? The same thing'll happen as before if you keep leaving. Phyl . . . please don't go anywhere tonight. Stay here; *I'll* be here. We can talk about this and—"

"I can't stay here," Phyllis said, rising from the sofa.

"But why not?"

"I just can't!" Phyllis snapped, then quickly calmed herself. "I'm sorry. I mean . . . it's going to be dark soon. I just can't be here tonight, okay?"

Roxanne sat in silence for a few moments as Phyllis disappeared into her bedroom to begin packing. Then she stood up quickly to follow her roommate to the doorway.

"Phyl—"

"I already know the answer," Phyllis interrupted, "but have you ever tried meditation?"

"Yeah, I have," Roxanne said. "Uh—why are you asking about that?"

"What's it like?"

"I thought you've done it before."

"I haven't."

"Oh," Roxanne said, "I could've sworn you have."

"What's it like?"

"Ummm . . ." Roxanne said, straightening up. "It depends on what you're trying to do. To be honest, I haven't really meditated in a while. No time, unfortunately. Usually I'd . . . relax with it, but mostly to focus myself. My thoughts and feelings."

"Have you ever done anything like . . . slow down your heart, or stop breathing or anything like that?"

"Ummmm . . . I don't know," Roxanne said. "I mean, yeah, that happens when you're relaxed enough, anyway. You want to slow down your heartrate?"

"S—s—s—something like that," Phyllis said. "I just wanted to know if you've tried to control your body while meditating. Mind over matter. That kind of thing."

"Oh." Both women were silent for a time. Roxanne watched blankly as Phyllis finished shoving clothes into her knapsack.

"I don't want you to leave tonight," Roxanne said finally.

"Staying here tonight would be even worse," Phyllis said. She gently pushed past her roommate. "Trust me. I'm not sure why, but I just know this."

"Why?" Roxanne said, ignoring that last comment. "Of course staying here tonight wouldn't be 'worse.' It's Michael, isn't it?"

"No, I already said it wasn't about him," Phyllis said. "I'm just going to go to some . . . motel or something. Maybe I'll even camp out somewhere."

"Here? No way, that's too dangerous. Not by yourself, and not in L.A."

"I'm going to be okay," Phyllis said. "Jesus, I need a friend, not a mother."

"I'm not—!"

"The longer I stick around here, the worse it's going to be, so please!" Phyllis said in frustration. "I swear that I'll be back tomorrow morning, okay? Okay?"

"Yeah," Roxanne said quietly. "Fine, whatever. Go on, whatever it is you're doing. You going to have cops take you home again, or will you get here by yourself?"

Phyllis thought of a response, but it was getting late, and she didn't want to leave angry. She glared at Roxanne briefly, however, then mumbled a goodbye and a promise to return. If Phyllis was willing to discuss her new problem with anyone, it was Roxanne, but she couldn't bring herself to tell her much of anything—not until she knew herself what there was to tell.

Fourteen

Phyllis had a vague idea of where some mountains and canyons were. Those would be the closest things to uninhabited areas in Los Angeles on such short notice. She had only mentioned a motel to Roxanne in order to stave off any further argument or delay. Fortunately Roxanne had not had the time to force Phyllis to call the apartment once she had reached whatever she was trying to reach.

Phyllis's original plan had been to stay locked up tight in her bedroom for the night and try to work through this whole mess. Or not work through it; ideally, ignoring it would make it go away. Then her mind flashed its memories of that smashed-up door at the club, the bizarre dreams that always ended with her waking up half-naked in some remote, almost-godforsaken place. If something was happening to her that made her strong enough to smash down doors, staying at the apartment would do no good. And what of her roommate? No, no one was safe who would be near her. Even so, she should have been heading for the shrink, not the mountains. Unfortunately the shrinks would charge a lot of money before they would tell her that she was crazy; she would probably find this out for free at the mountains.

Having left in the early evening, Phyllis expected the usual traffic, which was bumper-to-bumper. The bulk of it had resulted from rubberneckers catching a glimpse of someone being given a ticket. Such sights were so uncommon on southern California's freeways, after all.

She took the off-ramp that would eventually lead her to Griffith Park. It was the best place that she could think of on such short notice. With more time, she might have gone as far as San Bernadino, but this would have to do. But would it be large enough? It took her a good half hour to wind her way through twisting back roads. She had no idea if there were any official campgrounds at the park, so anywhere smack in the middle would have to suffice.

She pulled her jalopy off of one of those roads and began driving through and dodging trees and large brush. Any nearby police would have been pleased; what fun it was to haul in reckless drivers! Sunset was nigh, but it was already dark because of the trees. She parked amidst the tallest and thickest of them, flicked on her flashlight, and set to work setting up her essentials.

She was supposed to be afraid now. After all, this business went against everything that she had been raised to believe: don't be anywhere alone at night. Stay in the car. Murder statistics. Rape statistics. Wild animals. Don't be anywhere alone at night. . . .

She was not afraid. When the sun went down, others would need to fear *her*. She couldn't be sure whose or what's blood had been on her hands two mornings in a row, but she was sure that it wasn't hers. A "big, hairy ape-guy" was on the loose. It ran through the streets of Hollywood and tossed people left and right. It tore attack dogs to shreds. It tore some other things to shreds, too. Phyllis was not afraid tonight, except for those who might come near her after she blacked out. *If* she blacked out. What if she didn't tonight?

Phyllis finished arranging her gear. Her car's back seats had been pushed down to make a decent-sized sleeping area. She had a sleeping bag spread out, some food, drink, magazines, flashlight, kitchen knife (just in case) and her Walkman, of course. She sat cross-legged in the back seat and pulled out the magazines to flip through. Not that she was reading any of them, but it was comforting to pretend to. She did read the generic horoscopes that promised new and exciting things, especially regarding marital status. Sometimes she amused herself by reading every other word of several different horoscopes at once, usually finding that they made just as much sense that way.

Bored, she flipped on the Walkman and opened a bag of chips and a diet drink. It was officially dark now. The sun had finished setting, and there was no light save the beam of her flashlight. The trees did a fine job of blocking out even the city lights. She did not finish the chips or drink, but set them beside her as she lay down flat onto the sleeping bag and shut her eyes.

Her only plan of action that night was to try something repulsively "L.A."—meditation. Clear her mind of all thoughts and feelings, and perhaps the madness and bad dreams would leave her just this one night. Perhaps she would wake up whole and alive, lying flat on her back in her car with nothing on her hands. She pictured herself sitting cross-legged on the beach, the waves lapping at her toes occasionally, their sound keeping time to her breath. She pictured herself taking in deep breaths of the salt air, and she opened her eyes, but only in her mind, and looked out along the horizon. It was night in her mind as well. She pictured herself following a reflection in the water, following it up to its source, which was the moon, bright and round as her flashlight beam.

This was supposed to be soothing and relaxing. This was supposed to be meditation, yet even this mental image of the moon made her shiver. She found herself unable to look away, nor could she open her eyes for real. She felt herself shaking, followed by sweat. The car was too stuffy; it was too hot, she couldn't breathe. She pushed her bedding away from herself and tugged at her shirt.

Clear your mind, clear your thoughts, she chanted to herself. Listen to the ocean; it's soothing. It's cool, it keeps you cool! The ocean breeze—it'll keep you cool! Stop sweating! Calm, cool, clear your thoughts, clear your—

"Miiiiiiind!!" she shrieked, her eyes shooting open. She sat upright and banged her head against the car's roof. The bump wasn't painful; this heat was painful. She tore off her shirt and tangled up the Walkman's wires along with it. With a yell she ripped those away and smashed them against the window.

From outside, passersby, if any, might have thought that two people were inside the car and were giving in to nature, but would not have thought it was only one woman trying to fight against it. In a last ditch attempt, Phyllis forced herself to take slow, deep breaths and to clear her thoughts. She breathed erratically as before, then a little more slowly, a little more rhythmically. Was it working? It seemed to; the heat was leaving, a little. The shivering calmed itself some. Her mind *was* emptying itself of thought. She kept up the slow, rhythmic breathing, and dared to open her eyes. The darkness was as thick as ever. She could not see herself, but brought her hands together to feel them.

Phyllis the woman was allowed one shout before Phyllis the woman went to sleep until morning. It may have been for the best. Her hands and arms no longer resembled Phyllis the woman's, anyway.

The woman's arms were never as long, lean, strong, and hairy as they were now.

Phyllis had only eaten rabbit once before, and remembered that she had thought it was extra-small chicken until someone had told her otherwise. It would never have occurred to her that she would remember the smell of a rabbit, but this was what she woke up to on this bright, shiny, and warm morning. She kept her eyes shut for a long time, for various reasons, after regaining consciousness. One was that she was comfortable. The air was warm and clean; she could feel the sun poking its way through treetops to caress her cheeks. The ground was noisy, but soft. She ran her arms up and down slowly, listening to the leaves crinkle and snap, as though making a snow angel in the middle of summer.

Another reason was that she was afraid of what she would find. More blood? More torn-up clothes? A body, and human this time? She opened her eyes and shielded them from the sun while she turned over. There was blood on her hands, right on schedule. She ran an arm across her mouth. Now her arm was bloody. Leaves had stuck themselves to her body where the red glue had smeared. Some of it had dried; some of it hadn't. She picked them off and was by now not surprised to find tatters where her clothes used to be. This was why she had put spare clothes in the car.

Her car—! It could be anywhere in this nigh-desolate place. Where had she ended up this time? Was she still in the park, or had she run all the way to Sacramento? Something caught her eye just then. Phyllis found herself staring at a pile of dead animals, mostly squirrels and one rabbit, before looking away in disgust. She stood up and hoped to run from this mess, but almost smacked her knees against a car's bumper. A car bumper? *Her* car bumper. She had transportation away from this place, and without any miles-long hikes or lifts from helpful authority figures.

Then it *had* been rabbits that she'd dreamed about. She could still taste their juicy, but stringy meat, especially since some of it was still in her mouth. She wiped the other arm on her mouth, and now that arm was bloody, too. Brushing the last of the leaves from herself, she went to the car's side mirror and checked out the blood, scratches, and small bruise on her cheek. That was from . . . from something hitting her. She remembered now. She had hit her face against a tree branch while in hot pursuit of one of her meals. She had been chasing a "four-legger." That's what it was. That's how she perceived them. And people—they were "two-leggers."

She remembered much more from this night than from the other two nights, yet she still had no memory of hurting, or worse, killing anyone. If it could only stay that way while she sorted out just what had brought about this insanity. She had no desire to be a news statistic—to be the girl who had been "so quiet . . . until she started killing everybody, of course."

Phyllis popped the hatchback of the car open and climbed in after her duffel bag. It was foolish of her to stand outside with barely even rags covering her body. Murders and rapes took place in the daytime, too, but her madness only came at night. She grabbed her bottle of water and drank half of it, then poured the rest onto a washcloth and wiped it all over her body. The washcloth was pink when she finished, but only a shower could finish the job. She squirmed into her clothes, crawled over into the front seat, yanked out her purse from under the seat, fished out the keys, and had just barely gunned the motor before shifting into gear and peeling out from her parking spot to speed for a road.

Fifteen

Phyllis forgot to have her keys ready before reaching the door. She wiggled the doorknob silently, then dug around in her purse after it proved to be locked. The door flew open, startling her, and there stood a much paler version of her roommate. Roxanne held the door open in silence and glared accusingly.

"Um . . . thanks," Phyllis said breathlessly, pushing past her roommate. Roxanne shut the door behind them in silence while Phyllis headed for the bathroom.

"I hope I didn't wake you," she called from there.

"No, I was up," Roxanne mumbled.

"Have you gone running yet?"

"Actually . . . no. I waited here to make sure you got home okay."

"Oh, you did?" Phyllis said, washing her hands and arms as quickly as she could in the sink. "You didn't have to do that. I told you I'd be home okay."

"Yeah, well . . . some people just worry too much, I guess."

Phyllis finished in the sink and wiped herself with some hand towels. Roxanne had followed her to the bathroom and stood in the doorway.

"Are you okay this morning?" Phyllis asked.

"I'm okay," Roxanne answered. "I'm just wondering about you, that's all."

"Why? I told you I'd be okay," Phyllis said. "Look," she said, spreading her arms. "I'm not hurt. You didn't have to worry about me."

"Well, maybe I did anyway. I didn't sleep much."

"Roxanne," Phyllis said, stroking her friend's cheek briefly, "You shouldn't worry so much about me."

"Where were you last night?"

"I was just . . . at different places."

"Why didn't you call?"

"Jeez, Rox, do you call *me* every time you take off somewhere? I don't worry when you go off to Linda's."

"But I always *tell* you when I'm at Linda's," Roxanne said. "I just—all these things that have happened to you these past few days. Getting lost. Not knowing where you'd been. Cops taking you home. Why wouldn't I be worried to death about you this time?"

Phyllis glanced at her friend, then looked down and stifled an embarrassed laugh. She rubbed the back of her neck absent-mindedly.

"Oh, boy," she whispered, then looked up. "You really do like to worry about me, don't you?"

"I care about you," Roxanne said. "You're the best roommate I've ever had, and I'm worried about what's been happening to you. I've been thinking about this, even though I don't like where it's leading, but I have to ask you. Whatever's happening to you, I want to help you."

"I know," Phyllis said softly. "You always do."

"No, dammit, I mean it this time," Roxanne said. "I

know that—that you've been under so much stress lately. No steady work, that attack, the bills, the—"

"It's nothing new with me, I suppose," Phyllis said.

"This is different," Roxanne said. "This other stuff that's been happening. It's not like you."

"So what have you been thinking about?"

Phyllis watched her roommate try to form words, but the effort looked almost painful to Roxanne.

"I was wondering if—" Roxanne began, "if maybe . . . maybe you've—gotten involved with something. Something like—like—"

"Drugs?" Phyllis offered. Roxanne looked surprised, then relaxed her features and nodded quickly. Phyllis looked down and fought a smile.

"Sometimes I wish it were something that simple," she murmured.

"Hunh?"

"Nothing," Phyllis said, and shook her head. "No," she said. "It isn't drugs. That would make things easy to fix, though, wouldn't it?"

"Since when are drugs 'easy to fix?' "

"Do you have to be anywhere this morning?"

"I canceled a job," Roxanne said. "I don't have to be anywhere."

"What? Why did you do that?"

"Because I wanted to make sure I was here when you got back."

Phyllis had no response at the moment. She was touched and angered by her roommate's efforts to find her, and momentarily disappointed in herself. It was possible that Phyllis would not have made that great a sacrifice just because she thought Roxanne went off somewhere one night.

"Jeez, I didn't think you'd be so upset that you'd cancel a job," she said quietly.

"Well, it was done," Roxanne said with a sigh. "So maybe you can tell me what happened. It's something you can tell me, isn't it?"

"I told you what it was before," Phyllis said. "After the first night. About those weird dreams? God, has it only been three days?" she whispered to herself.

"You dreamed about being big and strong and running through crowds, or something like that," Roxanne said. "Right?"

"They weren't dreams," Phyllis said. "They were real. It happened last night, too."

"What? What happened?" Roxanne asked in frustration.

"I turned into an animal," Phyllis said. "For three nights in a row, I've been . . . blacking out, but not really. I remember what I do, but it's always hazy, like it was a dream. *Like* a dream, but after last night, I know that I'm not just dreaming this.

"Did you say you changed into an animal?" Roxanne asked. "As in . . . changed?" she added, spreading out her arms as though that would make a better picture.

"I turned into a wolf," Phyllis said. "Since that first night, I've been changing into a big . . . big, hairy *wolf* and running around and . . . and . . . God, I don't know what. Killing things, I think."

"What?? Killing things? Like people?"

"But that's the problem," Phyllis said. "I remember . . . running in crowds, and pushing people away, and hitting them, but I don't know if I've killed anyone! I've hurt *some*thing every night, though, because I always had blood on my hands when I woke up in the morning!"

"Blood?—*real* blood, like—"

"What other kind of blood would I have?" Phyllis said. "Look," she said, reaching for her roommate's hands, "I know this sounds bizarre, but it's true. Last night I—I—" she began, then stopped to switch her train of thought. "Every time I've changed, it's been painful. *Very* painful, and very hot. It's the heat that hurt the most. It always felt like I was going to burst into flames. Seriously! But last night, I went out to the woods—or the best thing that L. A. has for woods—and tried to meditate. That's why I was asking you about it. I figured maybe I could figure out what was happening to me if I relaxed, and kept my mind clear, and you know what?"

"Um . . . what?"

"It worked, but to a point," Phyllis said. "It started to hurt, and get incredibly hot, but I kept trying to calm down and clear my head, and it stopped hurting. I was warm, but not hot, and I was able to . . . well, to 'stay awake' longer than the other times. The last thing I remember is looking at my arms. They were . . . they were like—" she said, examining her arms again as though expecting the same thing, "They were bigger, and longer, and so was the rest of me. And furry! I swear to God there was fur all over me!"

"Fur? What kind of fur? You didn't do something horrible like buy a fur coat, did you?" Roxanne asked.

"I didn't," Phyllis said. "It was *my* fur. I tell you I *changed!*"

"But into what??"

"A wolf!" she said. "I swear I turned into a wolf! What else could I have been?"

"Um, yeah, what else . . ."

"So how can anyone help me?" Phyllis asked. "I figured I was going crazy from these weird dreams and the waking up naked in God knows where, and . . . and cops everywhere I go. Do you think I like getting rides home from cops every morning?"

"Is that what happened this morning?"

"No, I drove myself home this time. And get this! I woke up next to my car! In fact I . . . remember trying to get back to it. . . ."

"This is too weird," Roxanne said, shaking her head and backing away.

"Do you think I *don't* think this is weird?" Phyllis asked, moving toward her.

"Well, no, I . . . just . . ."

"You're afraid of me now, aren't you?" Phyllis asked quietly when her friend kept up her backward pace. Roxanne stopped and fumbled for words.

"No, I'm—" she said, "Of course not, I'm—I'm confused," she finished. "People don't 'change' into other animals. They *act* like them most of the time, but they don't *become* them."

"Looks like they do now."

"But how?"

Phyllis shrugged. "One hair at a time?" she offered.

"How can you be so . . . cool about this?" Roxanne said. "You said you think you might have killed somebody! You can joke about that?"

"But I don't *know* if I've killed anybody, or even hurt anybody," Phyllis said. "I remember attacking other animals. Small animals . . . some dogs . . ." The memories became more vivid, and more disturbing for her. She remembered enjoying the hunting, and the killing, and especially the blood, but now that her human feelings had returned . . .

"No people," she said quietly, shaking her head. "I don't remember killing anyone, please believe me."

"I'm trying to . . ."

"Ah, Gawd, Rox, if I make any jokes it's because I'm scared to death!" Phyllis said. "I don't believe in any of this shit! I know that there are people who *do* act like animals, but nobody turns into one! Nobody gets all furry and huge and—and grows huge teeth! So how can this be happening to me?"

"I-I don't know. . . ." Roxanne said feebly. It was only now that Phyllis noticed the pools of sweat on her roommate's face. Roxanne *was* afraid of her, even if she was trying not to be.

"I-I think maybe . . ." she offered, wringing her hands, "maybe you *should* see someone. See someone about this. You know: a professional of some kind, who could help you figure this out. I've been trying, but I don't know how to help other than that."

Phyllis smiled sadly and put a comforting hand on Roxanne's shoulder.

"How is some 'professional' supposed to help me?" she asked softly. "What can a therapist do to cure a werewolf?"

"A w—? You actually think you're a werewolf?" Roxanne asked.

"It sounds ridiculous, but I guess that's the only thing you can call someone who changes into animals," Phyllis said. "How is a psychiatrist supposed to help me with that?"

"I-I don't know, I just thought—maybe he could help you . . . figure out why," Roxanne suggested. "Why you've been having these dreams about—err, why you've been . . . 'changing.' "

Phyllis turned away from her friend and became lost in thought. Roxanne resumed wringing her hands nervously and fought for other suggestions, or even words of comfort.

"Full moons make me change," Phyllis said, but mostly to herself.

"Hnh? What was that?"

"I said," she said, turning toward Roxanne, "full moons make people turn into werewolves. We've had full moons for the past three nights, haven't we?"

"Uh, I don't know," Roxanne said. "I guess so. That is, I haven't been paying attention to it."

"Well, I have," Phyllis said. "I haven't had much of a choice. Now I remember some more. The first two nights, I was looking at the moon, and that's when things always started getting fuzzy."

"Did you . . . see it last night, too?"

"I don't remember," Phyllis said. "But I don't think I need to to change. It just has to be there, that's all."

"Oh. I didn't know that," Roxanne said.

"And that's my problem, too," Phyllis said. "I don't know. I don't know *any*thing about werewolves except from movies, and I've only seen one! I gotta find out as much as I can."

"What are you gonna do? Rent a bunch of movies?"

"Movies? They won't tell me shit," Phyllis said. "I'm

gonna go to a bookstore. I'm—no, not even that. I'm gonna try the library."

"You're gonna read a bunch of werewolf books?"

"Well, things *about* them," Phyllis said. "Like, maybe *Everything You've Always Wanted to Know About Werewolves*. I don't know, but I need to do *some*thing to figure this out! There has to be something that'll help me get rid of this!"

Roxanne had nothing to say for a long time. There was nothing *to* say, until one small question popped into her head.

"Everything You've Always Wanted to Know About Werewolves?" she said.

"So what are they saying?" Roxanne asked after many long minutes. Phyllis did not look up from her books.

"Hm?" she grunted. Roxanne looked around nervously, then shook her head. She had insisted on accompanying her friend to the library, but was regretting the decision more and more. She was bored, for one thing.

"Nothing," Roxanne mumbled. She passed away some more time by reading the comments that bored scholars had penned on their desks. She was soon disgusted by the abhorrently and unapologetically sexist and racist comments, and sat back to try and lose herself in her thoughts. Phyllis looked up from her books and, seeing her friend's furrowed brow, put a consoling hand on hers.

"Roxanne," she whispered, "you don't have to do this with me. All I'm doing is reading. I promise not to do anything . . . weird or anything."

Roxanne took the hand on top of hers and squeezed

it gently. She opened her mouth to speak, then turned away a little. Phyllis's comforting smile faded quickly.

"What's wrong?" she asked. Roxanne shook her head and stood up.

"Nothing," she whispered. "You're right, I'm . . . you'll be home soon, right?"

"Yeah," Phyllis said. "I think I'll check these two out. Wait . . ." she added. Roxanne hovered hesitantly. "Don't leave yet," Phyllis said. "I can check these out now. We'll go home together, okay? Okay?"

Roxanne shrugged. "Sure," she said. "Okay."

Sixteen

"Check this out," Phyllis said, shoving her open book across the table. Roxanne, who had been lost in thought, snapped to attention. Phyllis pointed to a passage.

"This describes a lot of the stuff that's been happening to me," she said. "Look at this: it talks about the transformation. This is *exactly* what's been happening to me!"

Roxanne rubbed her eyes before taking the book wordlessly. She had trouble finding the passage until Phyllis pointed it out. Phyllis watched her read, looking for some recognition or understanding, but Roxanne's face was blank. She finished and looked up.

"Looks great, Phyl," she said, scooting back the book. Phyllis took it and shut the pages. She watched her friend, who began to fidget nervously.

"I'm not sure what to say about it," Roxanne said.

"Just say you understand it," Phyllis said. "Just say you believe me. And I know this all sounds too bizarre, but it's true. I wouldn't be doing any of this crap if it weren't! Look at me! When was the last time you saw me with a book?"

"I-I don't know . . ."

"Probably never," Phyllis said, forcing a smile. "Listen

to me: I need to get help somehow. I don't know if I can do this myself."

"Oh, good," Roxanne said, sitting up. "I-I mean, I'm glad that you want to get help. You know I'll do what I can, but you need someone who . . . who's a professional about this stuff. Someone who knows how to help you—"

"I'm not talking about a shrink, Rox," Phyllis said. "I don't know *who* to look for, but there's gotta be someone who's like some authority on . . . monsters."

"You're not a monster," Roxanne said half-convincingly.

"Werewolves are considered monsters, aren't they?"

"I don't know," Roxanne said, fidgeting. "I've never met one, I guess," she added, laughing nervously.

"You have now," Phyllis said. "Me, remember?"

"Okay, okay," Roxanne said, standing up abruptly, "Wait, wait, wait, waaaaaaait a minute," she said. "Phyl, please . . . *please* listen to me. I don't know how much longer I can listen to this. I swear I've—I've been trying to, I swear I have! But how can you expect me to? What would you do if I was telling *you* this stuff? Would you believe me?"

"I guess this means that you don't, huh?"

"Good God, what do you think?" Roxanne cried, tugging at her hair. "If you told me that you were having weird blackouts and sleepwalking, I could believe you, but this—! What proof do you have of this?"

"Look at this!" Phyllis said, pointing to her open book.

"Well, what about that?? What if I read some medical book and told you that I had every disease listed in there? People do things like that all the time!"

"This isn't a 'medical book,' this is—"

"Everything You Wanted to Know About Werewolves, I know."

"Well, not exactly, but if you'd just look at—"

"What about the tryout?" Roxanne said. "Shouldn't you be trying to work on a routine? Or maybe . . . maybe you've been working *too* hard."

"Are you talking about the Tamara Taylor thing?"

"Yes, that, and any other job that comes our way. Look, Phyllis . . . you know that I'm just trying to help you. What you *really* need to help you is to get out of this slump!"

Phyllis responded by sighing loudly and leaning back into her chair. She closed her book and rubbed the top of her head.

" 'Slump?' " she muttered. "Yeah, this is one hell of a 'slump.' It just keeps getting better and better. I know what you're gonna say when I say this, but—"

The phone interrupted the discussion. Roxanne was closest and motioned to her friend to hold her words. It wasn't until she reached the kitchen that she remembered about their new answering machine. She answered in an unusually surly manner, then calmed down once Linda announced herself. Roxanne's face brightened, and Phyllis decided to resume her research.

Her concentration was broken by a tap on the shoulder. She turned around to see Roxanne, the phone cradled in her hand.

"Um . . ." she said, shuffling back and forth, "I was kind of wondering if . . . if it'd be okay for Linda to come over tonight."

"Fine," Phyllis mumbled. "But I'm not leaving tonight."

"Oh no, no, no, see . . ." Roxanne said quickly. "See, I figured she could come over tonight, and then we could . . . I don't know, keep you company tonight. Is it okay if we do that? Could she come over?"

Phyllis did not voice her first thought. Her roommate—her friend—was afraid of her, and wanted someone with her to protect her against the Big Bad Werewolf. She blinked her eyes slowly and fought off tears while speaking.

"She can come over," Phyllis whispered, then turned back to her studies and bit her upper lip hard. She tried to continue her reading, but soon gave up and gathered her books to head for her room and shut the door.

She tossed the books onto her futon and slumped down next to them. She shut her eyes and tried to piece through the still-murky memories of the past few nights, but all that was left were dreamlike images. After a few moments of empty thoughts, she sat up and rolled off of the futon to check her schedule. Her true intention was to check her calendar for the little full moon symbol that most of them had. This one was no different; the full moon was noted, and from two days ago. If last night hadn't been a full moon, according to the calendar, then why had she changed? Phyllis kicked herself mentally for not checking out anything about the moon. It was late afternoon now. Roxanne probably had great reason to be so afraid.

Roxanne was just hanging up the phone when Phyllis bolted from her room. Roxanne started and almost dropped the phone. Phyllis stopped in her tracks.

"Aaah!" Roxanne cried. "What is it? Is something wrong?"

"Uh . . . uh . . ." Phyllis stammered, then calmed her-self. "No," she said, straightening up. "I was just think-ing of something, and I figured that I should leave right away, but—I think tonight will be okay. I think there won't be any 'repeat' of those other nights. It's just a feeling. But what if I'm wrong?"

"Um . . ." Roxanne said, moving slowly toward her friend, "Linda says she'll be here soon. I told her we don't have much food or anything. She might pick some-thing up on the way over."

"She doesn't have to do that."

"She made a casserole last night, and . . . and . . ." Roxanne said, but her voice faltered away to a squeak. She sniffled once then looked away. Phyllis put a hand on her shoulder, and Roxanne whirled around suddenly to fall into her arms, sobbing.

"What . . ." Phyllis said, startled, "what is it? What's wrong? Is it Linda?"

"No, it's not Linda," Roxanne said. "It's *you,* you goof! All this stuff that's been happening to you and . . . and I don't know how to deal with it! Are you sure it isn't drugs?"

"No, it's not drugs . . .

"Please tell me the truth, Phyllis!" she sobbed. "We don't mess with each other's minds like this! Let me help you . . . please?"

"Of course I'll let you help me," Phyllis said. "I *want* you to help me. But I should warn you that it could get dangerous, big time. I don't want you hurt, but I don't think I can do this without somebody's help."

"Do what?"

"Cure myself, of course," Phyllis said. "Cure myself

from . . . from this!" she said, parting from her friend and watching her hand.

"What are you doing?" Roxanne said after a few moments of puzzlement.

"I don't know if I can do it," Phyllis said. "I don't know if I *want* to do it. But those books . . . they talk about different kinds of werewolves, different ways you can become one, and what happens after that. Did you know that some people turn into wolves by putting on something made from wolf skin?"

"Uh, no, I didn't."

"And the kind who change under full moons," she continued. "Maybe I'm wrong, but I got the impression that those are the least common kinds. Most of the ones they talked about could change on their own."

"Wh—why would anyone want to do that?" Roxanne asked nervously.

"I don't know," Phyllis said. "But maybe . . ."

Roxanne waited for her to complete the thought, but Phyllis turned away to sit cross-legged onto their sofa. She pulled her legs in tighter into a lotus position, and shut her eyes. Her roommate approached her cautiously.

"Um . . . what are you doing?" she asked. Phyllis said nothing, but brought a finger up slowly to her lips. After some hesitation, Roxanne moved to the smaller sofa opposite Phyllis, and settled in as quietly as possible. She watched her roommate nervously, looking behind herself occasionally, perhaps hoping for Linda to knock on the door at any moment.

Phyllis looked almost asleep; her face was completely calm, her breathing slow and steady. Then, very slowly, she began lifting an arm. Roxanne watched, and waited, and widened her eyes at a new sight. Phyllis's fingers were twitching, but not in a way that indicated tenseness. Unless she needed glasses, Roxanne watched the fingers appear to be getting smaller. Phyllis normally kept her nails neat and short, but not this time. They grew longer and sharper—much sharper. Phyllis's arm took up the quivering begun by her hand, but it was more controlled. At first glance it appeared to be turning gray, until the hairs became longer and more prominent, covering her arm with a brown fur.

Roxanne cringed back into her seat, holding her own arm out as if to stop it, and tried to call out, but could only manage some inaudible squeaks. Inaudible to her, that is; she could have sworn that Phyllis's still human ears pricked up. Phyllis opened her eyes and looked at her friend, whose face was frozen in fear. She looked at her arm and grimaced as it quickly shifted back to its more familiar form. Then she took another deep breath and straightened her legs. Both women sat in silence until Phyllis sniffled, and Roxanne looked to see her eyes reddening.

"Phyl?" she said. "Phyllis? You okay, hon?"

"What do you think?" Phyllis mumbled, wiping her nose. "I can't believe I even did that. How can I do that? Why is this happening to me?" She was fighting them, but Phyllis's tears were gaining strength. Roxanne gathered the courage to roll out of her seat and sit next to her friend.

"Shhhh," she said, trying to rock Phyllis, who resisted such movement. "It's going to be okay, Phyl. Linda's going to come here and—"

"And do what?" Phyllis snapped. "Cure me?"

"No, she isn't," Roxanne said. "What I meant was, was we want to help you. What about those books? What did they say? Didn't they say anything about . . . about this problem?"

Phyllis forced a quick laugh. "This 'problem?' " she said. "Yeah, they said all sorts of things."

"Tell me about them," Roxanne said. "What did they say about . . . well, what about becoming a werewolf?"

"God, there was so much crap in there . . ." Phyllis mumbled to herself. She seemed to be lost in thought, then pushed away a little from Roxanne and stretched her legs. "It told me how I got this way," she said. "That's part of why I was crying. It listed about eighty different ways to become a werewolf, and I get it the way everyone knows about."

"You were bitten?"

Phyllis nodded. "Yeah," she said. "Could I be attacked by some dog or a bear in Wisconsin? No, of course not. I have to be ripped up by some . . . fucking werewolf!"

"You think so?"

"What else was it?? No one even saw the thing but me, and I was hit too fast to get a decent picture of it. That's what killed Uncle Bill. That's what ripped through his fence and tore open his llamas and . . . killed him. Some fuckin' vacation. *Rabies* I could deal with. Maybe even AIDS, but—this!"

"Well, didn't it say anything about getting cured?"

"I couldn't find anything that made much sense," Phyllis said. "But I'm not letting anyone shoot me with any silver bullets, I'll tell you that much."

"I wouldn't even know where to get any," Roxanne

said. "Uh—! I meant, not that I'd shoot you! I meant—uh . . ."

"Never mind," Phyllis said, smiling. "I should probably do it myself."

"Don't say that," Roxanne said. *"Please* don't say stuff like that."

"I'm not going to," Phyllis said. "Unless I have to. First, I have to get back to Wisconsin."

"How are you going to do that?"

"Why, by borrowing from you, of course," she said, then smiled. "Nahh I can't afford another plane trip, so I'll have to drive."

"Drive? You think your car can make it?"

"Well, I drove it *here,* from New York," Phyllis said. "Wisconsin's about half the distance."

"But that was years ago," Roxanne said. "You shouldn't drive that thing so far now. And who's going with you? You shouldn't go on a trip like that alone."

"Why not?"

"Well, because it's too dangerous, that's why."

"For who? Me or the guy who tries to rape me when I turn into a big monster on him?"

"I'm serious," Roxanne said. "How do you know you'll be able to defend yourself? Besides, do you even have money for gas and things?"

"Gas won't cost that much," Phyllis said. "I can save money by sleeping in my car."

"No way, you can't do that," Roxanne said. "That's way too dangerous. You know, I had a friend who was driving to Florida to visit her fam—"

"You know someone who's been attacked for every situation," Phyllis grumbled.

"But this is true—!"

"Would you rather wait for the next full moon to change your mind? I can't stay here!"

"But . . . but I thought you could control it now. I saw you making yourself change, then you stopped it."

"Look; look, Rox," Phyllis said, stopping her friend's next sentence. "This isn't something I can just sit around and hope will go away. This isn't like a bad cold or a flu; if this is a disease, it won't kill *me,* it'll kill other people! It may already have! I just wish I could remember more details. That's why I have to get back there."

"How do you know you can find this . . . guy that did this to you?"

"It could've been a girl, for all I know," Phyllis said. "It's a start, though. Maybe I can sniff them out like a dog now, I don't know."

"You're not a dog."

"Only during the daytime."

"Wait a minute," Roxanne said, standing up abruptly. "You're not gonna change tonight, are you?"

"I don't think it's a full moon anymore," Phyllis said. "There couldn't be one for more than three nights in a row, could there? I mean, how many phases does the moon have, anyway?"

"I have no idea," Roxanne said. "Maybe four?"

"Forget it," Phyllis said, waving her off. "I'll have to look it up somewhere. I'll have to look up everything I can find about this 'problem' of mine. Meanwhile, I don't think you and Linda should be here tonight. It's too dangerous."

"No," Roxanne said. "We're going to stay here tonight

with you. You wouldn't hurt us, even as a . . . wolf. I know you wouldn't."

"How do you know?"

"I just know. You wouldn't hurt us; you love us, remember?"

"Maybe, but I thought you always hurt the one you love. Right?" Phyllis asked.

Roxanne had no answer.

Seventeen

Before Linda showed up, Phyllis made Roxanne promise not to bring up "that subject" anymore. They could talk about Phyllis being ill, but not specify the illness. Phyllis excused herself early in the evening to retire to her room and read. Roxanne made a small protest, hoping that company might give her friend some comfort. Phyllis spent the time staring out her window before hitting the books.

It occurred to her to call up Aunt Joanie to "warn" her of her visit. The phone rang for a while, and Phyllis realized that she had woken up her aunt. She never could keep her time zones straight.

Joanie was grateful for the call and surprised at the news. Things were going as well as could be expected at the ranch. A new stud had been brought in. She already had customers for it. But why did Phyllis need to come again? she asked. Phyllis would only tell her that she might have caught something from that animal, and Joanie accepted this explanation, albeit with professed concern. Eventually she agreed to take Phyllis in when she could get there.

The thought did occur to Phyllis to arrange for her absence with her employers. At the moment she was still

on temporary leave from the health club, but had jus
resumed her work at the restaurant. Asking for another
"vacation" might not be met with great understanding.
Phyllis enjoyed her work at the health club, but waiting
tables was waiting tables.

Phyllis spent the rest of the evening packing her ne-
cessities for the trip; arranging time off would come later.
Roxanne and Linda interrupted her briefly. As far as
Linda knew, Phyllis was only "sick," but Roxanne may
have been checking to make certain that Phyllis hadn'
grown any extra hair or teeth that night. Idle chitcha
broke out occasionally until Phyllis became increasingly
distracted by her packing, so Linda excused herself firs
from the room. Roxanne paused at the door after Linda
rounded the corner to the living room.

"Phylly?" she said quietly.

"Yeah," Phyllis said, still somewhat distracted. There
was a long pause before Roxanne spoke up.

"Be careful," she whispered. "Okay?"

Phyllis looked up from her open drawer of lingerie,
then stared at her friend. She stepped forward to pat Roxanne's shoulder, then pulled her toward herself into a
brief half-hug.

"I will," she whispered. "When I come back, I'll be
normal. I swear I will."

"No!! Shit! No!! Shit! No!! Shit! No—!!"

"All right, all right, just shut up a minute, willya?"

"You don't understand, this can't happen to me *now*,"
Phyllis said. "You don't understand how important this—"

"Try it now!" her neighbor said. He set down his hammer on Phyllis's air filter. Phyllis cursed to herself once more, and tried the ignition. The car made a spitting noise, and nothing else. She tried again, then again, and again, until her neighbor got her attention enough to stop.

"What the hell is it?" she demanded. "What the fuck is wrong with it??" Her car gave no reply. She listened to the neighbor whack at her starter with the hammer and ran her fingers through her hair in frustration.

"Try it again!" he shouted. Phyllis muttered threats to her car and tried again. It spat at her in response. She cried out and slammed her fists against the steering wheel and didn't care when the horn occasionally went off.

Her helpful neighbor, Marty, went to her window to calm her down. She was ready to tear the seats apart, but for his sake, Phyllis calmed herself down and climbed out of the driver's seat. Marty smiled weakly, shrugged his shoulders and shook his head.

"Hey, I'm sorry," he said. "My starter's gone out before, and you just whack it a few times when that happens, but I guess yours is really out."

"Fuck," Phyllis muttered to herself, then turned to Marty. "I know you were trying to help. Thanks for trying, man. Old Faithful was going to lose its faith someday. But why the hell did it HAVE TO BE TODAY??" she yelled, kicking the car door. "How much do these things cost, anyway?" she mumbled.

"You mean a starter?" Marty asked. "Oh, at least a hundred bucks. That's just for the part, too. They ain't cheap."

"Noooo, they aren't," Phyllis said, pacing slowly now.

Then she slapped her thighs and straightened up. "I guess I'll just stay here and be doomed, then."

"Doomed to what?"

Phyllis waved him off as if she'd just told a bad joke. "I've been trying to leave L.A., uhhhh, you know, take off for—I'm just kidding," she concluded. "But hey," she said, patting Marty on the shoulder, "really, thanks for trying to help."

Marty held up the hammer and smiled.

"No problem," he said. "If you need someone to whack at something with a hammer, I'm your guy." He smiled and waved at her awkwardly while going back into the building. Phyllis waved back and briefly wished that he really were "her guy." Too bad he was already his wife's guy.

This had been about a week after the first full moon. The restaurant manager would not allow Phyllis another hiatus for at least a few months, even though she had gone back to work since the untimely death of her car. To both Phyllis's and Roxanne's delight and relief, there had been no "relapses" since the third night of the full moon. Since the third night, Phyllis had checked out a book on the moon and had gained superficial knowledge of lunar phases. The most important thing she learned was that there are indeed three nights to each phase of the moon, including full moons.

Roxanne came home one night to catch her roommate in a most unusual position. The sparse furniture had been pushed against the walls, leaving an open area in the living room. Phyllis was on the floor, as were various open books spread about herself. The most unusual part was that she sat in the middle of a crudely painted pentagram, with each point of the star covered by a lit candle.

"Oh, my God," Roxanne whispered, dropping everything that she had been carrying. Phyllis looked up. Roxanne barely remembered to shut the door behind her.

"It's not what you think," Phyllis said quickly, jumping to her feet. "I thought you were gonna be home late tonight."

"Um . . . um . . . I was just . . . picking up some stuff, and . . . um . . ." Roxanne stammered, unable to pull her gaze away from the pentagram.

"Look, I-I know this looks like some Satanist thing or something," Phyllis said, "but one of these books was talking about this as maybe a cure. I just wanted to try it, to try *any*thing."

"Um . . . what . . ." Roxanne said, now able to divert her attention to Phyllis, "What others things have you tried?"

"This is the first thing, actually," Phyllis said. "Well, next to meditating. Yeah, I was trying that, too."

"Has it helped?"

Phyllis let out a heavy sigh and scratched her head. "It might," she said. "I don't know. I tried it that last night that I changed, you know, when I took off for Griffith Park. It made it less painful, but didn't stop it. I don't just want to learn how to control this, and leave it at that. I want to *stop* it. I want a full cure!"

"And . . . *this* is supposed to do that?" Roxanne asked, indicating the mess of their living room.

"That's what I want to find out," Phyllis said. "I pretty much just sat down when you walked in."

"I don't like all this," Roxanne said. "I don't like . . . devil stuff. Isn't that a sign for summoning demons? What if you can't wash that paint off? I don't want a pentagram sitting permanently in—"

"I used watercolors," Phyllis said. "I already tried it off in a corner somewhere and it came right off. Believe me, I don't want this thing on our floor forever, either."

"Well . . . what exactly are you supposed to do in that thing?" Roxanne said, now stooping over to pick up her dropped items.

"Well, there's this poem, and—wait," Phyllis said, and raced off to snatch one of her books and bring it back. She pointed to the passage that described the ritual. Roxanne took the book and skimmed it. She glanced over at another page.

"What's this about virgins hitting you in the face?"

"Huh?" Phyllis said, snatching the book away. "Oh, that. That's another thing. If this doesn't work, I might have to try that, too. Except, I don't think I know any virgins. Do you?"

"I know . . . one person," Roxanne said, trying to remember. "Wait a minute, I can't believe I'm trying to help you with some magic spell."

"I gotta try something," Phyllis grumbled.

"Look, you know I'm anything but some rabid Christian," Roxanne said, putting her load onto the eating table, which was now pressed up against the counter. "But . . . occult stuff makes me nervous. Even ouija boards scare me!"

"Oh, those things are fun . . ."

"Well, they aren't to me!"

Phyllis started to smile, but it was halted by Roxanne's

tone and piercing gaze. She was not joking. Phyllis closed the book quietly and placed it on the table.

"I'm sorry," Phyllis said. "Seriously, I thought you wouldn't be back for a while. I was fully planning on cleaning everything up before you even got here. But please try to understand how . . . how desperate I am right now. I've got barely two weeks to the next full moon, and I don't have enough money to get to Wisconsin now."

"What makes you think getting there will help?"

"I don't know," Phyllis said, falling onto the couch with a sigh. "I'm hoping maybe that I could find the guy . . . well, the thing that did this to me, and . . . maybe make him cure me. If that's even possible. But I do know that I can't be around here at all the next time."

"Um . . ." Roxanne said, scratching her head, "you said that the full moon is two weeks away. Did you remember that Tamara Taylor has her tryouts in one week?"

"I remember."

"Oh, good. That is, I was wondering if you'd been working on your choreography. That's your real strength, and—"

"I haven't been," Phyllis muttered.

"Haven't been what?"

"I haven't been working on a routine."

"You haven't? My gosh, what have you been doing? Do you mean you've been reading about werewolves all this time?"

"I have to learn about them somehow," Phyllis said. "I don't trust the movies."

"But what about your work? You can't go into an audition and improvise the whole thing!"

"I've done that before," Phyllis said. "So have you."

"Yeah, but have you ever gotten a job that way? I haven't."

"Look, I haven't exactly been able to think about try-outs or auditions or anything else for awhile, okay?" Phyllis snapped. "I'm in trouble here! I have to take care of this little problem before I can do anything else, you know?"

"What 'problem?' That you're a werewolf?"

"No, that I can't get the stains out of my sweater," Phyllis grumbled. *"Yes* that I'm a werewolf! And yeah, I can see you don't believe me, but I don't know how to prove it to you except to change, and no way will I let that happen again!"

"So . . . you're telling me that you're not going to the tryout, right?" Phyllis said calmly.

"Not if I don't find a cure by then. I can't go to any tryout, no matter how great a break it would be. I have to . . . have to figure my way out of this." Phyllis gathered up her books in silence and avoided meeting Roxanne's gaze when she next spoke.

"I don't expect you to believe me," she said. "And right now, yeah, I do look crazy, especially with all of this 'occult' stuff lying around. If it helps, I haven't gotten into drugs, and I'm not a devil-worshipper."

"I don't know what to think about this," Roxanne said quietly. She, too, gathered up her belongings from the dining table. "I was planning on spending the night at Linda's tonight. Unless . . . do you need me here?"

"Go to Linda's," Phyllis said. "Don't worry about me. You will, anyway, but try not to."

"You're not making it easy."

Phyllis smiled bittersweetly, then went to her friend to put a comforting hand on her shoulder.

"I've never made it easy on people," she said. "And, take this for what it's worth, but I'm going to make a promise. Whatever happens, no matter what I end up changing into, I promise never to hurt you."

"That's . . . a nice promise," Roxanne said uncertainly. "I think I'm more worried about *you* getting hurt, though. I don't want *you* hurt. And this thing . . ." Roxanne said, pointing to the pentagram. "Who knows what'll happen if you start messing with stuff like that? I've heard too many bizarre stories from people. From people I *know*, who used to be friends."

"Gawd, where do you find these people you keep talking about, anyway?" Phyllis said. "Oh. I guess I'm one of them now, huh?"

Roxanne said nothing.

Eighteen

"We've been through this before," Phyllis said. "There's no way I can do this."

"You can't afford not to do this," Roxanne said. "Reality says that you need a way to pay the bills!"

" 'Reality' says that I need to get out of town! Besides, so far, the waitressing has been paying the bills."

"You didn't come here all the way from New York to become a waitress!"

"I didn't do it to become a werewolf, either!"

"Enough of the 'werewolf' story already!"

"I already said that you didn't have to believe me! Just trust me on this, okay? You don't want a demonstration!"

There was a brief silence before Roxanne broke it with a sigh.

"Do what you have to do, then," she said. "If you want to throw away everything you've ever wanted, then don't do anything. Don't dance, don't teach, just serve people all day and run away to the woods at night. I guess that's what you want."

"Look, this is not the most important tryout in the world!" Phyllis said. "It's not going to be the only chance I have!"

"It could be!" Roxanne said. *"All* of our chances are, you know that! That's the first rule of this business, and you know it! Any break could be the big one: *any* break. And there's something else I've been thinking about. If you won't let *me* help you, then . . ."

"Then what? Oh, not the therapists again . . ."

"Well, I don't know what else to say," Roxanne said in growing frustration. "Maybe . . . what about a priest?"

"A priest?" Phyllis said warily.

"Well—I meant just—you know, somebody," Roxanne said. "Anybody, I don't know. Just . . . get help. And um . . . you really sure you want to cancel this one? We don't have much more time to get there."

Phyllis looked down in thought. She started shaking her head, then looked up and cocked an eyebrow.

"Fine," she said. "Yeah, I'll do it. But you know I haven't even been able to work anything out. I'll have to improvise."

"It's better than not going at all," her friend advised.

"I suppose it is," Phyllis said. "Come on, let's go."

Roxanne smiled and hugged her friend briefly before gathering up her purse and leaving, with Phyllis bringing up the rear.

Security was quite tight, which only mildly surprised the two women. A bouncer at the only entrance to the stage had a list of names. No name, no entry. Many people were turned away. Phyllis had been to auditions like this before, and never could understand the logic of them. This was the way of the entertainer, however; most of the time what mattered was not how good you were, but how good your agent was.

Both women expected a stage packed with hopefuls, but there were surprisingly few people. That is, it was possible to take a deep breath and not be crushed by a mass of bodies. At first there was no sign of Taylor, until the double doors leading from the lobby burst open, and she appeared, already deep in conversation with an entourage. Phyllis remembered reading something about how Taylor was down-to-earth and disliked the pomp and circumstance of fame; this scene made her shrug to herself. No doubt, avoiding a mob of one's own employees was sometimes unavoidable.

Taylor and her manager, producer, publicist, boyfriend(?), friends, and perhaps her third grade teacher, as well, reached the front row of the theater and seated themselves. The man next to Taylor never stopped talking, except to call out "Next!" Apparently he would be calling the shots.

Phyllis found herself strangely indifferent to everything that was going on. She did not stretch out or practice any moves as most of the hopefuls did, but stayed far back in an offstage corner. She stared at her hand for a long time as though expecting it to change. If the calendar was correct, the full moon was not even a week away. Strange things could happen before that time, then. Abruptly her senses returned to her. Nothing was going to happen. She was going to give a knockout performance whether she was prepared or not, and no wild animals would destroy the moment. Yet, if this had been a full moon night, Phyllis's confidence would not have been so firm. She knew this.

She decided to rejoin the group and wandered up to watch the latest hopeful. Roxanne was at the other end of the stage, but neither friend made a move toward the other. Everyone who deserved to be there was there, and no one else was allowed inside, but Phyllis turned around as a cool breeze hit her back, as if someone had just opened the door. The door was shut as firmly as before, and no one appeared to be near the exit. The bouncer had stationed himself outside long ago. Phyllis gave this mystery only a moment's thought before turning back to the music.

The list of names used to call up each dancer was in no discernible order, so no one dared go anywhere until his or her name was called. Phyllis was almost bored with all of this. Of auditions, she liked it least when no one could go outside to get fresh air. All of these sweating bodies onstage and in the theater seats were making the air unbearable.

Wiping away some sweat, Phyllis felt someone touch her shoulder. She looked back briefly, but saw nothing. In fact, she stood in the far rear of the group, so no one was ever behind her. She told herself repeatedly that this meant nothing, but nevertheless found herself inching her way toward the other side of the stage where Roxanne waited. Roxanne smiled at Phyllis and patted her shoulder briefly before returning to the "show."

Again there was no one directly behind her, but Phyllis sensed that someone was, and he (she?) was staring at her. She whirled around.

"Phyllis Turner!" Taylor's manager shouted. Phyllis fought the urge to keep searching behind herself, and pushed quickly through the crowd, fighting a racing pulse and cold hands. Simply the jitters? Perhaps, but Phyllis had never known stage fright like this. She handed the sound man her music tape and shook herself out while waiting for the music to begin.

"Name."

Phyllis finished her trek to the front of the stage, but remained silent.

"Name, please."

Her eyes fought to pierce the darkness that always covered the director's face.

"Loraine," she said. Behind Phyllis/Loraine, Roxanne's eyes went wide, and her jaw dropped.

"Uhhh we called up Phyllis Turner," the director said.

"Oh, yeah, that is me," Phyllis said. "I'm using . . . a middle name."

"Oh," the director said. "Okay, Loraine . . . Phyllis. Whoever you are. Whenever you're ready."

Phyllis nodded in comprehension. There were a few seconds of silence as her music was cueing up, until the melodic strains of "Moondance" filled the stage. Before this time Phyllis had never used any music other than the most recent and "hip-hoppenist," but today she needed to hear something somewhat more personal.

A chill then crept down her spine. Whoever had been watching her before was doing it again. Phyllis could pretend that the other dancers did not exist, but not this new presence. There was no opportunity to confront it once the music began, either. She had been unable to work on a new routine and had no choice but to improvise. That may have been to her advantage this time; her attempts to remember a routine would have been destroyed at this audition. No matter which way she faced, something was behind her, watching her, trying desperately to unnerve her.

If this was the mysterious presence's intention, it eventually failed. Phyllis was unnerved, and frustrated, and even a little frightened, but somehow, this time, she took this growing negative energy and focused it into a dance that took her to limits she had never before dreamed of reaching.

Almost anyone else attempting her stretches, spins, contortions, flips, and leaps—not merely hops, but stage-length bounds—would have shown far too much strain, but not even a bead of sweat appeared on her forehead. At one point she spun for a full ten seconds, then immediately flowed into a forward flip that only moved on to more feats of aerodynamics. Few are allowed to complete a dance at tryouts, but Phyllis was allowed to complete it, and then some. There was a silence after she struck her final pose.

It was too dark in the theater to truly see the faces of the spectators, but Phyllis clearly saw the bright flash of Tamara's smile. She was leaning over and whispering excitedly to someone. Phyllis fought the growing urge to smile as brightly.

"Um . . ." came the director's voice, "Um, thank you. Could you go and talk to Gordon, please?"

"No problem," she said, and bowed quickly before rushing over to "Gordon," a bookish man who had always stood far off in the shadows of stage right. So far only two other hopefuls had talked to him on their way out.

"Hi," Phyllis whispered. Gordon nodded to her and smiled politely.

"Hello," he whispered back. "Congratulations. They'd like to see you in a call-back. Now, you are—?"

"Yes!" Phyllis whispered. "At last, at last!"

"Shhhh," Gordon said as the next hopeful's music began. "I need your name."

"Oh, yeah! It's Phyl—Um, just Loraine," she finished.

"Last name?"

"No last name," she said. "Yet," she whispered to herself.

"Okay, no last name," Gordon said to himself as he scribbled. "Address . . . ?"

Loraine startled the security detail outside as she burst through the doors, beaming brighter than the sun. The bouncer quickly shut the doors behind her and attempted to silence her. There was no longer a need, as Loraine was already out of earshot, having somersaulted her way to the main sidewalk. She finished off her tumbling with a great cry and a six-foot leap straight up, to the surprise of an impromptu audience of passersby.

She strutted down the street to her inner music, only to yelp at one point and whirl around to face . . . no one. A man who had been walking behind her frowned as he swerved to pass her quickly. Loraine watched him pass, then looked back down the sidewalk. Somebody had been right behind her—close enough to feel his (her?) breath on the back of her neck; then it was gone.

Loraine's "secret admirer" had not returned by the time she made it back to the apartment. It was not unusual for either roommate to leave an audition without the other, but now she sorely regretted not waiting for

Roxanne to finish. Loraine bolted the door tightly and clicked on the television. She hadn't felt the "presence" for nearly a half an hour now. Perhaps the noise of the television would keep it away for good. Hadn't primitive people danced and yelled and screamed to frighten away evil spirits? Don't civilized people do that, too, in their own way?

Loraine considered taking a shower, but she was resuming her work at the health club by teaching a beginning dancercize class that night. Roxanne had raised Loraine's ecological awareness at every opportunity—in this case, to save water whenever possible. It was after she had clicked on the TV that she noticed the answering machine's blinking light. Playing it back revealed one hangup and one unexpected call, from Michael.

"Um, hi," his voice said. "Phyllis, I hope this is still your number. If it is, thank God you finally got a machine. Ummm, anyway, this is Michael, and I'm at lunch right now, so if you hear this before one o'clock, here's my work number. They should be able to page me or something. Um, 555-6281. But, if you don't, call me at home like after seven. They're going easy on me today. Usually I get home like ten, but, um . . . anyway, I hope you still have my number. I'd . . . like to talk to you again. I know it's been awhile, but . . . you probably think I'm lying, but I'm not seeing anyone right now. Not since we broke up, I mean. Anyway . . . please call me today or tonight, and . . . and then we can talk. Okay? Bye, Phyllis. Oh, say hi to Rox for me!"

"Ahhh, boy," Loraine muttered to herself. There were no other messages. She let out a loud sigh and scratched her head. It was after one, so she would need to call

Michael at home. *If* she called him. Under normal circumstances she might have called him back, but this was
not a good time. She did want to talk to him and even
see him again, but not if it meant trying to explain what
was happening.

Roxanne had not checked in by the time Loraine had
to leave for the club. She usually went straight to Linda's
after an audition; lately she had been spending more time
than usual there. Loraine was no fool; she knew that she
was largely the cause of her friend's increased absences.
She probably would have done the same thing.

At the club Loraine caught herself a few times doing
too much for her class. This was a beginning class, but
no one in her advanced class could have kept up with
her if she hadn't reined herself in. Loraine's energy had
not diminished since the audition; if anything, it had increased. She tried to diffuse it some by teaching the class
some extra steps involving leaping and kicking, but this
only frustrated her. This soon became the longest class
that Loraine had ever taught—or rather, it seemed to be.
Afterward there were always some stragglers who wanted
to chat with her, so Loraine deliberately kept her answers
brief and hurried to pack up her things.

Eventually everyone had left, only to be replaced by
early arrivals for the next class. Loraine only remembered
that it was a martial art of some kind. There were only
six people in the room now—five students and Loraine.
She was hunched over her bag, slamming clothes into it,
when she felt a familiar sensation of somebody breathing
down her neck. She started and whirled around, attempting to smash her bag into who/whatever was behind her.
The bag swung at empty air and came loose from her

hand. It slid halfway across the floor, to the surprise of most of the pajama-clad onlookers. At least, they always looked like they were wearing pajamas.

Standing up slowly but breathing heavily, Loraine apologized meekly as she shuffled over to fetch her bag. She briefly entertained the thought that one of these kung fu fighters had tried to spook her, but none of them had been at the audition. Whatever person or presence had been at the tryout had followed her here. Loraine glanced at her watch. She didn't actually care what time it was, but the motion of the watch hands helped her think about the date, and how many days were left until the next full moon.

Nineteen

As of Tamara Taylor's initial tryout, four days remained until the next full moon. With the callback at two days after the tryout, that left two. Loraine had no intention of being anywhere near the city then, whether she was finally picked or not. In the meantime, besides the work and money, she had a new reason to keep trying for a position: she was either becoming paranoid, or somebody was watching her every move. It was possible that she could still leave town, and her "secret admirer" would follow, but she would just as soon confront it here than out in the middle of the desert or the woods. Another question for her was: Why now?

It was always in the back of Loraine's mind that Roxanne was right. The human brain was capable of coming up with the most bizarre images and make them seem real. It was completely possible that her hand had never actually grown fur and claws, but—she was suffering hallucinations from spiked aspirin or food. Stress could be doing this; perhaps a therapist could uncover some post-traumatic "flashbacks" of that wild animal's attack. She would have to look into other possibilities, then, other cures. After she got back from the desert, of course.

"Hello, everyone," Tamara said, yanking back Loraine's distant thoughts. "I guess you all know who I am."

Five of the six lucky callbacks chuckled to themselves. Loraine was still trying to bring herself back to reality. This was her first callback in far too long and was no time to be daydreaming.

"Even if you do, I'm Tamara Taylor," she continued, "and you may not know that this is the last stop I'm making to get some dancers. I never wanted them all to be from one place. Out of five, there's actually only two positions open for a dance troupe, and one of them could be the choreographer, too."

Enthusiastic cooing came from the group.

"People were saying that I should start with the choreographer and let him or her do the picking, but I don't like that. I mean, I can dance, but I want to be able to do these moves, too! So, yeah, I've worked with choreographers in my videos, but I want someone I can . . . I don't know, I guess bond with her, or him. I have a rep as a perfectionist, and it's true. I am. But I think you guys are, too."

"Ummm," she continued, "well, that's enough for the pep talk. Like I said, you guys are the last group I'm going to look at, and I can only take two others. I hate this part—turning people down, I mean—but I can't take everyone, right? Okay! knock me out!"

Some of the hopefuls whooped and applauded to themselves, and all of them kept an eye on the competition while taking their places. Loraine had only learned the night before that Roxanne had not been called back. Loraine had offered comfort, but Roxanne had tried to pretend that it had been like any other rejection—a staple in their business. They both knew, however, that this had not been just "any" rejection; this truly would have been a major break for any dancer. Loraine even felt twinges of guilt for getting as far as she had. Roxanne had all but dragged her to the audition. Roxanne had been so excited about it, and Loraine, who had been so ambivalent about going, got a callback on an improvised dance.

The situation had changed little. Loraine still had nothing planned. She had tried to work out something the day before, but had found herself preoccupied with discovering her "secret admirer." She had also been wrestling over whether or not to return Michael's call, or rather, calls by this time. She would do this soon, but not just yet. She could just tell him that she had been on a vacation.

"Phyllis Turner!" a man's voice called. Loraine stepped up to center stage. Only one person had gone before her. Usually she disliked being up early, but this time, she wanted it over with soon.

"Ummm," Loraine said, shaking herself out quickly to loosen up, "I've changed my name to Loraine. Just recently, that is."

"We'll make a note of it," the voice replied. "Whenever you're ready."

Loraine had snatched up "Thriller" no less than five minutes before leaving the apartment, and prayed that no one would laugh. In her state of mind "The Monster Mash" would have been just as appropriate. The tape was not even cued up properly, and started in at just before the chorus.

Once again Loraine let her instincts guide her. The music was miscued, but she picked up instantly on the tempo and rhythm, and executed moves that put the Gloved One to shame. No one else existed as soon as she took her first step. She lived now in a world fifty feet wide by thirty feet deep, and called a stage. Friction and gravity also ceased to exist, allowing her to glide and fly across the stage at will. Even the music faded until only its beat remained. Loraine danced to the beat only, and would have continued even in its absence, except that the man's voice finally penetrated her mind.

"—nk you!" it said. "Okay, thanks! You were great!"

"Um," Loraine said, straightening herself up slowly, "um, thank you."

"Don't leave yet!" came Taylor's voice. "Just stay off to the side, okay, hon?"

"Yeah. Okay."

For now, this meant nothing, because everyone had been asked to stay until the end. Only then would Taylor make her decision.

Roxanne cried out and hugged her friend with glee. Loraine stiffened in surprise, then soon relaxed and returned the embrace.

"Heyyy, it's just a job," she said. Roxanne slapped her shoulder playfully.

" 'Just a job,' " she said mockingly. "This is a *great* job! Lead dancer *and* choreographer to Tamara Taylor?? So what would be a great job to you?"

"I'm just kidding," Loraine said. "Believe me, this blows me away! But I've . . . there's just so much on my mind. . . . This happened so fast . . ."

"Well, when are you supposed to start?"

"In, um . . . a week," Loraine said as if coming out of a daze. "Yeah, a week. There are other people that are flying in from . . . New York? At least one girl is from New York."

"Two, if you count yourself."

"Nah, I've lived here long enough to be an 'Angeleno.' But hey; you don't have to pretend not to be pissed at me for 'stealing' a job from you."

"I'm not pissed at you," Roxanne huffed. "I'm happy for you; I'm not faking this!"

"I know, I know," Loraine said, forcing a smile. "I'm just . . . fucking with you, I don't know."

"Okay . . . Roxanne said, leaning forward against a stool and nodding her head slowly. "So . . . why am I happier that you've made it than you are?"

"You know why."

"Not really, no."

"It's what you keep saying I need to see a shrink about, that's what. Or, what was another one? A priest?"

"I didn't mean to bring up a priest; I don't even know what I was thinking," Roxanne said.

"I think you meant it, though, even if just a little bit."

"It doesn't matter what I mean," Roxanne said. "I just want you to be happy. If even this new job doesn't do that, I . . . I don't know what to say." She picked up her purse and shouldered it.

"Are you leaving?"

"Just to Linda's."

"Wait a second," Loraine said. Roxanne stopped, but did not face her friend completely.

"What?" she said. "Oh, Michael's been calling lately."

"I know. I'm going to call him back, but I can't until a few days from now. See, I have to leave, too."

"Where? Is it for the job?"

"No, it isn't for that," Loraine said. "It's before the job that I have to leave. I have to get out of town, or . . . go somewhere. *Any*where, as long as no people are around."

"Why?"

"Because . . . I want you to see something first."

"What?"

"I've been expecting too much from you. I owe this to you, I think. I'm gonna show you the whole thing. Not just a hairy hand, but the whole thing. My whole body. Do you think you could take it?"

"What are you saying?" Roxanne asked. "Oh, Phyl; please don't tell me that you're going to change into a werewolf."

"But that's just what I have to do!"

"Hey, uh . . . really; that's okay," Roxanne said with a nervous smile. "You don't have to change into anything if you don't want to."

"Quit being all . . . sarcastic and stuff," Loraine said. "I don't want to do this. Do you think it doesn't scare the shit out of me, *making* myself change? But it's probably the only way I can make you believe me!"

"Um . . . y-you don't have to prove anything, Phyl," Roxanne said, backing away slowly. "I mean—oh, did I call you Phyl? Oh, man, I can't even remember your new name."

"Loraine."

"Loraine," she repeated. "I know you don't owe me,

but I was. you know, wondering why that particular name."

"I hate the name Phyllis."

"Oh, I know," Roxanne said. "It was just a matter of time before you changed it. But in the middle of an audition?"

"It just came to me, really," Loraine said. "And it wasn't until I got home that I remembered that it's Joanie's middle name."

"Your aunt?"

Loraine nodded. "Funny how we never really met until maybe two months ago, other than our two seconds at her wedding. We were like instant friends, y'know? She's the way I wish Mom had been. You should go with me back to Wisconsin. You'd love her. She's so sweet and . . . and warm." Loraine seemed lost in thought a moment. "Huh," she said, "Yeah, my deep subconscious, I'm sure. Obviously I want to be just like her and live on a farm and cook pot roasts every day."

"I doubt if it's quite that extreme," Roxanne said. "You admire her, that's all. There's nothing wrong with—"

"I'm still going to show you," Loraine said. "I have to."

"Have to what?" Roxanne said. "Wait—you mean you're still serious about changing into a wolf?"

"I don't blame you for freaking," Loraine said. "I know this makes me look . . . obsessed, I guess, but I need to prove this to myself, too. Just stand over by the door."

"You don't have to do this," Roxanne said. Loraine stepped forward to usher her friend to the door. "Phyl—um, Loraine, it's okay," Roxanne protested meekly. They both stopped at the apartment door. Loraine opened and shut it very quickly.

"Just keep your hand on the knob, and if anything happens . . . I mean, if you think you're in *any* danger, then get out and run like hell."

"Now you *are* scaring me."

Loraine looked her friend in the eyes.

"I'm sorry," she said softly. "Please do this for me. All I'm asking is that you stand there and watch. It's all I'm asking."

Roxanne nodded her head slightly as Loraine went to the far end of the room. Roxanne's palm that held the doorknob was already sweating. She watched Loraine shake out her arms and legs and take several slow, deep breaths. Loraine blew out one long breath as she shut her eyes.

There was some silence, and Roxanne continued to watch. Her hand began unconsciously twisting the knob back and forth. Loraine then appeared to tense up. She began to grit her teeth and let her head tilt forward. Her hands curled up into fists as her concentration intensified. Loraine held this position a few moments before her body began to quiver. The quivering never became shaking or convulsions, but it was enough to partially conceal the beginnings of the transformation.

Loraine opened her eyes and looked up briefly. It was in that moment that Roxanne first noticed the change in eye color and the entire shape of the face. Of course, it couldn't *really* have been growing outward. Loraine's arms weren't actually growing hair, nor were the hands compressing into paws, or the ankles stretching out into animal legs. Roxanne's hand had stopped fidgeting with the doorknob. Her whole body was immobile, while Loraine's appeared to be quite fluid. Loraine's limbs stretched and flowed into non-human proportions. Hair appeared to be falling onto her to cover her otherwise perfect skin. Fangs that could tear open any throat glistened in a mouth lined with black lips. Roxanne watched her friend reach up and tear open her clothes like paper. There was a brief struggle, but the clothing lost and was immediately tossed away.

Loraine dropped onto all fours; four true legs held up her body now. She was now standing and not taking the clumsy crawling position that humans took. Roxanne was still frozen in place; if anything was to happen, she would not be at all prepared for it. It appeared that Loraine's change was complete; there was now one human and one wolf in this apartment, but the wolf continued to quiver. It pushed up several times on its front legs, until it pushed hard enough to stand onto its hind legs. The bones of the hind legs flowed into new proportions, as did its front legs. Paws stretched out into claws. Once again the she-wolf had two arms and two legs, but it was not human.

The wolf/human creature looked up at the frozen two-legger at the other end of the room. It appeared to be studying her a moment, then curled its black lips into what, under other circumstances perhaps, Roxanne would have thought was a smile. Then a slow, low growl came from its throat. The growl became something like a bark. It made different barks that Roxanne heard, but did not react to. The creature cocked its head and . . . shrugged? It growled again.

"Now—doo—yoo—bleeve—meee?" came the words again in quick, painful bursts. The creature waited for

Roxanne's response. She responded, but not the way it had expected or hoped. Her eyes rolled up. The last part of her body to fall was her hand which had, until then, been gripping the doorknob.

The creature barked and fell forward onto its hands and knees. It tried to sit up, then collapsed and shivered. The sound of each gasping breath became higher and less harsh, until it was clearly the sound of a young woman gasping in pain.

As soon as she could move, Loraine struggled to her feet and scrambled the rest of the way to her fallen friend.

Loraine had only just touched her friend's forehead with a wet washcloth, when Roxanne bolted upright. "Is it still here?" she asked.

"No, it's gone," Loraine said. "Shhhh, it's okay. Lie back down."

"It's gone?" Roxanne asked. "Are you sure? Did you look? Where did it go?"

"Shhhh, it's okay, hon, it's okay," Loraine said softly. "It's gone. Really. It's gone."

Roxanne allowed herself to be laid down once more. She rested her arm on her forehead and blew out a breath.

"Why am I lying here?" she asked. "Was I asleep?"

"You fainted," was the answer. Roxanne responded with silence. Eventually she let her arm drop onto the sofa and opened her eyes.

"That was you," she whispered, "wasn't it?"

"Yeah, it was," Loraine whispered back. A brief silence followed.

"Shit."

"I didn't want to do that," Loraine said. "God knows, I was more scared than you were. I didn't know if I could do it, and . . . and still be sane. I was scared to death that I'd . . . hurt you."

"You were scared to death . . ." Roxanne muttered.

"I almost fainted with you, but it hurt too much."

Roxanne began to sit up.

"It hurt?" she asked. "Like, you're in physical pain?"

"Sometimes," Loraine said. "It hurts more to . . . become that thing than to change back. Maybe it's because I'm always fighting it. But then, I'm not about to just let it happen."

"Please don't."

"I won't," Loraine said. "Like I said, I'm not going to go running off into the woods every month. I can't even be happy about this great new job I have. As soon as it's over I'm going back to Joanie's."

"You mean Wisconsin? What if . . . what do you think is there?"

"I keep telling you, the thing that did this to me," Loraine said. "Even if I learn to control it, like today . . ." Loraine shook her head quickly. "No. It's not worth it."

"I was wondering about something," Roxanne said.

"What?"

"Well, the . . . the stuff you did at the tryouts," Roxanne said. "All that leaping around and . . . come on, everything you did was . . . was . . ."

"It came from the wolf," Loraine said. "I know it does."

"No, that can't be it," Roxanne asked. "It came from you, not from—"

"Do you want me to change again and show you that t's true?" Loraine cried.

"No!" Roxanne said, curling up into a ball on the couch. "No, really, you don't have to do that again."

"I'm sorry," Loraine said, reaching out to her friend. 'I didn't mean that. I won't ever do that in front of you again."

"Why don't you just not do it again, period?" Roxanne suggested.

"What do you think I'm working on?" Loraine snapped. "Sorry. I'm just trying to figure out what the hell I need to do. I have two days to figure it out or get out of town."

"Two days?"

"Until the next full moon. If I can't find something that can help me, I'll—go to the desert or something, I don't know. Somewhere where there are no people."

"But what about Tamara?"

"What about her?"

"Well, doesn't she have you coming back in a few days now? How can you do that it you run off to the desert? Oh, there's got to be a better way to do this. You can control it, can't you? I just saw you do that."

"I'm not gonna stick around here to try and meditate myself out of changing. What if it doesn't work, like it didn't last time?"

"Well . . . well, keep practicing," Roxanne said, shrugging. "You don't have to change; you can control it, right?"

Loraine met Roxanne's query with a long silence. She appeared to be stifling frustrated laughter. Loraine bit her bottom lip and shook her head to herself.

"This is changing the subject," she began, "but I wa
wondering it you've noticed something lately."

"Like what?"

"Well . . ." she said, scratching her chin, "it's kind (
hard to explain. At the audition, did you notice anythin
weird about it?"

"Like what?"

"Like . . . someone was watching us while we trie
out?"

"But someone *was* watching us.

"I meant besides Tamara and her entourage, and th
rest of the dancers and . . . I guess I'm not making
strong case for myself. Let me try this: when I was a
the first tryout, I felt somebody . . . watching me. It wa
different than the feeling I got from everyone else. It wa
like someone, or even some*thing* that was watching me
but I couldn't see him. It could have been a her, though
A she, I mean. Am I making sense?"

"Um . . . um . . ." Roxanne fumbled.

"Never mind, you've answered the question," Lorain
said. "Thanks for trying, though."

"Uh . . . anytime."

Twenty

Loraine had happily given notice to the restaurant manager, now that she finally had a job that really would pay the bills. She was in her room packing for a short trip, when Tamara phoned and asked Loraine to meet with her at her Los Angeles office. She had until the next morning before the bus to Barstow left, so Loraine left her packing on hold for the moment.

"I want us to work together before everyone else gets here," Tamara announced as soon as the formalities were out of the way. "This is my first major tour, and I wanna look *good,* you know what I'm saying?"

"Uh . . . uhhh, you want to start right now?" Loraine asked. "This minute?"

"Yeah," Tamara said without a qualm. "You said you didn't have anything major going on right now, right?"

"Uh . . . well, no, not this—I mean . . . yeah," Loraine said. "Yeah, let's do it, then. What did you have in mind?"

Tamara began pacing around her office as she spoke. A man sat quietly and immobile on the soft couch that wrapped around half of the room. Loraine had only just realized that he had been there. She did not recognize him from the tryouts. He could have been her manager,

boyfriend, bodyguard, or anyone at all. Tamara did no
pay any attention to him during their conversation.

"See, I can dance," Tamara continued, "but not lik
you, of course. Not that good. Your job is to make sur
I *do* look good."

"Of course."

"I want simple, but fresh moves, you know what I'r
saying? It has to . . . has to be choreographed, but I hat
stuff that *looks* choreographed, you know what I'm say
ing?"

"Uh-huh."

Nothing that Tamara said was boring, but Loraine
needed all of her powers of concentration to keep under
standing and remembering everything that she heard. To
night's moon was one day away from full. This knowledg
brought back memories against her will. Even now th
room seemed much warmer than when she first entere
it. Her hands fidgeted on their own, as if to check for an
change or imperfection. Thankfully, they remained a
smooth and hairless as they had ever been.

"—you know what I'm saying?" Tamara's voice brok
in. Loraine had always appeared as though she were pay
ing full attention, but until now Tamara had not stare
at her as though electing an answer. Loraine stared back
then smiled nervously.

"Um . . ." she said, "I'm sorry; I didn't hear that las
comment." Tamara cocked an eyebrow.

"I was just saying that we should start thinking abou
the routines now. Right?"

"Um . . . um, I've been thinking about a few things,"
Loraine said, wiping away some sweat. "Do you have
heater on in here?"

"I don't think so," Tamara said, looking over her shoulder at the man, who shrugged, then at Loraine. "Are you hot?"

"Kind of. No, not really. I'm okay. But—before we keep going, I have to be honest with you. I know that I said I wasn't really doing anything, and . . . I'm not really . . . but see, I had this trip planned before your try-outs, and . . . I'm still kind of packing, and . . ."

"A trip? Now? How long is it gonna be?" asked Tamara, concerned.

"Oh, just a few days," Loraine said hastily. "Seriously, just a few days. I'll be back before Friday. Before everyone gets here. It's just that—I can't really do much with you before then. That's all."

"Oh. I see," Tamara said. "How come you didn't say that before?"

"Well, I wasn't sure what you needed to talk about when you called. That, and . . . well, you *are* my boss now. And you're a star!"

Tamara smiled as though embarrassed.

"Ahh, Gawd, I didn't mean it that way," Loraine said. "We're suppose to be cool in L.A. about 'stars,' but—*geez*, you have two hit records and . . . now I'm your choreographer, for Godssake!"

"Hey, I feel lucky to have found you," Tamara said. "And . . . I know I can kinda overwhelm people, like today, I suppose—"

"Oh, no . . ."

"Sometimes I'm a bitch, too," Tamara continued. "But I don't want to be the 'boss' of the group. In this case I can tell you what I don't want to do, but I'm still your student."

"Huh. I never thought of it that way. I guess I *am* your 'teacher.' "

"So where you going?"

"Hm? Oh, just . . . just out to the desert."

"Ohh, you mean Palm Springs? I've never been there. What's it like?"

"Not Palm Springs, Loraine said. "Uhhh, more inland. But . . . um . . . I guess I really should finish packing tonight. Is that okay?"

"Yeah, that's okay."

"I know you wanted to get started right now, but—"

"Hey, I said it was okay. I was just being impatient."

"I'll work out some routines while I'm there."

"Is this a business or pleasure thing?"

"Um . . . business."

"Well . . ." Tamara said, tapping her foot, "don't stress out about this, then. It's only a few days. Just be sure you're back by Friday morning."

"No problem," Loraine said. "I just . . . have this thing that needs to be finished, and then I'll be back no later than Thursday night."

It was just past noon by the time a familiar, but disturbing feeling came over her. Loraine instinctively looked at her hands, but they were as hairless as always. It was that *other* feeling—the one she had felt during the tryouts, and on the way home. She was already at the back of the bus, so this feeling of somebody watching her from behind had to be simple nervousness. Regardless, she stood unsteadily and gripped the seat backs for support as she lumbered slowly up the bus's aisle. Also on board were two couples, one with a baby who expressed its discomfort often throughout the trip, a fat woman who was trying to sleep, a young man whose attention was buried in his newspaper, two silent black men, and a teenager who could very well have been a runaway.

She glanced at each passenger as she passed, hoping to sense something stronger as she came near them. Some threw back glances at her, but then immediately returned to their previous business. Finally she reached the driver. Nothing registered from him, either. She turned and walked back a little faster, and then stopped near the end. The only one beside Loraine now was the fat woman, with the young man and his newspaper just in the seat ahead of her. Loraine hesitated only for a moment, however, before disappearing into the cramped unisex toilet room. She sat down, her hands clasped together as though in prayer. The feeling of being watched had been with her as she had moved up and down the bus, but she had not been able to pinpoint it. Now it was gone, and somebody on the bus had caused it to do this.

Loraine did not allow herself to use a hotel in Barstow. She could not afford to be in a populated area tonight, so she rented a car, got directions to the desert, and sped away as soon as possible. She never explored the town itself much past the bus station. Her cargo consisted of as much camping gear as she could scrounge up, which in this case meant a sleeping bag, flashlight, matches, food, and drink. She also brought extra clothes—one outfit for each day.

If it was illegal to drive out into the middle of the

desert and set up camping, Loraine did not know or care. Better to get a ticket than to wake up with bloodied corpses by her side. The sky was already turning red by the time she had found a suitable spot to park. Once stopped, she busied herself pulling out the food and flashlight. She scooted into the back seat, which was only slightly more comfortable than the front, and shuffled some of her bags around as though taking a count. Looking at the sleeping bag almost made her laugh; it seemed unlikely that she would be doing any sleeping tonight. Hope never killed anyone, however.

She brought magazines but was afraid that reading them now would wear out the flashlight. Instead she set to work eating as much of her luke-warm food as possible, in the hope that the wolf's hunger might also be sated this way. The sky was growing darker, and the desert heat disappeared as quickly as the sun did, but Loraine would never have noticed this. She was always warm on nights like this. Soon enough she would be sweating waterfalls from the heat. She also found herself increasingly dissatisfied with her food. She had canned fruit, water, diet drinks, corn chips, and a chicken sandwich. First it was everything but the meat that offended her; now it was the meat itself. It was not tender enough, not juicy enough, not . . . rare enough. But chicken needed to be well-done, she reminded herself. They had diseases otherwise.

By the time she finished the last of the sandwich, Loraine was pulling at her collar. Outside the desert had dropped its temperature considerably, but Loraine found herself sweating. Near panic now, she ripped through her bags in search of more food. If she could just eat enough, perhaps she'd be so stuffed that the wolf would lie on the side of the car all night, picking at its fangs and burping.

She tore open another bag of chips, then groaned and leaned over in pain. It was her stomach this time, which was not surprising, except that the terrible heat accompanied the pain. Ignoring the pain, Loraine grabbed for more chips and shoved them into her mouth just as an explosion erupted from her belly. She had left the car windows shut, and they were now dripping with a multicolored goop of barely digested junk food. Loraine's first thought was the extra cost of cleaning this stinking mess, when the pain struck again. Her mother had always criticized her for eating too quickly. This felt like more than just a reminder of childhood scoldings, however. It was as if her own body were thwarting her plan—as though it were clearing the way for the wolf to feast on whatever it cared to.

Loraine growled at these thoughts, and at her new discomfort. She held her gut and slumped over onto her side, where another supply of vomit blasted from her gut, this time covering the back of the passenger seat.

She felt weaker this time, as though she had feasted on a sick animal and had been poisoned for it. Yet life was so scarce here; there were scents of creatures on the wind, but where were they? The wind did not follow a straight path. It blew, then seemed to circle back, and may have circled back yet again. How could a hunter follow a scent this way?

She was ready for a two-legger now, but the scent of

none traveled on the wind. Except . . . a scent lingered from inside the shiny behemoth by her side. She peered inside carefully, and sniffed. The stench sent her into a coughing and sneezing fit. A two-legger had been there before, but something intolerable was in there now, and a trace of her own scent was also within. Sensing no further use to the behemoth, she began the night's hunt.

There *was* life here—a lot of it—but most of it was so small. Some scents definitely came from warm-blooded food, while others were unfamiliar. This new land also brought unfamiliar sounds. Something once hissed at her as she raced by, or rather, sounded as though something were shaking a handful of gravel at her. She retraced her steps, but could not find the source of this "rattle."

The moon was at its apex, when a very familiar sound filled her ears. Far away, perhaps miles away, something else was howling. She was uncertain if it was wolf or another creature. With renewed speed and strength she raced off to its source. The wind seemed to be striking her from all sides. The howling began again, and it, too, seemed to come from all directions. The howl sounded closer, however. She howled back, and there was silence. The silence lasted longer than she liked it to. There was no way to tell if she was still going in the right direction; there was not even a scent to follow.

Suddenly the howl was nearly in her ears, and she yelped and leaped off to the side, allowing herself only a split-second to be off-balance. Silence followed once again, and still no scent blew in on the wind. She stood her ground and braced herself for an assault. She bore her fangs, brought out her claws, growled, snapped, and barked at the unseen enemy. Then she dared to take forward steps—slowly at first, but always cautiously. Eventually she reached the spot where she had last heard any noise, and shifted into her erect form. The balance of her two-legger form was so awkward compared to all fours, but for now, it seemed a familiar stance to her. She was used to it for some reason.

There was no sound or motion now save from the wind. Except . . . something warm brushed the nape of her neck. She tensed and almost whirled about to attack, when strange odors filled her nostrils. Her muscles relaxed, and she felt her balance shifting to that of four legs once again. Was something holding her up throughout this? She felt warm limbs caressing her own, but she never thought to touch them back and see if they were real, after all. She was on all fours again, and crouched down even more as a heaviness came upon her back. Her legs tensed, especially the hind ones, and she breathed in these wondrous scents that made the heaviness seem to float away. Now *she* seemed to float away, and yet her paws were firmly planted on the ground.

She shut her eyes and let her head arch back until her snout pointed skywards. Warm limbs continued to hold and caress her from behind, when a loud grunt sounded next to her ear. Her eyes shot open, and all senses snapped back into crisp focus. She jolted forward and felt something heavy slide from her back and fall to the earth with a soft thud. Snarling, she whirled about and squared off against the intruder. There was a brief silence before a snarl not her own joined the roaring of the wind.

Twenty-one

Erotic, but violent dreams faded quickly soon after Loraine opened her eyes. All that soon remained were impressions of a chase, a struggle, and a Pyhrric victory. The ground was hard and very cold. This was something that baffled Loraine. She could not fathom why a desert could be so cold at night when it was so blistering hot during the day. That was the least of her concerns for now. She rose slowly to her feet and struggled to hold together what little remained of her clothes. Perhaps it would be wise from then on to strip before the full moon rises completely. But what of when she awoke in the morning? She wondered if the wolf would keep on a backpack throughout the night.

While dusting herself off, Loraine found more blood, except that it hurt to brush it away. A little bit of spit and gentle wiping revealed that these were *her* wounds this time. There was one large scratch on her shoulder, two small ones on her side, and several on her face, but she would need a mirror to properly locate them. She then caught herself sniffing the air before she thought to look for any unwelcome visitors. A murky memory of fighting something remained from her "dream." What, in this desert, could attack her while the wolf was dominant? A pack of coyotes, perhaps, if any dared to approach her. She knew that coyotes were known to carry off people's pets, even in Los Angeles. But a full-grown wolf? She shook her head vigorously as if that might clear away any cobwebs, but it was of no use. She never remembered her dreams for long.

The sooner she escaped to civilization, the better. Far, far away she caught a glimpse of something that could have been her car. It wasn't easy walking barefoot in this rocky terrain. Gravel and spiky plants and bushes poked at her feet. The sudden thought of coming across some nasty creature—a scorpion or rattlesnake, perhaps—spurred her to walk faster, however.

The glimpse of something was her car. It appeared to be undamaged, except for the remains of half-digested food that had dried onto the back of the seat. Holding her nose, Loraine donned her clothing for the day and held her breath while climbing into the driver's seat. She then opened all of the windows but the soiled one.

Her first stop in town was at the car wash. It took one hour and a half of her spending money to clean out the vomit. After this was a trip to the market to load up on more supplies. A different approach to fighting the wolf was necessary tonight. Intense concentration and meditation did not seem effective enough, and binging on junk food only created a mess.

She made several attempts at collect calls to home, but answering machines cannot accept phone charges. After the last attempt she considered calling Joanie again, but did not have her phone book with her. This, and what could she say? That she was out in the middle of the desert in order to avoid killing people? Loraine would probably not be able to explain her situation once she finally reached Wisconsin, either.

With little else to do but wait once again for the night, Loraine wandered aimlessly through the town for about half of the day. For the other half, she discovered a small library—the only library for all she knew—and searched inside for a private spot. A brief search revealed nothing useful in the way of lycanthropy lore. She settled for a magazine that she never actually read. Too many thoughts were shooting about in her brain now. Unfortunately all she had at the moment were questions and no answers.

The more she considered her situation, the more of a paradox it became. She still did not believe in real monsters such as werewolves, yet she believed herself to be one. Of course she was one; what else could explain her actually becoming a wolf before her friend's very eyes? This was not Loraine's greatest concern, however. The most disturbing thing, she realized, was the ease in which she had come to believe in and almost accept this curse.

What was keeping her sane throughout all of this? She had never enjoyed horror films because they inevitably gave her nightmares. She was not having nightmares now, but her dreams were always very strange when the moon was full. If the wolf's actions were becoming Loraine's dreams, then the wolf had to be some subconscious part of her that had managed to—literally—manifest itself. What, then, of her actions? Did the wolf have dreams about drinking diet soft drinks and sitting in libraries?

Suddenly there were no more questions. The most important one had been answered. She was calm and rational about the curse because the wolf wanted her to be that way. She had been fighting a battle that, until now, she had no idea that she had been losing. The real curse was not the physical change, but the mental. This led to a thought; Roxanne had once suggested counseling for her problem, but only because she didn't believe Loraine. Counseling did not sound as offensive this time. Her body was not the only thing being violated; it was her mind most of all.

Loraine chuckled out loud to herself, then silenced herself in embarrassment. No one had seemed to hear her, fortunately. She was laughing at the mental image of herself, lying on a sofa and discussing her flea and tick problems with a skeptical shrink. No, Loraine didn't need someone who would waste all of her time trying to convince her that no curse existed, except in her fantasies. Briefly she also considered finding a psychic or a parapsychic or a superpsychologist. She couldn't remember what they were called, so she settled on "ghostbuster" for the time being.

This "secret admirer" who had been haunting her was no outsider, after all. Loraine would have bet her soul that the wolf had been her "ghost" all along. It had been following her, watching her, trying to intrude on daylight hours. Loraine felt herself shiver in spite of the great heat outside. She was not cold, but afraid of what her answer could be to a new question: Did she want the wolf to stop? After all, what had caused her to get not only a new job, but a great new job—herself or the wolf?

The sky was turning red. It was time to see if this new knowledge would be of any use.

* * *

Two days now and no police had hauled her away for camping in the desert. Perhaps it wasn't illegal, after all. On the other hand, a night in jail might be the safest way to spend the second—and strongest—full moon. If the police didn't shoot her while she was trying to rip the bars from the cages, that is.

Loraine brought more water than food with her this time. She hadn't eaten or drunk very much that day, and was feeling dehydrated. She spread her sleeping bag across the back seat and attempted to sit in a lotus position. This proved to be impossible, so she settled for leaning back into the seat and stretching out her legs as far as possible. Then she cleared her throat and closed her eyes.

Okay, she thought, no meditation shit this time. I know you're in there. Hey! I said I know you're in there! Talk to me!

" 'Talk to me,' " she mumbled. "What the hell am I doing?" Going crazy, she thought. Too late! Already there!

So since I'm already crazy, she thought, who cares if I'm trying to carry on a conversation with an animal? You're going to come out sooner or later, so you might as well come out now! It doesn't matter if you can't 'talk,' you can at least growl or something.

"This is bullshit," Loraine mumbled, opening her eyes. She sighed loudly and leaned against the door. Then she sat up again abruptly and tried to prick her ears. Somebody coming? The wind? Or had she really heard rough laughter? Animals don't laugh. It was either the wind or some homicidal maniac who specialized in lone campers. But the laughter was coming from within.

What's so funny to *you?* she thought hard to the beast. I was here first! You're just some fake monster that used to show up all over the movies and TV, but nobody cares about you anymore! Didn't you know that? Nobody believes in werewolves, and neither do I! Stop laughing, you asshole! You're not going anywhere tonight! You're gonna sit inside of me all night, or better yet, go away completely! I don't *have* to accept you, you know!

She took off her shirt from the heat.

I've figured out what you've been doing! You've been trying to make me accept all of this, and believe that it's true with barely any proof! Well I *don't* accept you and *don't* believe in you! You're nothing but a delusion, so get out and take your fucking laughing with you!

She opened the door beside her and kept it ajar. She tensed up in rage and fought for new fighting words, but burst out laughing instead. There was a loud, shrill voice shouting at her from within, but the louder she laughed, the smaller the voice became, until it was as if a mouse had crawled into her mind to squeak its rage at the goliath.

There was as little hunting this night as before. The animals were too small, too well-hidden, and too difficult to see by their warmth. The wind blew in too many directions to truly follow a scent, but one direction revealed some tiny lights far into the distance. She remembered that two-leggers liked lights, so she bolted off in their direction. The wind whipped around her ears and fur haphazardly, until a familiar sound broke away from the din and forced her into a dead stop. The wind died a little as if stepping aside for the quick growl—almost a bark— that sounded close by. As always the sound fascinated her, and yet this time it also annoyed her. Her preferences had been made clear two nights in a row now, so she fought the compulsion to remain, and crept toward the lights, picking up speed slowly.

By the time she was at a quick trot, she felt her as-yet-unseen companion nearby, matching her steps. If it was another wolf, she no longer cared. She had no more wish to confront this cowardly presence. It could follow her all the way to the lights if it wished; she had had her fill of it.

The lights were becoming brighter and larger. Shapes coming into view reminded her of the caves that two-leggers lived in. She was in a full run by this time, her "friend" still matching her every step. Her heart quickened at the thought of escaping her shadow and finding some two-legger meat for the first time. There seemed to be so many different shapes and sizes to these creatures that it was bound to be a true feast. If one was too stringy, a plump one might make up for it easily.

An intruding thought made her slow down and stumble somewhat. She was able to keep running, but a sudden revulsion had accompanied her previous thoughts. Strange that it would come while she was thinking about food. It came again at that moment. There was a brief image of her own paws becoming pale and hairless as she was feasting on a two-legger; in effect, she became a two-legger feasting on her own kind. This was only a thought, and not reality, but it was enough to make her trip over herself.

She tumbled headlong into the dirt, her hind legs flying up and over, until after several flips she landed on her back. Only for an instant, however, before she scrambled back onto her feet and shook the dirt from herself.

A very solid presence slammed into her from behind, causing her to flip over again, but she did not manage to climb back onto her feet. A warm, but heavy weight was pressed onto her back, as it had attempted to do on earlier nights. She did not have the leverage to force it off of her this time. She could feel the fur from its body and the hot breath on the back of her neck, but it would take time to break away from this attack. In the meantime she snapped and barked and squirmed, but to no effect so far. She also howled, but it was a strange howl. It was not like a wolf's at all, but more like some two-legger trying to imitate a wolf. Sadness, fear, and rage came from this howl, as well. She gathered her strength, howled again and squirmed forward with all her might until the weight fell away from her back. She darted far ahead of her assailant, then doubled back quickly, stood her ground, and snarled.

Loraine awoke with a yelp on a cold, hard desert floor. If the desert did not seem all alike to her, she might have remembered this as the same place as she had awoken to the day before. Once again her dreams had been haunted by violence. They were less erotic than the ones the night before. There was a brief, fading memory of someone or thing trying to join with her, but the rest was slashing and snapping, and the smell of blood.

This was the first time in years that she had made a

noise while waking up. She remembered waking up screaming as a child after a particularly terrifying nightmare. Her mother had come in, but was angry that Loraine had woken her up. That was all she remembered of that. And this time? She didn't remember a horrible nightmare, but there was a remaining feeling of fear and frustration. Yes, frustration. She had been shouting or yelling or something in frustration. She didn't remember why. Loraine yelped again, but this time in pain as she discovered more wounds. Perhaps it would be wise to buy a first aid kit in town today.

She settled for bandaids after discovering just how much a first aid kit would cost her. After ministering to her wounds, Loraine walked through town again. As before she did not pay much attention to her surroundings, except when she briefly amused herself by counting as many garish motels as she could find along one of the main streets.

Loraine found a used bookstore and browsed for possibly an hour before attempting to strike up a conversation with the proprietor. He was a wiry, hyper, middle-aged man with a smoker's face and a voice to match. She had only asked a few innocuous questions, but it seemed enough to send him off on an avalanche of facts, tidbits, and trivia about whatever topic happened to come up. And opinions. He had opinions about everything, including werewolves, who at one point were compared to "goddamned cockroaches." Loraine had brought up the subject first by asking about horror in general, and then monsters.

The proprietor shot out obscure lore about lycanthropy as though it were common knowledge. Many of his comments were punctuated with a shrug. Eventually Loraine noticed that the store held more than just books. Besides posters and historical photos lining the walls, a small section of the store displayed knickknacks ranging from collectible tin toys to medieval armor. Loraine discovered these artifacts after following the proprietor around as he busied himself with restocking and rearranging, all while never missing a beat in their one-sided conversation. Her gaze skimmed along the shelves several times, trying to take in all the details. After three such passes, she noticed a box with what appeared to be very shiny bullets.

While the proprietor continued his diatribe against lycanthropes, Loraine crept closer to the box. She was reaching out for it, when a hand and arm shot in from the side and snapped the box shut.

"Hey, sorry," the owner said quickly. "This ain't supposed to be out."

"What were those?" Loraine asked. "Were those bullets?"

The owner had already set the box aside by the time she had asked her question.

"Huh?" he said. "Oh, yeah, yeah. Guy ordered them a while ago. Damndest thing. They're silver, you know."

"Silver?" Loraine said skeptically. "Silver bullets."

"Yeah," the owner said, nodding quickly. "Listen, are you gonna buy anything or you just following me around? I'm married, you know."

"Huh?" Loraine said as the owner was turning his back on her and disappearing into the piles of books and collectibles. It took her several moments to absorb his parting words before she let out a nervous chuckle and left the store hurriedly.

* * *

The bookstore owner had not actually told Loraine anything about werewolves that she did not already know. If there were some other way to a cure than a silver bullet in the chest, he had not offered one. There was no way for her to tell if those bullets really had been silver, who had ordered them, and how long ago. It could have been her "secret admirer," after all, who had followed her here in order to hunt her down. No, she knew now that the "secret admirer" was actually the wolf within her, trying to intrude on reality.

For the third and last time there would be a full moon. Camping in the Mojave was no Hawaiian vacation, but at least it was safe. She would take the bus back to a fabulous new job in Los Angeles and renew the cycle of working for a month before taking another three-day vacation. This was not going to work. No employer should be expected to allow it; Loraine would certainly not have.

She tried a form of "angry meditation" this time. It was much like the shouting match with the wolf that she had attempted earlier, but more focused and better prepared. The wolf wasn't going to laugh at her this time. She cleared her mind of all thoughts but angry ones and "spoke" to the wolf in the form of an intense mantra: You are weak, you are nothing, I am strong, I am everything, I belong here, you belong nowhere.

Loraine repeated this and variations of it to the wolf, each repetition building in intensity and anger. She strayed from the mantra more often as the moon moved higher into the sky. Sometimes she degenerated into another shouting match, but always went back to the chant.

As always her temperature began to rise, and she opened her eyes often, but there appeared to be no physical change. But deep within her body, she felt a swelling begin, as though a balloon were being blown up inside of her. Loraine instinctively held her breath and shut her eyes hard, but the swelling would not disappear. She would have sworn that her body was blowing up like that balloon, but she dared not open her eyes to see.

Then the swelling stopped attacking her entire body, and shot down to her feet. She reached down and felt them; they seemed as small as ever. Her hands followed it as it seemed to travel along her legs. As before, only the feeling of swelling was there, but touching the affected places revealed nothing. It swept up her legs and into the torso, seeming to circle around her midsection, only then to shoot straight into her head. The shock caused Loraine's head to fly back and her eyes to shoot open. Her sleepless night began just as she realized what the "swelling" had really been.

Twenty-two

Loraine awoke with a stiff neck, sore feet, and bruised arms. She rolled over in the sand and almost gave her thigh a charley horse. Last night had been the oddest "dream" yet. Her body had been severely weakened. Her strength, her stamina, her senses—none seemed to work well, she recalled. She remembered being constantly frustrated. Her "dream" had also been very cold, as though her fur had not been thick enough for warmth. Last of all, she remembered being angered and repulsed by somebody's pale skin.

Loraine stood up slowly and examined her arms as she did so. As she poked at the bruises near her wrist, she briefly remembered hitting something. She had been trapped and had been trying to break free, and had struck something repeatedly. The memory disappeared now, as most of them did after such nights. The sight of ghostly pale skin remained in her mind, though. Whose skin had it been? A victim's?

There was no blood on her hands or anywhere else this time. Her clothes were intact, except for her missing shoes. Much closer this time than the last two nights was the reflection of her rented four-wheel drive. She hobbled off in its direction, then hurried when she remembered that there was a bus to catch that morning. She tore off her socks after they quickly became bogged down in sand and bristles.

Loraine barely made it back in time to return the rental and make the bus. She was in a hurry even after she was safely aboard, and was slow in regaining her breath. The ride back seemed to take much longer than the trip to the desert. Absent this time was that maddening feeling of being watched, but the anticipation of its appearance made the trip no less uncomfortable.

It was evening by the time she returned. The moon was due to appear, but it would be in the next phase now. She had already called for a ride from Roxanne; the two rode home in uncustomary silence. Loraine realized this and apologized after they reached the apartment, citing exhaustion.

"I'm sure you are," Roxanne said, carrying Loraine's heaviest baggage to the bedroom. Loraine followed solemnly with the rest of her gear. They almost bumped into each other on the way out, but Loraine did not smile.

"Um . . . I don't think there's anything in the fridge," Roxanne said as they made their way to the living room.

"I'm not really hungry," Loraine said. "I ate some stuff on the bus."

"You sure? I thought maybe you'd want to . . . go somewhere, but I guess you're too tired, huh?"

"Yeah," Loraine said distantly, then appeared more alert. "Yeah, I know it's early, but maybe I should just go to bed."

"Your thing is tomorrow, isn't it? With Tamara Taylor?"

"Ahh, God, that's right," Loraine said with a groan.

"You mean you forgot?"

"No . . . no, I didn't forget," Loraine said. "It just wasn't exactly in the front of my mind."

"She's called twice. You talked to her before you left, didn't you? What's she like?"

"You were at the tryout, too, remember?"

"Yes, but she didn't say very much. She sounds like a New Yorker; you know, a real fast talker, in a hurry."

"Yeah, she's like that," Loraine said vaguely, then looked up at Roxanne and smiled slightly. "Yeah, I'll make sure you get to meet her."

Roxanne beamed.

"Hey, I wasn't going to ask," she said.

"Yeah, you were. I would've. I would've begged you to. I would've hated you, too, but that's another thing."

"You would not."

"I know, I'm just—" Loraine yawned and stretched, "Ahhhh, I'm just kidding you. I guess I should call her back."

"You 'guess' you should?"

"I should. I will." Loraine went to the phone and began punching numbers, then frowned and groped around the counter for her address book. She redialed, then noticed Roxanne watching her. "Don't worry, I'll ask her to talk to you." Roxanne beamed again.

"—Five six seven eight!"

For the umpteenth time the sounds of Tamara Taylor

and her music blared over loudspeakers. Tamara herself was dancing to it, as were five other dancers. Loraine stepped back and kept time to the music while inspecting the performances. For two weeks she and these five other dancers had memorized every word and note of at least half of Taylor's songs. Some of them were beginning to hate this particular song—"Let Me Not"— because of the number of times that they had had to stop it. Tamara was surprised that she could follow Loraine's moves on this song while two others could not. Eventually Loraine called a break and went to confer quietly with the two, but Tamara seized the opportunity to interrupt with a pep talk after the spectators' applause had died down.

"Hey, are all you guys as sweaty as I am?" she shouted to the room. Some muttered "no," but most agreed loudly with Taylor. "I don't know about me, but you guys are great!" More applause. "Loraine, a break for lunch, okay?"

"Hm? Oh, uh—yeah, we'll take lunch," she said. "Nothing heavy, you guys! Hour-and-a-half!" she called out to those who were already leaving. Tamara ignored her manager and approached Loraine.

"I just want you to know that I love what you're doing here," she said. Loraine allowed herself an embarrassed smile before shaking her head.

"Sometimes I feel like I'm cheating," she said.

"Whadda you mean, 'cheating?' " Tamara said. "How can you 'cheat' what you've been doing?"

"I guess I didn't mean cheating," Loraine said. "I mean it's—I guess I still think that it's too good to be true. You know . . . working for you and all that."

"Ah," Tamara said, waving her off. "So . . . where do

you wanna eat? I'm buying. Speaking of which, some guys left before I could offer. I was gonna take everyone out."

"But you always do that."

"Not 'always,' " Tamara insisted. "But you know," she added, lowering her voice, "when I do, it's a business expense."

"Huh!" Loraine said. "I don't know where to go, though. We have to eat light, but I want a steak sooo bad."

"So do I," Tamara laughed. She didn't realize, of course, that Loraine always wanted a steak—or any meat.

Los Angeles treated its celebrities one of two ways: a star could be mobbed by fans or ignored by them when showing herself in public. Tamara was approached by only one person while in the restaurant, but she could feel the eyes of rubberneckers upon her at all times. Loraine could, too, but was much relieved that someone else was being watched this time. She had not felt her "secret admirer's" presence since her time in the desert. The wolf was weakest during a new moon, perhaps.

Loraine poked at her food while Tamara ate steadily and chatted with Paul, her manager. Tamara only noticed Loraine's silence after she asked Loraine a question.

"Hey, girlfriend," she said, waving her hand in Loraine's face. "Wake up."

"I'm awake," Loraine said. "I was just thinking about . . . my car. It's being fixed, I mean."

"Oh," Tamara said. "Will it live?"

"Huh? Oh, yeah, I think it will. They keep finding stuff that's wrong with it. I need that thing bad, though."

"Don't we all." Tamara pulled aside a waiter to order more iced tea, then shook some pepper onto her salad. "So whadda you think?" she asked. Loraine was lost in thought again. "Loraine?"

"Hm?"

"I was wondering about 'Let Me Not,' " Tamara said. "Rene and Danny keep having trouble with your moves. Do you know why that is? I mean, I figure if I can do them, anyone could."

"I started talking to them, but you called lunch," Loraine said. "I guess—"

"Oh, I wasn't trying to interrupt you," Tamara said. "I didn't see that you were talking to them."

"I don't think it'll be a problem after a few times," Loraine said. "They'll get it eventually."

Tamara nodded, and her eyes went up to follow the man who was approaching their table from behind Loraine. He seemed to recognize her. Another one, she thought. The man put his hand on Loraine's shoulder. She sat up straight and almost swallowed her food the wrong way.

"Excuse me? Aren't you Phyllis Turner?" She turned around. He wore dark sunglasses, but she had no difficulty recognizing him. "Could I have your autograph?" he said.

"Michael!" she exclaimed. "What are you doing here?"

"Well, I'm—"

"I mean—" she broke in. "Well, you know what I mean."

"Believe it or not, I'm on vacation," Michael said. "My character has 'mysteriously disappeared' for the next few weeks, meaning I get a break. I'll probably come back with amnesia or something."

"Is that the only way you guys can get any time off?"

"No, they can kill off our characters, too," he said with a wink. "I didn't mean to interrupt if you're . . ."

"Uh, no, not really," Loraine mumbled.

"Did you say you have amnesia?" Tamara asked.

"Hm? Uh, no, see I'm—" Michael stopped and leaned forward, removing his glasses and lowering his voice, "I work on a soap opera. Their plotlines can sometimes be . . . you know, unusual."

"Oh, I think I've seen you now," Paul said. "Uh . . . I don't remember which soap, that is. Probably on a magazine cover."

"Yeah, suuuuuure," Tamara said, nudging him.

"I believe I've seen your face on a cover or two," Michael said, holding out his hand to Tamara. She took it and shook hands weakly. "Tamara Taylor, right?"

"Yeah," she said. "Oh! Not *too* loud, okay?"

"Oo! Sorry about that," Michael muttered. He put his sunglasses back on.

"Um, Michael?" Loraine's voice came softly.

"Yes?"

"I . . . changed my name," she said. "It's Loraine now. Not Phyllis."

"Loraine, huh?" he said, nodding his head as though giving it great consideration. "I like it."

"Thanks."

"I was wondering when you'd finally do that, actually. You've hated 'Phyllis' since I've known you."

"Long before that," she said. "Uh—well—I was surprised to see you here, and, uh—well, it was nice seeing you again."

He looked at her with a gentle smile.

"It was nice seeing you again, too," he said quietly. He patted her shoulder. "Maybe we'll run into each other at some more restaurants."

"Yeah," she said. "Maybe we will."

"Well!" he said, bringing his hands together. "I'm sorry if I interrupted you all. Ms. Taylor, it was a pleasure meeting you."

"Nice meeting you, too."

"I'll leave you all alone, then," he said. "Phyl—uhh, Loraine. See you around, I hope."

"Yeah."

Michael waved briefly and let his hand linger on Loraine's shoulder as he did so. He let it slide off slowly as he finally took his leave. There was a brief silence after he had gone out of earshot.

"He was my boyfriend," Loraine said.

"Ohh," Tamara said. "Not anymore, huh?"

"Nah, we, uh—we actually broke up not too long ago. That is, I broke up with him."

"Oh, sorry."

"Yeah, well, he's called me a couple of times," Loraine said. "They were always at bad times, like when I couldn't call him back."

"He'll get the hint eventually," Tamara assured.

"I guess," Loraine said. "Except that I broke up with him, because he wouldn't commit. I wanted to move in with him, and he 'wasn't ready.' So it wasn't like some couples who fight all the time."

"Oh," Tamara said, nodding. "I've been through something like that, too. I know what you're saying."

Paul looked at his watch and tapped Tamara's shoulder. "We need the check soon," he said. The two women now looked at their watches.

"Damn," Tamara muttered. "Lunch always goes so fast for me. Hate it. Back to the music, huh?"

"Back to the music," Loraine said.

Loraine had been very close to expressing her misgivings about remaining with Tamara's troupe, until Michael had interrupted her thoughts. She had actually come close to quitting her position since her first day on the job, besides not accepting the job in the first place. Once she began dancing, though, she was always swept away by the music, the movement, and the emotion. But whenever the music stopped, Loraine returned to her somber state of mind. If Tamara had noticed Loraine's mood swings in the meantime, she had not mentioned anything.

The lunchbreak had done everyone some good. Rene and Danny, the two who had been having difficulties with some of the moves, finally fell into place and never fell out again. A minor difficulty with some of Tamara's moves was dealt with, and the day was finished. Loraine was drinking the last of her mineral water, when she felt a hand on her shoulder. She didn't need to turn around to know that it was Tamara.

"You were great today," she said after Loraine turned around.

"Thanks. Everyone was."

"Tomorrow I wanna work on " 'True Minds,' " Tamara

said. "Except, I don't think I like everyone being out there. I mean, maybe just two of us onstage would look the best. Me and two others, I mean."

"No problem," Loraine said, gathering her gear.

"Yeah. Well, see ya, Lor," Tamara said, and left to join Paul, who wasted no time discussing business. Loraine was at the door, though, when Tamara called to her.

"Hm?" Loraine said, and waited. Tamara broke away from Paul to join her.

"I was just wondering something," Tamara said, her voice low. "Are you okay?"

Loraine seemed confused by the question, when in reality a knot was tying in her stomach.

"Oh, yeah," she said cautiously. "How come?" Tamara responded briefly with silence.

"No reason, I guess," she said eventually. "You seem like you're . . . down a lot. When you're not dancing, I mean. But . . . you're probably just tired, huh?"

"Yeah," Loraine said distantly. "I'm just tired."

"Sorry 'bout that, girlie," Tamara said. "But . . . if you're ever . . . 'not tired,' you call me, okay?"

"No problem."

Twenty-three

Tamara's concern for Loraine, now finally revealed, was mostly for professional, but also personal, reasons. Any problem that could affect a performance needed to be disclosed to Tamara. This, and she genuinely cared for her "people." Once the thrill of working for a celebrity wore off, Tamara expected Loraine and the others to become friends. Loraine had not yet revealed her unusual problem to Tamara, but in less than two weeks it would become necessary to.

That night after rehearsal, Loraine spent almost an hour sitting on her futon, holding the scrap paper upon which she had scribbled Michael's phone number. Roxanne was not at home. Loraine did not know if she would come home later or would stay at Linda's for the night. For a brief time she contemplated practicing on controlling her monthly change, then discarded the thought. She could not afford to give the wolf any opportunity to come out.

Loraine reached instinctively for the phone when it rang, then decided to let the answering machine do its work. After the message ended, she went to the kitchen and replayed it. A hang-up. Just then the phone rang again, so she answered it this time.

"Hello?" she said a second time. Silence. Loraine hung up quickly without another thought. Everyone got crank calls like that one. They were annoying, but never frightening.

She went to the couch and slumped in, when the phone rang again. Growling now, Loraine dragged herself from the couch and snatched up the phone.

"Hello!" she said.

"Wh—? is this Loraine?" a male voice said. "Oh, I mean—"

"Michael?"

"You said it's Loraine now, right?"

"Um—um, yeah," Loraine said. "Do you like it?"

"Yeah, I do," Michael said. "It's better than Phyllis. That is, not that I hated it, but you always did."

"Well, Phyllis is an old lady's name," Loraine said. "So when I'm an old lady, I should change it back."

"Yeah," he said, chuckling. "Yeah." An awkward silence followed.

"You didn't just call earlier, did you?" Loraine asked.

"When?"

"Just before now," she said. "And didn't say anything?"

"Not me. It must have been a wrong number."

"I guess so," she said. "So . . . what is it? I mean, what's up?"

"Oh . . . nothing, really," he said. "I was just . . . it was nice seeing you again, that's all."

"It was nice seeing you, too."

"Yeah," he said. "And . . . your friend, too. You didn't tell me you and Tamara Taylor were best buddies!"

"We're not 'best buddies,' " Loraine corrected. "I work for her now."

"No kidding? As a dancer?"

"Her choreographer."

Michael whistled, impressed. *"Nice* work, Phyl—uh, Loraine. Jeez, I'm sorry. I'm trying to remember that."

"That's okay," she said. "You didn't find out until today."

"Uhhh, I know," he said. "I'll just remember that you look more like Loraine Bracco than Phyllis Diller."

"Gee, thanks."

"Oh, you know what I mean," he said. "I'll think of some way to remember. But—congratulations, anyway! Tamara Taylor is really hot now!"

"She's going on tour in a few months," Loraine said. "That's why she's getting a dance troupe together."

"Outstanding," he said. "You were way overdue for a break. I know that you really love dancing—"

"True."

"—and people who love what they do shouldn't be frustrated all the time."

"Like you?"

"Me?" he said. "Well, not anymore. I'm on a soap, remember? But . . . yes and no, to be honest. It's not like soap acting is the epitome of the craft."

"Nicely put," she said. "Um . . . Michael . . . I was wondering . . . if you're on vacation, why would you still be in L.A.? Not that I'm saying 'get outta town,' but— you could probably afford a trip around the world by now, right?"

"Um . . . probably," he said. "But that brings me to the real reason I called. Last week I was out of town, but this week I promised to do these benefit dinners in town, and, um . . . of course, this new job must be keeping you exhausted, but, um . . . well, I . . . I wasn't sure if you'd even be interested in a benefit dinner. People give long speeches and toasts and . . . the food is usually good, though."

"When is it?"

"Um . . . Thursday night," he said. "Seven o'clock. I know this is real spur of the moment, but . . . I've just been thinking about you lately. You never return my calls, so I guess you're not thinking of me, but I'm thinking of you."

"It's not like that," Loraine said quietly. "I do think about you. It's just—"

"Just what?" Michael said after a pause.

"I doubt if you'll believe me," she said, "But I do want to see you again. I really do. But—this is a terrible time for me right now. You have no idea."

"Is it—is it your work?"

"No," she said quickly. "Work is fine. It's something I've been going through that—I don't want you getting involved in."

"Um . . . oh," Michael said. "I think I know what you mean now."

"I doubt it."

"Well, it's another guy, right?"

"I could give you a million guesses right now, and you wouldn't get it," she said. "No, it isn't another guy. That I could deal with."

"Then what is it?"

"I said I don't want you getting involved," she said, but unconvincingly.

"You don't have AIDS or something, do you?" he asked. " 'Cuz if you do, I—"

"Michael, please," she said. "I don't have AIDS, it's not another guy, it's—it's just not anything you can help me with!"

"But now that I know that something's really bothering you, I can't just hang up and forget you said anything," he said.

"Michael—"

"Maybe it isn't something I can 'help' you with," he continued. "But—I don't know. I could try to cheer you up, couldn't I?"

Loraine smiled, but out of frustration.

"Couldn't I?" he asked again.

"I can't tell you what it is," she said.

"Then don't," he said. "At least, not until you're ready. I won't even ask."

"You'll just get hurt," she said. "I'd die if you ended up—hurt."

"I've already been hurt."

"Not the way you could be."

"Loraine," he said, "tell me now. Do you ever want to talk to me again? Ever see me again? If you don't, then say it now. If you don't, then . . . I'll leave you alone."

"I—" she started, then needed to stop and take a breath. "I want to see you tonight. I just need somebody to . . . be here."

"I'll be right there."

Loraine thought of banging her head against the wall. How could she be so weak? She paced the living room floor endlessly, wondering why she couldn't summon the courage to call Michael back and cancel their "date," or why she had asked him to come in the first place. Not too long ago she would have easily found the strength to refuse him, to . . . protect him.

It was night, but Michael appeared at her door with sunglasses on. She hesitated at first, struggling over whether to allow him inside or to send him right back home. She allowed him inside. He removed his sunglasses as he entered.

"Hi," he said as she locked the door behind him.

"Hi," she said. They stood face-to-face now. He shifted back and forth while she fidgeted with her hands, and then the two fell forward into an embrace. Loraine rested her head against Michael's chest before looking up to kiss him. She wanted him never to leave, even though he would have to, and soon. Perhaps forever.

"Hi," he said again, and looked quickly around the room. "Is your roommate here?"

"Uh . . . um, no," she said, her thoughts returning to her. "I don't know where she is."

"Do you want to sit?" he said.

"Yeah," she said, but stood tiptoe to kiss him again. He would have to leave. He would be hurt, or killed, if he stayed.

Michael put his arm around her waist as they went to the couch and fell into its cushions. Loraine leaned close to Michael as he rubbed her shoulder gently.

"Did you still not want to talk," he began, "or did you want to?"

She shook her head.

"You still don't want to?"

"I don't. I can't."

"Okay," he said. "If you still don't want to talk, I just want you to know that I can at least just . . . sit here and be here with you. If it helps."

"Maybe it will," she whispered. "I'm glad you're here, though." She was horrified that he was there. She was disgusted with herself for being so weak. She sat back up.

"But I'm a terrible hostess," she said. "Do you want me to get you something?"

"I'm fine," he said, waving her off. "C'mere. You're the one who needs comforting, right?"

"I'm . . . I'm just using you," she said. "I mean, asking you to come here just so I can cry on you?"

"That's all right," he said.

"It's not fair to you, though," she said. "Especially since I can't even tell you what's wrong."

"Well . . . well, does anyone know? Can't you tell anyone what's going on?"

"Roxanne knows."

"So it's . . . girl stuff, right?"

"Uh, well, I wouldn't say that, exactly."

"So . . ." Michael stopped, then sat up straight. "Loraine, " he said, "are you pregnant?"

"Like I said, I could give you a million guesses and you wouldn't get it," she said.

"Well, are you?"

"No. Please don't ask me, Michael. I might tell you, and then you'd think that I'm crazy."

"Oh, I knew that a long time ago."

"What?"

"Just kidding!" he said quickly. "Just joking. You

know, since I don't know what's wrong, it's all I can do to keep things light. You know?"

Loraine watched him before smiling sadly. She sat up straight again and fidgeted with her fingers.

"I guess it'd be safe to go to that thing on Thursday," she said. *Tell him to leave.* "Or actually, I forgot to ask Tamara about it. In case she wants to do 'overtime' or something."

"Why don't you call her now?"

Loraine rose from the couch to do just that.

"And tell her I have all of her albums," he added.

"You don't have *any* of them."

"Well, I'll *get* all of them!" he called. She smiled, but very briefly, and called Tamara's private line. An unfamiliar male voice answered and took Loraine's message that Tamara return her call.

Michael had turned on the television before Loraine hung up. She almost asked him to turn it off, then realized that it would be a good way to avoid conversation. She returned to her place beside Michael and watched the television screen flip from channel to channel. Michael's tendency to "channel surf" had often been an irritant to Loraine, but now it was a comfort. It allowed her to keep from concentrating on any one subject.

Apparently satisfied, Michael leaned back after settling on one station. It seemed familiar to Loraine.

"What is this?" she asked.

" 'The Exorcist,' " he said. "I haven't seen this in—"

"No," she said, snatching up the controller to change the channel. "No monster movies. No scary stuff. I don't need that right now."

"Oh," he said. "Sorry. Guess I wasn't thinking. I'll find some sitcom. Ohhh, 'Star Trek.' Do you mind?"

"No," she said. He could have turned on any show, save another horror movie. Loraine watched the show, but absorbed nothing of what was happening. She leaned close to Michael, wrapped her arms around his, and shut her eyes. His gaze was glued to the television, until she began nuzzling his shoulder. She kissed him twice on the shoulder; Michael then tore his gaze from the space show and responded in kind to her affections. By the next commercial break they had tossed the throw pillows and back cushions from the sofa, and were doing some "space exploration" of their own.

Twenty-four

Loraine was jolted from sleep by a bang. Or rather, a slam. Somebody had slammed the door. Michael, his head under the pillow, groaned and rolled back and forth. Loraine rubbed her eyes and groped for her underwear. Michael fumbled with the pillow and seemed surprised after he finally pulled it away from his face. He forced his eyes open and watched Loraine as she pulled on her nightshirt.

"Did that wake you, too?" she whispered.

"What?"

"You didn't hear that? That loud noise?"

"Oh, is that what that was," he mumbled. "My pillow was almost smothering me. How'd it get on my face?"

"The way you crawl all over the place?" she said. "I'm surprised your head wasn't down there," she said, indicating the foot of the futon. "I think that was Roxanne."

Loraine made to climb out of bed, but Michael held her gently in place and tried to kiss her. She gave in for a few moments, then pulled away and rolled into a sitting position. He tried again to entice her to stay by scratching her back. For a moment she gave in to this as well. Michael stopped himself when he noticed her leg bouncing up and down. The faster he scratched, the faster her leg bounced. He was quite amused, but stopped and watched Loraine behave as though emerging from a trance.

Movement was heard beyond the door, so Loraine rose from the futon and found a robe to wear. She opened the door and peeked outside. Roxanne was moving about quietly in the kitchen. Loraine stepped out of her room and shut the door behind her.

"Hi," Roxanne said. "Did I wake you?"

Loraine shook her head. "I should be up by now, anyway," she said.

"Are you working with Tamara today, too?"

"Yeah."

"She's got you doing some intense work, huh?" Roxanne said. "You've been out all day almost every day."

"Yeah," Loraine said. "But then, you've been gone a lot, too."

"Well, yeah, I've been at Linda's . . . uh, more often. Yeah."

"Were you there last night?"

"Yeah. Why?"

"S'just wondering," Loraine said, rubbing her eyes again. "You didn't get in a fight, did you?"

"No, why?"

"Well, you usually don't come here in the morning when you go overnight with her. That's all," Loraine said, glancing back at her door.

"We didn't get in a fight," Roxanne said. "I left some stuff here that I need this morning. But . . . we're roommates, but we've barely seen each other lately. You know, to talk. I don't even know how your job is working out."

"I like it. Best job I've ever had."

"Yeah, well, I was more concerned about . . . about, you know . . ."

"I know," Loraine said. "I'm a bit . . . 'concerned' myself."

"But how are you—?"

Loraine's bedroom door opened again, and a sleepy Michael emerged. Roxanne appeared less surprised and disappointed than Loraine expected. Michael smiled and waved quickly at Roxanne as he approached.

"Hey, Rox," he murmured.

"Roxanne," she corrected.

"Ah, Roxanne, sorry," he said. He stood behind Loraine and kissed her cheek before rubbing her shoulder. She smiled a guilty smile to Roxanne, who went back to her business in the kitchen.

"I just came back to make breakfast and get my work clothes," Roxanne said. "I won't bug you guys for long."

"Hey, it's your place," Michael said. Roxanne hustled out of the kitchen and into her room.

"She still hates me, I see," Michael whispered.

"Hnh? She never hated you," Loraine whispered. "She doesn't hate anybody."

"Okay, barely tolerates me, then."

"Michael . . ."

He chuckled, then leaned over to kiss her cheek again. She was still tense and took his kiss stiffly. He noticed, but ignored it as he began nuzzling her neck. Loraine would not relax until a few moments later, when she let her head loll to the side. She was just shutting her eyes, when Roxanne emerged from her room again, carrying a small bundle of clothes. Loraine pulled away from Michael. He was mildly frustrated, but said nothing.

"Well, I'll be leaving you now," Roxanne said from the front door. Loraine approached her. "I think I might be home tonight," Roxanne said.

"So, you have a job today?"

"Kind of," Roxanne said. "I'm helping Linda with one of her pieces. I won't get paid, though."

"A volunteer job, huh?" Michael called from the living room. Loraine leaned close to Roxanne.

"I hope we can talk tonight," she whispered as quietly as possible.

"I'll try," Roxanne whispered, then mouthed the words: "Does he know?"

Loraine shook her head. Roxanne seemed to consider this, then said aloud, "See you both later. Bye!"

"Bye."

Loraine went back silently to Michael and let him put his arm around her.

"You sure she doesn't hate me?" he asked.

"She doesn't hate you, Michael. She doesn't hate people. It's just . . . something else that's been going on."

"Oh."

"She actually cares a lot about you," Loraine said. "She cares a lot about everyone. She's just . . . concerned about my happiness," she added, then looked up at him and smiled. This was more than enough to distract him from the somber mood.

Loraine was fifteen minutes late to work that day.

"Michael called," Roxanne announced as her roommate stormed in. "Ah. I could be wrong, but it looks like you had a bad day."

"Fuckin' bitch," Loraine muttered.

"What?"

"Sorry. Not you. I meant Tamara."

"Really?"

"She won't let me have those days off!" Loraine said. "In less than two weeks, the full moon will be here! And she won't let me have those days off!"

"You mean you asked her to give you time off because it's the full moon?"

"Yeah, right," Loraine muttered. "No, I said that it was a family commitment and that I couldn't get out of it."

"What kind of commitment? Like, a wedding or something?"

"No, I was . . . I tried to keep it vague, you know? So she wouldn't try to trick me with weird questions."

"Maybe you should've come up with something more detailed, then," Roxanne suggested.

"I suck at excuses. You know that. I hate lying, too, but I can't tell her the real reason, you know?"

"Well, no. But—what are you going to do then?"

"No matter what she says, I can't be here those nights. I have to . . . maybe go to Griffith Park again or something."

"Or quit."

"I'm not gonna quit. It's a great job, why would I quit?"

"Because . . . you have this problem?"

"But you're the one who dragged me to the audition in the first place," Loraine said. "Now you say I should quit?"

"But you can't just *stay* here, either," Roxanne said. "You could—" she stopped herself and looked away momentarily. Her voice was low when she resumed. "You know what could happen."

"I'll have to drive away as far as I can every night, then come back here to work," Loraine said. Roxanne seemed deep in thought.

"Have you considered talking to somebody who knows about stuff like this?"

"You already asked. You mean a psychic, right?"

"Maybe more like a parapsychologist. You haven't talked to just a regular psychologist, have you?"

"No," Loraine said tiredly. "I'd rather not waste my time with someone who'll try to convince me that it's all just some fantasy, and all I really need to do is remember that I was raped as a kid or some bullshit like that."

"You were raped as a child?"

"Noooo, I'm just telling you what psychologists do," Loraine said in frustration.

"I'm just offering suggestions," Roxanne said. "You don't have to get mad at *me,* too."

Loraine sighed. "I know," she said. "I'm sorry. I just don't know what to do. I've tried to cure myself, to control it . . . I don't know what to do."

Roxanne had a knapsack waiting for her on the table. She picked it up and went to Loraine. Loraine was looking down, but smiled in frustration.

"I'll be at Linda's tonight," Roxanne said.

"Why are you the only one I've been able to tell?" Loraine said, her eyes moistening. "Why can't I tell Michael? Or Tamara? Or anyone else?"

"I don't know," Roxanne said. "You need to try, though." She pulled Loraine toward her into a tight hug.

"You have to get out of here, too," Loraine said. "On

those nights. You and Linda should leave L.A. and . . . go to Vegas or something."

"I'll see what I can do," Roxanne said, parting from her friend. "But I don't want to have to run every month, too, if you know what I mean."

"I'll find a way to get out of this," Loraine said. "And if I don't—"

"Don't talk that way."

"If I don't," Loraine said emphatically, "you're the last one who'll get hurt. I promise."

Tamara was getting used to Loraine's strange mood swings. That is, during rehearsal Loraine inevitably lost herself in the music and became almost the personification of Dance itself. Afterward, she became somber, even melancholy, and sometimes grouchy. Many other artists shared this quirk, even if Tamara didn't. She did notice that Loraine was becoming even more moody, however. So far it was not affecting her performance, but it could, and at the wrong time.

"Look, I don't like pulling a 'boss' thing on people, but sometimes I just have to," Tamara said after rehearsal. "I can't afford to have you go off somewhere right now, especially if you won't give me any details."

"Yeah, I know," Loraine grumbled. "Forget I asked."

"If you want," Tamara said. "But really, I'm sorry. We've all made a commitment to this, and we can't let anything stop us."

"Not even being sick?"

"If it's bad enough, yeah, but even a flu wouldn't keep me off stage. I've done it before."

"You've gone on with a flu?"

"Yeah," Tamara said. "I know I shouldn't have, but as long as I'm not flat on my back, I keep going."

"That's probably not a good idea."

"Everyone tells me that," Tamara said. "I can't help it, though. If I'm sick, it's like I forget that I am when I'm performing, you know what I'm saying?"

"Yeah. I 'know what you're saying.' "

Loraine was ready barely in time for Michael to pick her up for the charity banquet. She had nothing like a ball gown, but it was her prettiest dress, so it would have to do. Michael made no complaints, regardless of whether he had noticed or not. They spoke little on the way. Loraine's mind was racing to try to figure out what to do come the next full moon. She only came back to reality as a flash went off in her face: a photographer's bulb. It had not occurred to her that she was a celebrity's date, and was therefore as vulnerable to the paparazzi as Michael would be. They waded quickly through the barrage of flash bulbs and took their seats inside.

The noise was such that it was difficult to make even idle chitchat. They were seated with two other couples, two of whom seemed familiar to Loraine. They could have been actors or some other sort of performer; she wasn't certain. One of the women tried to speak to her, and Loraine leaned closer to her. The other woman's eyes widened for reasons unknown to Loraine, then she smiled and continued her conversation. Loraine barely remembered the conversation as soon as it was over, but the woman pointed to Loraine's ears.

"That's so weird," she said. "I've never seen anyone do that."

"Do what?"

"With your ears," she said. She cupped her own ears and moved her hands back and forth. "They were moving like this."

Loraine felt her ears quickly. From under her hands she felt them turning to follow sounds throughout the room. They felt human, but they weren't acting human. Loraine's face turned crimson, and she smiled at the woman, more afraid than embarrassed, but the woman could not tell. Loraine quickly moved her hair around to cover her ears as best as possible, and changed the subject.

"Uhhh, were you in a movie?" she asked. "You look familiar."

"Yes, I have been."

"With a French guy? You were married to a French guy? In the movie, I mean."

The woman seemed amused. "Uhhh, yes . . ." she said.

Loraine knew exactly who at least one of her dinner companions was now, but their conversation was interrupted by the evening's first speaker. Loraine had never been to a charity dinner before, and did not even know how much each dinner cost. Each course was served in between speakers and performers, guaranteeing a very long evening. It took her a very long time to relax enough to look around the room and spot other familiar faces. Celebrities were everywhere, but in spite of her love of movies and television, Loraine could never be accused of being starstruck.

She felt her ears pricking up from under her hair.

Loraine had been touching them all night ever since the actress's comment, but now there was a real reason for it. The full moon was a week away, yet she felt them changing shape. It was a small change, in the end; they became just a little more pointed, but it caused her to stand up abruptly and excuse herself. First she went the wrong way to the restroom, then almost knocked over a waiter's tray.

There were other women in the restroom, so Loraine locked herself into a stall and waited. Meanwhile she scrutinized her hands, arms, and face for any signs of extra hair. Seeing and feeling nothing unusual, she returned her attention to the ears and tried to fold them over as if this would cover the point. She heard herself growl quite inhumanly in frustration, then made herself cough to cover it up. Another feeling came over—a familiar one. Her "secret admirer" had returned. She looked up, for that was where the feeling originated, but saw nothing. She listened carefully to the women outside, but heard only gossip and girl-talk. She looked at her watch: 8:43 P.M. Then she—

Loraine rubbed her eyes. She felt as though she had been sleeping. A knock came at the stall door.

"Ma'am? Are you all right in there?" an unfamiliar voice said.

"Hnh? Uh, yeah," Loraine said, standing up and flushing the toilet, even though she had not used it. "Yeah, I'm done here." She looked at her watch again: 8:50 P.M. Didn't I just look at this? she wondered. A confused look was still on her face as she emerged from the stall. A woman appeared to be waiting for her.

"Oh, I didn't mean to bother you," she said. "You sounded sick. Like you were in pain?"

"I did?" Loraine glanced at her watch again. Still 8:50. "Uhh, yeah, I was just, uhhh . . . you know. Couldn't go when I needed to?"

"Oh! I'm sorry," the woman cried, now red-faced. Loraine was not laughing when she left, however. She felt her ears, which were round once more.

A comedian was entertaining the diners when she returned. Michael stood and helped her back into her seat.

"I ordered another white wine for you," he murmured, leaning close. "I hope you don't mind."

"I don't," she said. "Thanks. Uhh, do you think it's too late to get my order changed?"

"You wanted the lobster instead?"

"No, I just wanted to change how my meat is cooked," she said. "That's all."

"Sure, I'll look for our waiter," Michael said. "I don't think they'll mind if you want it cooked longer. Not for two fifty a meal; they *better* not," he added, then laughed.

"Yeah," she said. "I wasn't thinking about cooking it longer, though."

Michael looked at her blankly. If he was puzzled, he was hiding it very well.

Twenty-five

Loraine expected the bizarre dreams to come as the moon grew fuller. Usually they involved running in some unknown forest and hunting. The last one that she had before the first full moon caused her hands to shake even after waking. As usual she had been running through a forest and over hills, when she came to a dead stop in front of another wolf. It stood on two legs and held out its arms as though pleading with her to follow, then smiled and laughed. Loraine awoke just as she leaped at the beast.

Tamara let everyone leave early that night. Loraine was in too much of a hurry to thank her properly. She raced to her car, threw in her duffel bag, and sped away as fast as traffic would allow. Her plan was not to run away this time. She intended to drive as far away from populated areas as possible, but hoped that she would not be alone. Her mistake had been to believe her "secret admirer" to be her own, inner Wolf. But tonight she would find the one truly responsible for this curse.

Her apprehension grew along with her determination. After all, she had already tried to find the other wolf, but only seemed to encounter it in dreams. It had followed her to places that seemed to have no hiding places, and still avoided detection. Yet it was real, and she would spend the next three nights, or the rest of her life, trying to find it.

Traffic allowed her as far as the San Bernadino Mountains. Finding a place devoid of people proved impossible. Loraine was regretting that she had not retired to Griffith Park once again. She pulled into several secluded lanes, all of which led to rows of houses for the rich and snobbish. The sun had set a half an hour before she found a reasonably safe place. She peered over the edge of the steep incline beside which her car was parked. She appeared to be just another sightseer to the motorists who raced by on the curvy roads, ignoring the speed limits.

Sometimes she poked her foot over the incline as if testing the temperature of a pool of water. There was no water in sight, however. To guarantee other people's safety, she would have to climb down the cliff and hide in the woods until dawn. Loraine was no mountain climber, nor even a hiker at that. She could see virtually nothing past her own body; a flashlight provided little other illumination.

Fewer cars zoomed by now. From just behind a distant mountain, the night's sun peeked out. Loraine sat down cross-legged, took several deep breaths, and closed her eyes. Meditation had not worked yet, nor had physical resistance, anger, or even magic. Something was bound to work if she just kept trying, so she meditated. It took some time before passing cars did not startle her.

Loraine concentrated on daytime images. She had not tried this yet; perhaps filling her mind with the sun and daytime scenes would make the wolf forget about the moon. She imagined the warmth of the sun on her face, and the ocean lapping at her feet while she walked along the beach. She passed a happy crowd of volleyball players and frisbee throwers. Some children were working on a sandcastle. Loraine paused to watch them pat it down and reshape it into the snout of a howling wolf. She rejected this image and moved on hurriedly. More frisbees were thrown in her path. One of them was intercepted by a golden retriever, which leapt into the air, only to land on all fours, twice its size and covered in black fur. It looked at her and snarled or laughed—she could not tell.

A police car had pulled up close to Loraine's car. She was parked legally in a "photospot," but Loraine was not visible from the main road. She did not hear the car approach, nor did she hear the door slam as the officer stepped out of his car, flashlight in hand. He approached the front seat cautiously and shined his light back and forth, then heard a groan and a whimper from the other side. Resting his hand on his holster, he crept around the side of the car to see a woman lying on her side, quivering violently. She appeared to be having a seizure.

The officer ran back to his car to pull out a blanket and cushion from the trunk, then raced back to hear and see the woman's clothing ripping apart. He pointed his flashlight at her, then jumped back as the woman revealed a snarling, inhuman face. She stood up quickly, her clothing shredded, and snapped at the bright light that blinded her. The officer called out to her, asking her name, trying to reassure her, until the she-beast howled. Instinctively the officer pulled out his gun but let off a shot into the air. The she-beast jumped back from the noise and missed the ground with one of her hind legs.

She had unwisely chosen a two-legged form and flipped over the safety railing to tumble painfully down a steep hill. The fall was too swift and confusing for her to shift into the more stable four-legged form.

After many painful moments she found herself wedged between a tree and the ground; the terrain was on a slant, but the trees grew almost straight up. She almost broke her back squirming out of this trap, but had soon shifted to four legs, and was ready again to hunt.

Loraine had "dreamt" about bright lights in the sky, hovering and roaring from high above the trees, only to disappear for a long time. She had also been hunting. She vaguely remembered finding something, but it was most likely not her "secret admirer," if it had followed her this time.

Loraine's body was stiff. She awoke in a semi-fetal position, and recognized it as a way that dogs sleep. It had probably been quite comfortable when she had first fallen asleep this way. Now it was a painful effort to stretch out her legs. Her back was pressed against something warm, and a familiar smell filled the air. She sat up and sniffed some more, then turned around. Loraine screamed and leapt to her feet. The back of a slaughtered deer had been supporting her for most of the night. Flies were already making their home in its exposed innards, and Loraine looked down at the dried blood on her hands. She tried to swallow, but tasted something horrible and spit it out first. A chunk of deer flesh flew out of her mouth and disturbed a swarm of flies.

Loraine turned away and started to cover her mouth,

but was reminded of her bloody hands. She felt more ill now than she possibly ever had, and tried to—literally—expunge the horrible mess from her system. Movement came from some bushes nearby, which distracted her momentarily. She looked up to see something pale darting away into the woods. Calling out, Loraine chased after the fleeing figure, but could never manage to see more than glimpses, first of its back, then a leg, and last of all, an arm. A man! Or a woman? Whatever it was, it was too fast and seemed to know the woods as if it lived in them. Loraine fell to her knees in quiet frustration, then saw her hands again, which reminded her of the mutilated animal behind her. She whimpered, then cried, then vomited to start her morning.

Loraine was two hours late to rehearsal that morning. Possibly the only thing preventing Tamara from killing her was that Loraine had phoned earlier to warn her of this. Loraine's excuse was that she had been to the doctor because of a bladder infection. She left out the details involving losing her car in the mountains when it was impounded, and convincing the local police while dressed in rags that she was not crazy and did own the car. Tamara seemed to accept the story about the infection, and continued rehearsal until another early finish. Loraine thanked Tamara for letting everyone leave early again, but did not explain why.

She went to her car and unlocked the front door, when her "secret admirer" made its presence felt again. Loraine froze in place and listened. She heard nothing aside from the usual sounds of the city, so she looked about cautiously. Perhaps she expected to see another pale figure peeking out from behind the bushes. She didn't know what to expect, but knew that, tonight, she would track down this stalker and make him(her?) explain himself.

"Something wrong?" a voice said from behind. Loraine jumped and held her chest. Tamara laughed and walked up from behind her.

"Sorry," she said, giggling. "Didn't mean to do that."

"Yeah," Loraine said, catching her breath. "Yeah, I know. Nothing's wrong. I was just thinking of something."

"Mm," Tamara said, nodding. "Well—hey, you have plans tonight? I postponed a remix session tonight so I could just relax. I haven't been sleeping enough."

"Neither have I."

"Well, if you wanted to rent a movie and hang at the hotel, that's all I was gonna do tonight."

"Um . . . well, actually, I kind of had plans," Loraine said. "Thanks for asking, though. I-I don't know about tomorrow night, either, but after that I bet we could do something."

"Cool," Tamara said, letting her arms swing back and forth aimlessly.

"Oh—uh . . ." Loraine said, "My roommate. She'd really like to meet you in person sometime."

"Well . . ."

"Oh, she wouldn't impose or anything," Loraine said. "Actually, she was at your first tryout, but wasn't picked, but—she wanted to just say hello, and that kind of thing."

"Then kill me for not picking her?"

"Oh, no way, she's a total pacifist," Loraine said. Tamara laughed and slapped her shoulder.

"I'm just kidding," Tamara said. "Sure, she can meet

us for lunch, or after rehearsal. Something. Just let me know."

"Great!" Loraine said. An awkward silence followed. "Uh . . ." Loraine said to break it. "Well, I really gotta go. Uh, see ya tomorrow."

Tamara's eyes glinted in the late afternoon sun.

"Yeah," she said, slapping Loraine's arm. "Break a leg."

The worst part about Loraine's plan was that she had nowhere to begin. No one place had given her a stronger sensation than any other. Her only choice, then, was to leave her car behind . . . and hunt. No matter where she went before, she had been followed, but this time she would find a way to do the following. Even if she had to crawl on all fours, sniffing the ground.

The sky was orange and red by the time Loraine reached the streets of downtown Hollywood. She wore nothing but her clothing this time: no backpacks, no weapons, food, or even extra sets of clothing. She walked slowly, trying to make herself aware of every living thing around her. At first the world seemed no different than before—noisy and crowded—until the noise began separating itself. It became less of a monogamous din and more of individual sounds that Loraine could pick out and listen to. Snatches of conversations became full conversations, staying with her even when they passed out of normal earshot. Then she shut off that sound to zero in on another one. Usually it was passing conversations, and other times it was an entire song on somebody's car radio, or the ticking of somebody's watch.

Loraine heard what may have been a growl, and spun around, startling a passerby. She mumbled an apology while he gave her a wider berth. She felt her ears prick up, and covered them, but sensed something nearby. She made several unsuccessful attempts to pinpoint the "something" before finding a real trail. It led her past several blocks before she realized that her target was moving. It had to be the real thing now—the "secret admirer," her stalker.

Frustration grew as Loraine could never seem to get closer to her prey. She was getting tired and was no closer to catching up than before. Only after she'd stopped at a corner did it occur to her; it knew it was being followed. The wolf had been one step ahead of her from day one, and this hadn't changed even now. Loraine caught her breath and continued the chase, until she reached a particular intersection and ran the opposite way.

For a time she sensed nothing save the cacophony of the crowd. Then, intermittently, there was a tingling at the base of her skull that grew in intensity and frequency. She ran effortlessly through the crowds, bracing herself for the exact moment when she could confront her pursuer once and for all.

The streetlights made Loraine forget that the sky was dark by now. She welcomed the warmth and sweat that pushed her body forward even faster. She never sensed her pursuer's presence to come any closer, just as she could never gain on it before. She finally reached a slightly populated area and ducked into an alley. There were few places to hide, but Loraine was not interested in them. She leaned against a wall and waited. It didn't matter if her pursuer had seen her go this way; they would meet tonight sooner or later.

Loraine pulled at her sweaty shirt and stared at the light from a streetlamp. She had stopped running almost a minute before, but was still breathing hard and heating up. Loraine looked at her hands, which were quivering. She stared at the streetlamp again, then leaned over slightly. The full moon had been shining at her from directly behind it. She cried out and slapped her face.

Shit! she thought. Not now! I lost track of the fucking time! Shit!!

Leaning back until the streetlamp covered the moon did not help. Loraine had planned to be in the city when the transformation began, but not before she confronted her pursuer. She had been doing that already as the wolf. Loraine began to panic. She snuck a peek around the corner, but sensed nothing from any passersby. Her arms were quivering. She slid down the wall and held on tightly to her knees, fighting not to stop the change, but to postpone it. People did walk by, and did notice her, but none stopped to help or even to ask if she needed any. Obviously she was just another homeless junkie going through withdrawal.

Loraine rolled over onto all fours and grunted in pain. She tried to stand back up, but her balance had shifted to one appropriate to four legs, not two. Loraine howled and opened her eyes just in time to see the bare legs of someone just in front of her. Before her consciousness left, the legs covered themselves with fur.

Twenty-six

Loraine heard a faint commotion from a distance. She wanted to open her eyes, but couldn't. The commotion seemed to be the voices of many men, but there was no way to sort out what they were saying. Loraine thought she felt someone or something touching her. Her arms would not move to find out, though. Then something definitely touched her. Something soft and sweet-smelling was put over her mouth. It was apparently not to suffocate her, though, for she found it easier to breathe now.

The commotion became more clear. She understood some words and one of the voices seemed familiar. Was it? Loraine put all of her strength behind opening her eyes. She looked at a white ceiling. It was a rough ceiling, with some cracks, dirt, one long cobweb. . . .

Her apartment! Loraine sat up abruptly, startling the paramedics who had, until then, been trying to revive her. The oxygen mask fell into her lap, as did the blanket that had been covering her. Loraine gasped and pulled the blanket back up as many hands and arms groped and pushed at her, people called out, and one voice called out her name. Loraine ignored everything but her name, which had been spoken by Michael. He had been standing by a uniformed policeman but was now by her side.

"Mikey?" she said weakly. Paramedics continued to try to make her lie down. She ignored them because it made no sense that they were here. She felt fine, after all.

"Hon?" Michael said. "Are you all right?"

"Yeah," she said. "What are you people doing here? What is this?"

"Ma'am, will you *please* lie down?" a paramedic begged. Loraine swatted his hand away.

"No!" she said. "Get your filthy hands off me! Where are my clothes?"

Loraine was nearly overwhelmed by those in the room trying to talk to her: to ask her to lie down, to calm down, to explain what had happened, to ask her name, date of birth, social security number. Loraine screamed and waved her arms around frantically. The only one nearby who managed to escape the onslaught was Michael, who caught her up into his arms and rocked her back and forth until she calmed down. He turned to the swarm of paramedics, police officers, and photographers.

"Uh . . ." he said, "uh, can I talk to her . . . alone?"

The paramedics nodded and left their side, but nobody left the room.

"What the hell is this?" Loraine said. "Mikey, what—"

"Shhhhhhh," he said. "I called them here."

"What? Why the hell would—"

"Just listen a minute," he said. "Please. I came over this morning. Nobody answered when I knocked, so I unlocked the door myself."

"Unlocked it? How?"

"With my key, of course," he said.

"How did you get a key?"

"What do you mean, I've had one forever!" he said.

"Oh, jeez, that's right," she muttered. "I guess I never took it back when we broke up, huh? But where are my clothes?"

"You didn't have any when I found you," he said quietly. "You see, you were—I found you like—and Roxanne was—" he looked away, apparently unable to continue.

"Roxanne?" she said softly, then craned her neck to look past Michael. "Roxanne?" she called. "Where is she?" A policeman stepped forward.

"Uh . . . uh, Ms. Turner . . ." he said, but faster than anyone could react, Loraine was on her feet and racing to what appeared to be a large, plastic sleeping bag. Before anyone could pull her away, she zipped open the bag, then screamed. The inside was solid red from the bloody remains of her roommate—"remains" being the best word to describe what she saw. Strangely enough the face was nearly untouched, but the body was little more than strips of flesh held together only by the bag.

Several men grabbed Loraine by the arms and pulled her away, literally kicking and screaming, from what was left of her roommate. The coroner hastily rezipped the bag as the others struggled, unsuccessfully, to calm down Loraine. Even Michael's efforts failed. In spite of the pandemonium, one officer managed to make himself heard.

"You have the right to remain silent; anything you say can and will be used against you in a court of law . . ."

Loraine neither knew nor cared how fortunate she was to have her own cell. Her mind had all but shut itself off since the moment she'd been thrown into the squad car with barely even a robe to cover her naked, bloody

body. She didn't know it, but blood samples had already
been collected from her body and that of Roxanne
Loraine was the one who had gone to jail, however; Rox
anne had gone to the morgue.

Cell doors creaked open, then clanged shut. Loraine
reacted to neither sound. She let her hand hang out par
tially from between the bars while she stared at the wall
Michael's voice came from her side.

"You okay, hon?" it said. Loraine did not answer
"Loraine?" Michael said. "Come on, everything's
gonna . . . it's gonna be okay."

Michael could act, but not well enough to hide his
doubts and fears this time. Michael's police escort now
turned her attention to Loraine.

"You got one phone call," she said, and unlocked the
cell. Loraine stood up, but shook her head slightly
"Come on, let's go," the cop said.

"Honey, go on, it's your phone call," Michael said. "I
asked John to get bail for both of us, but he can't guar
antee it. You gotta call somebody! Anyone!"

"You want your phone call or not?" the cop asked
impatiently. Loraine looked at nothing and said nothing.

"It doesn't have to be a lawyer, hon," Michael said.
"It can be anyone who can get help! Like Tamara. You
know *her* number, right?"

"Last chance, princess," the cop said. Loraine watched
her glumly, then turned away to sit on her cot. The cop
sighed and locked up the cell again.

"Loraine!" Michael said. "What are you doing?"

"No one to call," she mumbled.

"Why didn't you call your agent?" Michael said.

That's what I did. He could have found a good lawyer for you."

"Don't know her number," Loraine mumbled.

"That's what information's for!" Michael said. "Why didn't you call Tamara?"

"Oh, yeah," Loraine said, then seemed to be awake for the first time. "No!" she said, sitting up. "I can't call her. She can't find out about this!"

"How—is she *not* going to?" Michael said. "Ah, God, how is *any*one not gonna know about this? They arrested us for suspicion of murder! Did you know that? That's why we're here!"

"Yeah," Loraine said.

"What the hell did they arrest *me* for?" he said. *"I'm the one who called them!"*

"Remind me to thank you for that," she muttered.

"Loraine!" he said, grabbing the bars that separated their cells. "Honey . . . I thought you were dead! I came in and . . . and there was blood everywhere and . . . God, what was I supposed to do?"

"Why were you there?"

"What happened, Loraine?" he asked, ignoring her question. "Did you two get into a fight? Were you both attacked by someone? Oh, God," he moaned, sitting down and leaning against the bars. "I was—I was just remembering what she looked like . . . Roxanne . . ."

Loraine curled up into a tight ball on her cot and bit her lip. She still tasted some of the blood there. Back at the apartment her entire body had been covered with the stuff. She vaguely remembered being washed off at the police station, but some of it remained, and had dried or

become sticky. Perhaps her new tears would wash awa
what was left of the blood.

"Roxaaaaaannne . . ." she groaned before the tear
made speech impossible.

The police had looked into and confirmed Michael'
alibi, and released him, by the time Loraine decided t
make her phone call. Michael vowed over and over t
"get her out of this shit" before the police and his agen
finally shuffled him away. Loraine almost called her apart
ment, then remembered, and needed to fight off anothe
fit of tears. She needed to sound calm before calling
Tamara to tell her that she was in bed with the flu.

"What's going on?" Tamara said, both worried and
angry. "You're way late. I cancelled the practice!"

"I'm—"

"What? You're what?"

"I'm in jail." Loraine winced and groaned. What made
her say that?

". . . Did you just say you're in jail?" Tamara asked
and Loraine burst into tears. It took some time for Loraine
to make herself coherent enough to explain her situation
Tamara broke in long enough to promise to get help, and
then a cop cut the call short.

Loraine was returned to her cell. She had answered
only a few questions earlier before requesting a lawyer
so all that was left was to wait.

Loraine had no visitors that day. Michael had promised
to come back later, or pay her bail, or something, but

her memories of most of the day were hazy at best. No lawyer came, and neither did Tamara. Loraine was relieved; she regretted having called Tamara in the first place, but keeping the news from her would have been worse. This was not some minor crime where she could be in and out of jail in one night, then never hear of it again.

She stirred the thick soup that served as her dinner, but ate only a few spoonfuls. She finished the roll and the vegetable mix, then set her plate aside and stared at the wall some more. The food reminded her too much of her hospital stay. She had found it slightly amusing that two cops had brought both of her meals: one to actually hand her the food, and the other to look intimidating. It did make sense, as she was a cold-blooded killer who had torn her roommate to shreds.

Loraine could almost manage as long as she didn't think about Roxanne. As soon as she remembered the bloody remains of what had been her best friend, it was all she could do to quiet her weeping. The lady cop who had, for some reason, taken to calling Loraine "Princess," also seemed to derive some sadistic pleasure in seeing her weep.

"Oh, so this is too much for you, huh?" she had said earlier. "Could've been a lot worse than this, Princess. A *lot* worse. You're lucky you even have a cell to yourself. Enjoy your lunch."

Loraine had said nothing to the cop then, as she had been in no mood to cater to a fool. Later in the day a jailbird a few cells away had tried to get Loraine's attention, but with no success.

Twenty-seven

"Lights out, Princess," Loraine's favorite lady cop said. The inmates actually had no control over the lights. Suddenly the hallway and all the cells in them were dark, and Loraine was left to pull her meager blanket over her.

Her eyes got used to the darkness quickly; she had never closed them. She expected the blanket to be as warm as tissue paper, but ended up dropping it to the floor when it got too warm. Even her flimsy jail clothes were making her sweat. She tugged at the collar a few times and wiped her brow, then shot up into a sitting position. Her breathing was becoming quick and shallow.

Loraine stood up on the cot and pulled herself up to the tiny window to the outside. The sky was lighter than usual, and not just because of the city lights. She craned her neck just enough to see the last round, full moon of that month. Loraine dropped to the floor and rushed to the cell door. She tugged at it, and then hit it, both to no effect. She grabbed the bars again and shook them with all her might; they barely even rattled. In a panic, Loraine rushed back to the cot and tried to pick it up. It was bolted to the floor.

The hairs on her arms and legs stood up now, and sweat flew from her brow with every move she made.

She jumped onto the cot again and tugged at the window's bars. Her nails were long and black by the time she pulled her hands away. Her clothing itched against the long, bristly hairs that sprouted all over her body. Loraine lost her balance and fell onto all fours, which now seemed a more natural position. She cried out in frustration and pain.

"GET ME OUT!!" she shouted. "PLEASE!! GET—ME—OOOOUUUUWOOOOOOOOOO!!"

Almost every night somebody screamed from one of the cells. Usually it was an addict going through withdrawal. Occasionally it was some spoiled kid who had never even seen the inside of a police station before, and was now spending the night on a DUI. Most of the night duty officers had heard every kind of scream, until tonight. Two of them made the first move; the others simply waited for the next step.

They each rested a hand on their guns and brought in flashlights. No one was asleep anymore. Some flinched as the flashlight beams passed over them. Some glared back, but most had the unmistakable look of fear in their eyes. At least one pointed farther down the hall.

"What the fuck is it, man? Shut it up!"

"Yeah, shut it up, man, whatever it is."

"Someone brought their fuckin' dog with 'em."

"All right, quiet, all of you!" one cop said. The hallway vibrated from the nerve-shattering howl that followed. Even the officers needed to cover their ears until it stopped. They moved in quickly and shined the light on a black blur that charged at the cell door. The ground shook from the impact; the bars creaked and groaned, but remained intact. One of the cops dropped his flashlight. He snatched it up as quickly as possible, but not fast enough to avoid the claw that reached out and yanked him into the outside of the cell. His head clanged painfully against the bars, but he was given no time to acknowledge the pain. Before his partner could even draw his gun, his right sleeve had been ripped to shreds, and the arm was about to follow.

A split second of hot breath and nothing more warned the cop before his wrist was bitten nearly in half. A flash of light—from a gun, not the flashlight—ripped through the hallway. Screams came from everywhere—from the wounded cop, frightened prisoners, and the blur that howled in pain. Five more flashes and thunderclaps filled the hallway. The wounded cop and his partner coughed from the smoke. The hall lights clicked back on. Five other cops ran into the room and contributed to the pandemonium that followed. One of them had fired six bullets point-blank into . . . ?

"Jesus Christ, that's one of the K-9's," a sargeant said. "Wait, is it?"

"No, not one of ours," another said.

"I'm not even sure that's a dog."

"What the hell happened here?"

"What is that doing in there? There was a suspect in here, right?"

"There was, but . . ."

"An APB, stat! We have an escaped prisoner!"

"But how? No one's come in or out of here since lights out!"

"Seal the station! Move!"

"It bit me . . . I swear to God, that thing bit me . . ."

"I couldn't help it. . . . I just . . . my gun just kept firing. . . . It looked like it was eating him!"

"Get him to a hospital now!"

"It was so strong . . . like a damned vice . . ."

"Suspect may be armed and dangerous; use extreme caution. . . ."

"Somebody call the animal control!"

The wounded officer was taken to the hospital, the station was sealed, an APB was sent, and the animal control arrived. They came ready with body bags, as there was no doubt that the animal had been shot too many times to survive. When they arrived at the cell, the animal had changed positions. Before, it had been a tangled, bloody mess, but it now lay on its side, breathing shallowly. Patches of blood spotted its fur, but no open wounds were visible. The two animal handlers looked at one another, then set down the body bag.

"Lovely," one said. "You didn't kill it, after all. How many times did you say it was shot?"

"I wasn't here," the cop said, "but we heard Bill empty the gun. Looks like they all entered it."

"Poor thing's probably suffering ten kinds of hell," the handler said.

"Bill's not the kind to panic," the cop said. "If he shot that thing, he had good reason. You should've seen what it did to Devon—to his arm."

"We'll check it for rabies," the handler assured.

"But how could that still be alive?" the cop wondered. "It was dead; it wasn't moving, breathing, nothing! How could something be shot that many times and still be alive?"

"You'd be surprised what condition some animals have been in and still were alive," the other handler said.

"And people," the cop said, unlocking the cell door. He opened the door very slowly, leading the way inside with his hand at his holster. The beast made no moves other than its breathing. The animal handlers had dropped their body bag for holding nets. They crept forward at a snail's pace until the senior handler was close enough to kneel down and touch the beast's side.

A claw barely missed all three of them. The older handler jumped back and stumbled over his partner. The cop whipped out his gun but only aimed it while the handlers scrambled across the floor and out of the cell. The cop backed up slowly, and his eyes went round as the beast rolled onto its feet, then onto two feet. Now it towered over him and took one step forward. Several cops from the end of the hall had already run down, and were urging their comrade to get out. The beast took another step forward as if testing his bravery. Self-preservation won this round; the cop ran out and bolted the cell door behind him as the beast made a strange noise that could have been laughter, but only humans can laugh.

Everyone watched in stunned silence as the beast paced back and forth, throwing a glance at its audience every now and then, then dropped to the floor and finished its pacing on all fours.

"What the hell is that?" the senior animal handler whispered. "What did you guys bring in here? *Why* did you bring it in here?"

"We didn't," the sergeant said. "Brought in a girl on

a homicide, and she switched this . . . thing with herself. We have an APB out now."

"Well, that's nice, but we thought we were taking a dead animal, not a very much alive and angry . . . whatever that is," the senior handler said. "We didn't bring the equipment to—"

The beast's claws darted out between the bars, barely missing the police sargeant. Half a dozen hands reached for their guns, until the sargeant ordered everyone out. The hands and arms of the other prisoners groped at them as they passed, and their pleas for release fell on very deaf ears. All sighed loudly in relief as the door was shut and bolted behind them. None present had any doubts that the cell would be strong enough to hold the beast. Still, no officers bringing in other felons that night went in alone.

"Get up," a gruff voice filtered into Loraine's haze of a sleep. She raised her head up slightly and let her eyes open into a slit.

"Mikey?" she mumbled. Something hard poked at her arm. Loraine yelped angrily and swatted away the pest. A rough hand grabbed her by the arm and yanked her up into a sitting position. She opened sleepy eyes to see two scowling police officers.

"Come on, let's go," the one closest to her said. He resheathed his night stick, which apparently had been the object poking her, and pulled her onto her feet. She protested in vain, then straightened her clothing and avoided their pokes and prods.

"What is this?" she said.

"Lieutenant wants to see you," was the only answer.

They led her down the hallway toward the main door. Most of her fellow "guests" were silent as they passed, but one of them rushed at the bars.

"Get her outta here, man!" he shouted. "She'll eat us alive!" One of the officers hesitated long enough to swat his hands away. "She turned into a fuckin' dog, man! She's a fuckin' dog!"

The lieutenant shut the door behind Loraine as she entered. He positioned himself next to a woman who may also have been a lieutenant, but Loraine knew nothing of police ranks or what signified them.

"Is this one of those times when I'm supposed to have a lawyer?" Loraine asked.

"I doubt it," the lieutenant said. "This has little to do with your charge. And I ask the questions, not you. Clear?"

"I suppose," Loraine mumbled.

"Why don't we 'suppose' this, then?" the lieutenant said, leaning forward. "Why don't we 'suppose' that last night, seven police officers, after viewing your cell, found not you, but some wild animal that attacked and wounded one of those officers. The animal was shot six times, apparently to death, but when the animal control was called, it revived itself and tried to attack them and another officer! And now this morning, we find you back in your cell after an APB was called, yet no one here admits to bringing you back in, and the 'dead' animal is nowhere to be found! Now . . . maybe you can't shed any light on this at all. I think we can all agree that it'd be a lot easier for you if you could."

"Maybe I'm a werewolf, and that 'wild animal' was me," Loraine mumbled.

"Funny kid," the woman said. "We're giving you the opportunity to explain yourself. Don't be stupid."

"I'm being stupid?"

"You can find yourself with a lot more charges than murder from this," the lieutenant said. "Jailbreak, for one thing."

"What jailbreak? I'm still here."

"You *weren't* last night," the woman said.

"Where did you go?" the lieutenant said. "Did you see anyone? Was sticking a rabid animal in your cell just a sick joke to you? One of my men was injured by it!"

"Was he . . . bitten?" Loraine said, now alert.

"All I know was that he's at home now after a night in the hospital, after getting stitches and rabies shots! Now I want to know what the hell you think this is—some kind of—of zoo? You think this is a game? I can push for no bail, you know! You'll be rotting in here until trial, whenever that may be!"

"Rabies shots don't work . . ." Loraine said distantly.

"Have you listened to a damned thing I've said?" the lieutenant bellowed. "Answer the question! Where did you go last night?"

"I want a lawyer."

"You went to a lawyer?"

"I *want* a lawyer," Loraine said. "Here, now, as long as you're just gonna sit there and yell at me!"

"Ohh, I haven't even raised my voice, kid," he said. "This isn't about your charges! This is about your conduct while in custody! You pull any other crap like last night, and you'll be in solitary!"

"I'm already in solitary!" Loraine said. "There's no one else in there but me!"

"You're not in solitary," the lieutenant said, a smile threatening to crack his face. "Believe me, it's not like your cozy little cell."

"I'm taking the fifth," Loraine said. "I told you what happened, and you didn't believe me, so that's your problem."

"That's *your* problem," the woman said. "You could've made things easier for yourself, you know."

"I'm not going to tell you anything else, so you might as well take me back to my 'cozy little cell,' " Loraine said. The two cops scowled to each other, then let out a collective sigh.

The lieutenant apparently made good on his threat; no bail was set for Loraine. Or perhaps it was due to the nature of the crime itself. Loraine neither knew nor cared.

"Visitor, Princess," a familiar voice said. Loraine appeared not to have heard, but eventually she uncurled her legs and stretched before standing up as slowly as possible.

"Come on, move it, let's go," the cop said, banging the bars once with her nightstick. Loraine glared at her as she glided toward the door.

"Enough of that 'Princess' crap," she growled. The cop responded by grabbing her arm.

"Come on," she said.

Loraine kept her gaze at the floor as she was led through

the visitor's area. She passed the backs of several inmates and glimpsed the somber faces of their respective visitors. Loraine's visitor was getting several glances herself from nearly everyone in the room. By contrast Loraine could barely force herself to look Tamara in the eye. They seated themselves at their booths and picked up the intercom phones.

"Hi," Tamara said. Loraine forced a weak smile.

"Hi," she whispered.

"How you been?"

"Uh . . . okay, I guess," Loraine said. Oh, not now. She couldn't think about Roxanne now. So far only a waver in her voice threatened her demeanor.

"Hey, I'm real sorry I couldn't make it 'til today," Tamara said. "You have a lawyer?" Loraine shook her head. "Soon as I heard from you, I called my own lawyer. He can get you somebody good. If you had your own, though, I'd call him off. So, they were gonna assign you one or something?"

"I guess," Loraine said. Tamara had been smiling, then let her face relax.

"You look scared," she said quietly. Loraine bit her lip before looking down and nodding. "Did they tell you what your charge is?"

"Yeah," Loraine said, struggling to keep her voice intact. "Murder. They think I killed—" Her face squeezed into a tight ball of grief and despair. She tried to look away to sob, but gripped her phone even tighter.

"Hey . . . hey, it's okay," Tamara's soothing voice came from the other end. It was almost as if she were starting to sing to Loraine. "You don't have to talk about it if it hurts too much."

"Thanks," Loraine sobbed. "And now I'm—now I'm fired, right?"

"Huh? Look, don't think about that, okay?"

"Well, am I?"

Tamara hesitated for just a moment. "No," she said. "Don't worry about your job. Getting you out of here is the thing to worry about. And since you didn't do it, you shouldn't worry."

Shouldn't worry, Loraine thought. She had never been more worried, and not because she was guilty, but because she couldn't remember if she was guilty or innocent. She had not made much progress in remembering that night's details—neither the results of her "hunt" nor even approaching her apartment, nor anything else after the change. Finally she forced a smile for Tamara. "Thanks," she said. "You're like—you're the best boss, Tamara."

"Our kind needs to stick together," Tamara said cheerfully.

"What kind? Killers?" Loraine said. Tamara looked as though she had been caught at something.

"Uh, no, I meant, you know, us creative folks," she said. "The entertainers. We're famous for not having any loyalty, but I don't believe in that."

"Hmph," Loraine said. They both wanted to say so much more, but their conversation was cut short by Loraine's "favorite" cop.

"Time's up," she said. "Say bye-bye to your friend."

"You'd be out of here by now, but I hear that they didn't set b—" That was all that Loraine heard before the cop snatched the phone from her hands and set it back in its cradle. Tamara hung up her own phone solemnly, then waved to her friend as she was escorted away.

Time slowed to half-speed in Loraine's cell. She thanked God for not sending her any cellmates so far, although the danger to them should have passed by then. Last night WAS the third full moon, wasn't it? Loraine was already losing her concept of time. What Michael was doing, she did not know. He hadn't visited since being released.

"You're real popular today, Princess," her usual escort called out. Loraine had barely the energy to make it to the visitor's area again. She was expecting Michael until she made the final approach to the cubicle.

"Oh, shit," she whispered. For a long time neither she nor Linda reached for their phones. Then Linda let her hand all but crawl to the handset and held it to her ear in silence. Loraine waited a few seconds before following.

"I don't blame you if you hate me," Loraine whispered.

"That depends," Linda said. "Cops have talked to me, you know."

"I didn't know."

"I'm, uh—I doubt if I'm in much shape to talk for very long," Linda said, her voice quivering, "So just let me know if you—if you did it, so I can get out of here."

"I don't—" Loraine said, but her own voice broke. "No," she said. "I didn't. I couldn't have. I loved her. Well, not like you did, but you know what I mean."

"She said you two had—some trouble," Linda said.

"What trouble?"

"You tell me," Linda said. "She just—" She broke down into tears at this point. Loraine had to look away or do the same. It was all either of them could do to keep their composures. Linda was able to continue, but in a very halting voice that was ready to break again at any moment.

"I thought I was okay," she said. "I swear I didn't even cry yesterday. I don't know why, but I didn't."

"Shock?"

"Maybe," she sniffed. "All I know is . . . is she was worried about you, but wouldn't say why. She said you were going through difficult times and—owed her money and—I don't know. She was scared for you."

"Scared?"

"Are you in trouble about something?"

"Yes, I am," Loraine said. "I've been arrested for killing my best friend. I think that's trouble."

"Before that—this," Linda said. "Why was she so worried about you?"

"I'd—been depressed for a long time. That's all."

"Why?"

"I told you I didn't do it," Loraine mumbled, barely able to make eye contact. "I couldn't have."

"You keep saying that," Linda said. "You couldn't have, like you don't believe it yourself. Just tell me yes or no. Please, Loraine."

"No."

"Then you didn't? Or are you just refusing to answer me?"

"You're worse than the fuckin' cops, Linda. What do you want from me?"

"You were there!" Linda said, her eyes filled with tears again. "I just want to know what happened! I just want to know . . . know why *her?* I want to know why she was scared of you!"

"Of me? Did you say she was scared of *me?"*

"I-I meant *for* you," Linda said. "She was worried and scared for you. But you owed her money, didn't you?"

"I didn't owe her any money!" Loraine said. "I found a great job! Why would I kill my best friend? I couldn't have killed her! I—I couldn't have." Now it was Loraine's turn to break down. "I couldn't have," she sobbed. "I couldn't! Couldn't! Couldn't!"

Two officers surrounded her, trying to calm her down and to end the visiting session. Linda pressed the phone even closer to her ear as if to better hear Loraine's cries of anguish as they pulled her away.

"WHY CAN'T I REMEMBERRRR!?!" were the last words Linda could make out before Loraine disappeared around the corner.

Twenty-eight

She ate little of her meal again, then settled down for another uncomfortable night in jail. She had disturbing, violent dreams, but nothing like the kind from the last three nights. No talks with an angry police lieutenant greeted her the next morning. After breakfast, a cop did come to her cell.

"Your lawyer's here," he announced. Loraine considered staying put, then pushed her meal aside and followed him to a private room. Inside was a middle-aged woman in a red power suit and lipstick to match. She smiled and extended her hand until Loraine finally took it in a limp handshake. Behind Loraine her escort shut the door and left them alone.

"Have a seat," the woman said. "I'm Maria Sanchez. Did the police officer tell you that I'm an attorney?"

"Yeah."

"I was recommended to you by Tom O'Malley," she said. "He mentioned that you work for Tamara Taylor, one of his clients?"

"Yeah."

"And what do you do for her?"

"Her choreographer."

"Mmmm, very nice," Maria said, clicking open her

briefcase to pull out a notebook. She shut the briefcase and set it onto the floor.

"You look like you want to get down to business," Maria said, flashing a quick smile. "So we will. Now I've read the police reports. Your name is Loraine, but it was changed recently?"

"From Phyllis," Loraine said. "A real butthole name."

"Really," Maria said, scribbling on her pad. "My daughter's name is Phyllis."

"Well, I didn't like my name."

"Were you made aware of your charges when you were arrested?"

"They think I killed my roommate," Loraine said. "She was my best friend."

"The report didn't say that you did, but I'd like to know from you if you answered any questions related to the charges against you."

"Uh . . . uh, I just, uh . . . my name and age and stuff," she mumbled. "Well, yeah, they *asked* . . . but I didn't say anything. I almost did, though."

"But you didn't?" Maria said. Loraine shook her head. "Good," Maria said.

"How much is this going to cost?"

"Pardon?" Maria said.

"How much do you cost?" Loraine said. "Like, eight hundred an hour or something?"

"Uh . . . uh, no, not that much," Maria said. "My understanding is that you and Ms. Taylor will be splitting the fees?"

"Wha—?"

"I really don't think you need to worry about that right now," Maria said. "I won't charge more than you can afford. And I'm confident that there's a strong chance for acquittal."

"What's that?"

"Acquittal? That you'd be found not guilty."

"Oh, right," Loraine said, and leaned on her arm. Maria patted her hand in an attempt to comfort her.

"The evidence is circumstantial," she said. "You were found at the scene of a murder. That's hardly grounds for conviction."

"What about all the blood?" Loraine said. "They found blood all over me. And her. Roxanne . . ."

"That's why I need to know what happened that night," Maria said. "I'm not the police; you can tell me everything, good or bad. But I need to know every detail. Don't leave anything out."

Loraine mumbled something, then let her head rest on the table.

"What was that? I didn't hear you," Maria said.

"I was naked and had blood on me," Loraine said. "Roxanne was . . . ripped up."

"That was in the morning," Maria said. "That's what the police found. But before that. What happened? What were you and your friend doing that night?"

"I was . . . doing something else then," Loraine muttered. "Or trying to. Don't know what she was doing."

"And what were you doing?"

"I don't know how I got to the apartment," Loraine said. "I wasn't trying to be there."

"What were you doing that night?"

"I was . . . looking for someone. I'm not sure if I found him, though. Or her."

Maria seemed lost in thought a moment. "Were

you . . ." she began, "Were you drinking that night? Or had some other substance?"

"No . . ." Loraine said, covering her face and sighing. When she pulled her hands away, she avoided eye contact. "Nooo, I don't do drugs. Or drink. I don't even like beer or wine. I was just . . . out, okay? I didn't even plan on *being* home that night. Roxanne was my friend. My *best* friend, and everyone thinks I killed her!"

"Did you?"

"What?"

"Did you kill her?" Maria asked. Loraine just stared. "No matter what your answer is, my job is to defend you," Maria said. "But I need to know up front: did you kill Roxanne?"

". . . I don't know," Loraine whispered.

Michael pressed his hand against the bulletproof glass that separated him from Loraine. Loraine did the same, until a passing cop recited the rule about "no fingerprints on the glass."

"Do you have a lawyer yet?" Michael asked into the phone.

"Yeah. We talked a little bit," Loraine said. "Tamara got her for me. I guess she must be pretty good, then."

"At least it's not some court-appointed guy," Michael said. "You have somebody who cares."

"Lawyers is lawyers to me," she said with a sigh. "You know, she says there's some other guy who's going to help me, like a detective. Does that mean I have two lawyers?"

"Uhhh, I don't know," he said. "I've never even played

a lawyer before, let alone know anything about the law. What else did she say? Is she sure that she can clear you? I mean, you didn't do it, so is she sure she can prove it?"

"Uh . . . I don't know, really," she said. "There's . . . you know, all that court shit to go through and . . . investigating and uh . . . isn't this just perfect?"

"What?"

"Nothing," Loraine said, then was quiet a moment. "I guess it's just that some people are picked out to be the toilets of the world. The world shits on them."

"You're not a 'toilet,' honey," Michael said. "I'm not going to lie and say things are great for you, but it's not going to get worse. They'll see that you didn't do it. You're going to get off. You'll be acquitted. I'll be right there when it happens, too."

"Thanks."

"And when you do . . ." Michael began, but his voice faded out.

"What?" Loraine said.

"Oh . . . I was just thinking, you know," he said. "When it's all over, we could . . . live together. When we were apart, I realized how much I missed you. I'm sorry I was so indecisive, but—"

"No."

"What?"

"We can't live together," she said.

"N—No?" he said. "But—that's what you've wanted for a long time. That's why you broke up with me before, because I wasn't sure about it. So why—?"

"It—just wouldn't be a good idea," she said.

"But why?"

"I can't tell you," she said. "I mean—it—I really wish I could, but it would take so long. Please just trust me, Mikey. You'd only get hurt."

"Have you . . . met someone else or something?"

"No . . ." she said. "No, I haven't. This isn't really the best time to talk about it, Mikey."

"Oh . . . yes, I'm sorry . . ."

"That's okay," she said. "I don't blame you for being upset, or confused. I might be able to tell you sometime. Just . . . not now."

Loraine's escort called "Time's up." He hung up her phone before she could say anymore, but she heard a quick rap at the window. Loraine turned toward Michael just long enough to hear him mouth the words "I love you" and to see him blow a kiss. Then she was pulled away to be led back to her cell.

Maria assured her that what followed was not actually the trial, but simply a deposition, or the presentation of evidence. They had a long way to go before the main event. She also assured Loraine that it was to their great advantage that no eyewitnesses could be found. Loraine was disturbed that any witnesses had been found at all, even if they had only heard things.

She had lived in her apartment complex for several years, but recognized no one. Nevertheless, the prosecution produced various tenants who were awakened or startled or annoyed or whatever by a loud commotion of thumping, banging, yelling, screaming, and everything else from Loraine's apartment. Not surprisingly, the only person who finally called the police was Michael, long after the commotion had stopped. He was also called to the witness stand to present his testimony.

Loraine sat as if in a trance and barely listened to any of it. It was the only way she could cope with being forced to relive her friend's death over and over again. The coroner's presentation was perhaps most devastating of all. The wounds that Loraine had were superficial at best, and most of the blood covering her had been Roxanne's. She remembered when they forced her to sit still while cleaning out her fingernails; some of Roxanne's skin and hair had been found, the coroner announced impassionately. Loraine was silent all the while, but wanted to ask out loud if they also found part of Roxanne in her stomach. Maria could say whatever she pleased, but Loraine *felt* "guilty." She considered saying why and let Maria try to get her off on an insanity plea. Anyone who would think that she was a werewolf had to be crazy.

The judge decided that there was enough evidence to proceed with an arraignment, which was scheduled for later.

Loraine had already met her "detective," or investigator. His job, she learned, was to accompany the police on their investigations and find evidence in her defense. He also worked without the police and worked with, but not for, Maria. It made Loraine feel a little better, but not much. Like Maria, he was also middle-aged and married, but seemed more detached from the case. However, he and the police were puzzled by the many deep scratch marks and rips in the floor and other objects around Loraine's apartment. Also, very heavy objects such as the couch had been pushed far from their usual spots. Loraine's memory of that night had not changed, however. She remembered much violence, but in murky detail at best. He and Maria were on their own.

Loraine finally obtained two temporary cellmates: two female gang members who were suspects in a drive-by shooting. They yelled at and taunted the two cops who brought them in, until the cops disappeared behind "The Big Door." Then, unsatisfied, they turned their attentions to Loraine, who ignored their cutting remarks about her "cutie-pie" looks. Then, one of them finally asked about her crime, and only then did Loraine look into her eyes and very calmly announce, "I ripped my roommate to pieces, then ate the pieces."

The two girls stared at her a moment, then huddled together quietly from then on. Loraine returned to her solitude. The crazy prisoner in the adjacent cell started talking to himself again. He tried to mutter, but she could always hear him arguing with himself, if his name was "Al," that is.

One visitor she did not miss was the "secret admirer" that had almost driven her mad. It had decided not to follow her to jail, apparently. It was not a stupid admirer, then. She did have other visits from Tamara, Michael, Maria, and the investigator, whose name she could never remember.

Three weeks after her arrest, Loraine stood beside Maria while the judge asked for their plea. "Not guilty," Maria said. Loraine would have just shrugged.

"I have to get out of jail," Loraine said during their meeting afterward.

"You will," Maria said. "I'm confident that there'll be an acquittal."

"I don't mean that," Loraine said. "I mean that I can't stay in jail any longer."

"I know how difficult it is to be in jail, but—"

"You're not listening to me," Loraine said. "I'm not talking about the final verdict; I need to get out of jail, period. Now!"

"No bail was set," Maria said. "It's more difficult than—"

"Then get a bail set, and pay it!"

"Now *you* have to listen to *me*," Maria said sternly. "I do intend to get you out on probation, but it's not going to happen in the next hour, you know. Not even the next few days. And even then your movements will be *very* limited. This is a murder charge. I can't even guarantee that I *can* get you out."

"You have no idea how important it is that I do get out, and soon."

"Well . . ." Maria said, and was lost in thought a moment. "Look, if it's some sort of unfinished business you have, give me the details and I'll see to it that it's done."

"It's not like that."

"What is it, then? Why do you have to get out *now?*"

"I guess all I could say is that it'll be that time of the month again."

"Look, this isn't the time for PMS jokes," Maria said. "If that's what you mean. I can't help you if you don't give me more information. And I don't mean to be harsh, but you haven't been terribly cooperative about this whole trial. You do understand what could happen if there's a conviction, don't you?"

"I thought you said I'd be acquitted."

"I still believe that there will be, but let's face it: it'll be in spite of your uncooperation. You haven't even given me a satisfactory answer to the only question that's at stake here: did you kill your roommate?"

"And I probably never will be able to," Loraine muttered.

"And why not? Will my defense be based on an insanity plea? That you did do it, but aren't responsible because you don't even remember it?"

"Is that my fault that I don't? Maybe I was hit on the head."

"The doctor who examined you made no mention of that."

"Well, why does he think I was unconscious?"

"I'd . . . have to reread his report," Maria said. "As I recall, he was unclear on that, too. But you know what?" she added, leaning back and folding her arms. She had an odd smile.

"What?"

"I don't entirely believe you," Maria said. "That's part of why I decided that you didn't do it. I don't believe that you remember nothing."

"Oh, really? And how did you come to this conclusion?"

"Unfortunately, that's all it is right now," Maria said, going back to a more relaxed position. "A belief. A woman's intuition, if you want to go that far. It's almost as if you don't remember every detail, but remember enough to be . . . protecting someone, maybe?"

"Like who? Roxanne? She ripped herself up and I want to take the blame? Maybe I'm protecting myself."

"Look, I'm not the enemy—"

"I know you're not," Loraine said. "You're trying to

defend me, and to help me. And I appreciate that. But if you can't help me the way I really need it right now, and that's to get me out on bail, or parole, or whatever the hell it is, by the next full moon, then I won't be responsible for what happens to whoever's near me. Just . . . trust me. Okay?"

"Did you say the next full moon?"

"Just trust me."

Twenty-nine

Her trial had been set for six months from then, barring any extensions from Maria. It could have been six years from then; all that mattered was that Loraine was still in her cell a week after the arraignment. Her two cellmates had been removed and replaced with someone else: another gang member who had supposedly shot her boyfriend for "dissing" her, whatever that meant. Loraine didn't care to ask for any details. The girl probably wouldn't survive the night, anyway. Loraine had begged the cops not to give her any cellmates, especially not this night. Her answer had been a stern warning against causing more trouble.

Loraine twisted her hands back and forth on the bars of the cell door. Wanda, her cellmate, was bundled up at the opposite corner. Their half-eaten meals lay side by side on the ground. The crazy prisoner in the next cell had begun yet another monologue. At least he wasn't arguing this time. Loraine took great pains never to make eye contact with him, of course. Her favorite cop came by eventually.

"Beddy-bye, Princess," she said. Loraine gripped the bars even tighter.

"You have to let me out of here," she said quietly.

"Oh, do I?" the cop said.

"Or move her to another cell," Loraine said. "Please. You can hate me all you want, but for the love of God, don't leave anyone in here with me. Please."

For once the lady cop's eyes seemed to soften. Only a little bit, but perhaps it was enough. She spread out her arms.

"We wish everyone could have their own cell," she said. "I'm sorry, but there's nowhere else to put you."

"There has to be," Loraine said, her voice rising. "You don't understand; it can't be tonight, or the next few nights, either. No one else can be in here!"

"No one else can be in there, either!" the cop said, pointing to another cell. "Or there! Or there! You're lucky you only have one other person as it is! Lights out!"

"I have to be alone! Put me in solitary if you have to, but—!"

"Hey, shut the fuck up!" another prisoner called out.

"This isn't a joke!" Loraine called out as the lights were shut off. "Hey! Please listen to me! Get back here, you . . . bitch!"

"Shut up!" came a chorus of angry voices. Loraine squeezed and tugged at the bars with all her might, which was not enough to move them even the slightest. Eventually she gave up and raced back to the barred window.

"Sorry if I *smell* too much for you," came Wanda's muffled voice. "Maybe I don't want anyone with me, either."

"You don't smell," Loraine whispered, irritated. She climbed up onto the bench and peered outside. A perfectly round moon lit up her face. She yelped and jumped toward the bars, then resumed her futile twisting and tugging.

"Will you fuckin' chill and go to sleep?" Wanda growled. Loraine turned around, slowly panicking.

"Cover yourself," she said.

"Huh?"

"Go completely under the covers," she said. "Um . . . hide under the cot, go into the corner, do something! Damn, there *isn't* a safe place here!"

"Shut! Up!" Wanda said. Loraine raced to her side, her chest already warming. The heat always started there, and then spread.

"You don't understand," Loraine whispered. "I tried to get you out for your own safety."

"Get your hands off me! Quit touchin' me, bitch!"

"If you don't keep as much out of sight as you can, you might not make it!"

"Guard!" Wanda said, throwing aside her blanket and stomping to the door. "Guard, get me away from this lesbo!"

The big door flew open, the lights came back on, and several angry cops stormed down the hall to the loud protests of would-be sleepers.

" 'Lights out' means lights out, people!" one of them said. "We don't want to hear another word out of here!"

"Hey, it's those two bitches that way," an inmate grumbled.

"This lesbo was all over me!" Wanda said. "Put me with the whores, I don't care! Just get her away from me!"

"Yeah!" Loraine said, running up to the door. "I want her. I want her bad, and I swear I might rape her if you don't take her away!"

"You hear that??" Wanda said. "Get her away from me!"

"That's enough!" another cop bellowed. "There better not be another word from any of you tonight or else! Now you keep your hands off each other, is that clear?"

"Hey, I'm not going near the bitch!" Wanda said.

"But I don't think I could—!" Loraine began, then winced and doubled over to groan.

"Oh, *now* what?" Wanda said, throwing up her arms. Loraine groaned and grunted some more, then forced herself to stand up straight.

"What's wrong?" the cops asked.

Loraine's eyes were shut tight, but she managed to grunt out a response. "I—" she said, "Just—far from me—keep away . . ."

Wanda backed away slowly. The cops asked again what was wrong, when Loraine suddenly stopped grimacing and grunting. She stood up even straighter and forced a smile.

"I'm fine," she said, wiping away a puddle of sweat from her brow. "I'm just—upset by everything. Being in jail and all that. I guess I went—crazy. A little."

"A fuckin' *lot* crazy," Wanda grumbled. A cop pointed to them with his nightstick.

"Both of you get to sleep, right now," he said. "No more disturbances. If you really are all right now—"

"I am," Loraine said quickly. "Everything's . . . just great."

The cops paused another moment before nodding to each other and heading back down the hall. In another moment the hall was dark again, save for the light of the full moon that shone into every cell.

Loraine held onto the bars with all her might, hoping that the wolf would be unable to let go. Her hands began to shake again. Sweat from her brow streamed down her face. Every smell, every sound began to get stronger or louder or sharper. High-pitched sounds seemed even higher, and sharp odors sharper. She heard something new now. Perhaps it was just a chorus of car horns, or very distant sirens.

"Do you hear that?" she whispered.

"Oh, God, shut up," Wanda's angry, but quiet, voice sounded from the darkness. Loraine's clothes were already soaked and sticking to her body. It itched from the fur that tried to push its way between the skin and false skin. Loraine did not move from her spot, not even to scratch. The "chorus" sounded again, and louder this time. Closer. How could anyone else *not* hear it?

She was unaware of her surroundings only a few seconds later. Even the mouth-watering smells that surrounded her no longer affected her. The sound was closer. *They* were closer. They were coming. That was all that mattered. She no longer felt her paws locked around the hard metal things, even though they had not moved from that position. She even remained in the two-legged form that she had woken up to. They were coming.

Crashes and booms nearby rocked the concrete and metal cages. Grumbles and cries of fear and pain echoed from near and behind the big door. There were bangs, crashes, screams, booms, and tremors assaulting the senses of every living thing there, yet only one knew no fear at that moment.

She felt something warm touch her limb, then pull away quickly. A quiet gasp blended in with the increasingly loud chaos from within and without the hallway. A living thing—potential food—made the sound, but she ignored it. They were here.

The big door slammed into the wall and made the ground shake. A blur of dark shapes poured into the hallway and whipped past the terrified prisoners, only one of whom managed to scream. Those who could see past the door spotted glimpses of chaos in the police station: cries of pain, residual gunfire, smoke, debris, bodies, and blood. Even the big door was smeared.

Her thoughts were filled of theirs. Until then she had been resisting their summons, but now welcomed it. A score of claws wrapped themselves around the bars and pulled while she pushed. In barely an instant the concrete and steel crumbled and bent, and the entire cell wall was yanked free. She fell onto all fours, as did they, and the entire pack raced back down the hallway. A mob of blue two-leggers blocked their way out. Deafening bangs and flashes of light came from them. All in the pack felt a stinging in their sides and fronts, but smashed right on through, sending the two-leggers across the bright room.

More of them met the pack in the bright room. Blood and pain were everywhere, but the two-leggers were tenacious. They formed a wall around the pack and pointed at them with their loud toys. The pack stopped only long enough to snarl before sending the beasts running for cover. In the distance they heard more banging and smelled the smoke, but the pack was long gone before anything could pursue.

* * *

Once again she thrilled to the pleasures of the earth

under her feet and the wind in her face. Until now she had always enjoyed it alone. Now a dozen of her kind surrounded her, guiding her toward a new home, perhaps. For an hour they raced through back streets and hills, seeking the parts least infested by the two-leggers. For an hour she ran happily with her new family. Then, little by little, murky memories filtered past their hold on her thoughts. She remembered much anger and violence. Blood, not from prey, but from herself or the other that had followed her everywhere. She remembered the last great confrontation, when she had howled in anguish over the death of a two-legger. It had not been like the others; this one had been special somehow . . . "protected." She would never have hunted this one, yet one of the pack had killed it.

She slowed her pace and began to fall behind the others. Eventually the pack slowed down to bring her back to the middle, but she slowed to a trot now. A quick bark from the alpha caused two of them to run directly behind her and nudge her forward repeatedly. She snarled at each poke, until finally she dodged to the side and fell over another, causing a chain reaction of stumbles and falls amongst half of the pack. She was the first to roll back onto her feet and plant her legs firmly to the ground. She flattened her ears and pulled back her lips so far that every wickedly sharp fang in her mouth flashed at them.

At first, there was puzzlement. The pack looked at her blankly, then one another, until the alpha wolf stepped forward. She snarled even louder and snapped once. The alpha stopped, surprised, then gave a silent signal for the pack to step forward. She was immediately surrounded, but the alpha remained closer than the others. She flashed a mental challenge at the alpha, who finally gripped the earth and flattened its own ears. Then she witnessed a remarkable thing: the alpha's body began to shift and change. Its hind legs grew longer and thicker, losing their fur, as its front legs and torso also lost theirs. The alpha pushed on its front legs until it was standing erect. A few seconds later a slender, naked woman stood before her. She blinked and looked around, and saw the rest of them in their own two-legged forms. She looked up and saw the moon shining in all its glory, and was puzzled.

A strange feeling came over her. Her own body was changing. She followed the others into their standing position, and was soon just as naked as they. She did not notice this yet. There were eight males and four females, including the alpha. A female alpha? This puzzled her. There was also something strange about her . . . about her body.

"Why are you doing this?" the alpha said.

"What?" she said.

"Why do you challenge me? Challenge the pack?"

"I'm . . ." she said, looking at her hands. "I'm . . . how can this be? The moon is out. I should be running and hunting."

"And so we would have, had you not challenged us," the alpha said. "We freed you from their prison; we offer you a new home, a new family. You understood this; we could sense it. Why turn on us now?"

"There was a reason I was in there," she said, turning away. "I was . . . there was a girl who died. A girl that I would never hunt . . . She died, but not by my hand. I was in the cage for that."

"We know she did not die by your hand," the alpha

said. "And only now do you remember it yourself. That is why—"

"One of you did it!" she said, now whirling to face the alpha. "One of you attacked me, and killed the girl instead!"

"You attacked him; it was not the other way around," the alpha said.

"You've been stalking me," she said, stepping forward, "Hounding me. Attacking me!"

"We've been calling you!"

"Who's the one who killed her?" she demanded, storming past the pack in a circle. "Eh? Who made me go to that cage instead?"

"He is not here."

"What?" she snapped, stepping to within inches of the alpha. "What do you mean, 'not here'? You will not deny me my vengeance!"

"We do not kill our own kind," the alpha said calmly. "We are not like the other creatures who infest this earth, who kill each other for the pettiest of reasons. No, our greatest punishment is to banish."

"Banish??" she said. "Exile him from the pack? That's the worst you do to anyone?"

"When you have run with us longer, you will understand how devastating that would be."

"And what if I don't want to run with you?" she asked. "You have denied me satisfaction! I want his fate to match the female's!"

"You want to fight him to the death, then," the alpha sighed. "That is not our way; you must understand that. He was banished from the pack for cowardice. He was sent to bring you to us, but killed your friend and took pains to make you appear to be the guilty one. Your anguish must have been unbearable."

"Until now I believed that I *had* done it," she said. "And now you deny me my justice."

"We were appalled by his actions!" the alpha said. "He did not deny them, so his punishment was quick. We do not bear such cowardice from our kind."

"Where is he now?"

"We do not know," the alpha said. "When exile is done, we also sever our thoughts with them. He is no longer part of the pack in any way, physically or mentally."

"Loraine," a male voice called from the side. She turned toward him, puzzled.

"You called me . . . Loraine?" she said. The male stepped forward.

"You're in her form now," he said. "But not in mind. You don't remember me, do you?"

She looked at him, shaking her head. He stepped even closer and brought his arm up to her face. She tried to jump back, but he held her close and covered her mouth, forcing her to breathe through her nose. Now she could smell the arm. His scent . . . it was familiar.

"You," she said. "I've tasted you. Not long ago."

"I was a policeman in that 'cage,'" he said. "My partner shot you after you'd bitten me. I went to the hospital, then went home that night."

"I bit you," she whispered. "I've . . . brought you over. I'm sorry . . ."

"They found me only two weeks later," he said, indicating the others. "Before I'd even changed. I felt their call but didn't resist as you did. I . . . suppose they've given me the family that I'd never had. I was even married and have cubs—uhh, I mean children—but—it's just something you must experience to understand. The pack *is* the ultimate family."

"So you left your wife and children and run with the pack now," she said.

"Open your mind and heart," another female said. "Only that way will you understand us, and accept us."

"Your life before us," the alpha said. "Was it pleasant? Were you fulfilled and happy?"

"I was . . . struggling," she said. "I was not happy. And no, I have no family."

"You do now," the alpha said. "Run with us, cub. Join us."

"Yes, join us," the former policeman said.

"What's back there for you?"

"Unfulfilled . . ."

"No family . . ."

"Imprisoned unjustly . . ."

"Wait!!" she said, throwing up her arms. "My life is no better because of you, either! That's why I challenged you. Would you follow *me* and testify on my behalf? Would you confirm my innocence?"

"We do not go to their cities unless we must," the alpha said. "Like tonight. The cities . . . are offensive to us."

"I get no pleasure from being a fugitive," she said. "I truly *will* have to 'run' with you always. I'll be *on* the run. That, too, is cowardice."

"What would you have us say? That we are a pack of werewolves, and one of us killed your friend while battling with you?"

"Yes!"

"What purpose would that serve?" the alpha said. "We will not reveal ourselves to mankind!"

"Then make up a story!" she said. "Tell them that . . ." she added, and then her voice died. The others looked at each other while she stared at the alpha. The alpha stared back.

"Tell them what?" the alpha said.

"Your body . . ." she said whispered, slowly lifting her hand to point. "What happened to you?"

"What?" the alpha said, looking down and shaking her head. "Nothing 'happened' to it."

"You have no breasts . . ." she continued. "You have. . . . Oh, my God. Is this what happens to you?"

Understanding now, the alpha ran her hands slowly along her torso, feeling each of its six nipples as they passed. It was true that the alpha had no breasts, not anymore.

She looked at each of the other females in the pack. None but the alpha had six nipples, but she could see the others in various stages of change. One had four, and two red spots. The others still had breasts, but very small ones and red spots marking where the others would soon grow. She felt her own body, which showed nothing unusual—so far.

"Eventually, wearing a bikini would be out of the question," the alpha said, a sly smile on her face. "This will happen to you in time."

"But I'm a dancer," she said. "I . . . can't be deformed like that."

"Deformed? You will understand how beautiful it truly is, in time," the alpha said. "Perhaps it will take more time for you. You are a dancer? This will be the ultimate dance for you."

"Having six nipples?"

"Dancing with us," the alpha said. "Running with us. Hunting. When your feet strike the earth when chasing your prey, does it not feel like a dance? Does the sand whipping up into the air as the moon sings to you not seem like a ballet? I was a poet almost a hundred years ago, and still am. Our world is a living poem. To you, it would be a living dance. To him, who was a sailor, it is an ocean of wonder. To her, who was a songstress, it is a song beyond compare."

"I . . . I have a life with . . . with them," she said.

"The humans?"

"I-I was human before," she said. "All of you were— um, are. We *are* still human."

"We are both and neither human and wolf. We have our own ways, our own laws. Our own world. The bond of the pack is stronger than even the bond between mother and child. No other family, human or animal, can compare. That is why banishment is worse than death to us. Even our thoughts are one, yet we have our own, as well. Open your heart, cub. You did see this. You felt it, even if only briefly. Can you truly say that you don't welcome it? Welcome us. Join us."

"But I'd be . . . It'd be like . . . I don't know," she said, shutting her eyes. "I had a new job . . . I was dancing again. Really dancing, and then . . . this . . ."

"You can dance forever now," a female said. "You will always be young, and strong."

"A cure . . ." she said, opening her eyes. "I was . . .

looking for a cure. How do I go back? Nothing I read or saw could help me. Tell me how to be human again!"

"You don't wish that," the alpha said. "That would be your death."

"No, there has to be a way besides that!" she said. "A silver bullet can't be the only way!"

"I didn't mean your death that way," the alpha said. "I meant you—" she pointed at her, "—would die. Could you kill half of yourself?"

"I don't . . . want to die," she said. "I can't live like this! Always in fear! Afraid to talk to anyone! Please! Don't let her kill me!"

"You are in such conflict with yourself," the alpha said. "We have never sought a 'cure' because we never believed it to be a disease. We have accepted both sides. We welcome the wolf. You fight against it, though it is a part of you now. You would no longer be complete without it. The harder you fight it, the harder it fights back. The moon is no longer our enemy. It makes us change, but we welcome it, and can control it if we must. Even now it is difficult to maintain your form because you fight against it."

"Then you're the reason I stand erect now," she said.

"Yes. And if you leave, you will return to your true form for the night. As we will, also, but because we wish to. There is still the hunt tonight. Come with us. Hunt. Your old life need never haunt you again. You will never know what true and total freedom is until you join us."

The pack sent up a chant of "Join us" as they moved closer to her, now surrounding her in a tight circle. Many hands reached out and caressed her as they circled around, still chanting. "Join us, join us, join us."

Soothing smells and touches soon brought her into a trance. She closed her eyes and breathed in the pleasant aromas slowly, then sighed. Warm hands and arms caressed and massaged her as they passed all over her body. She reached out blindly, and a hand took hers and patted it gently. It was warmer than usual. It was covered with fur.

She opened her eyes and gasped. The pale, naked bodies were now covered in brown, red, black, or gray fur. A score of green, brown, and red eyes peered at her from fanged, black-lipped, furry faces. She pulled her hand away and began to back up. She bumped into somebody's furry chest, then panicked and broke away from the circle. Her thoughts were bombarded with feelings of great puzzlement and concern. The alpha wolf stepped away from the circle, but Loraine/wolf held up a hand. It, too, was covered in fur, and her body was following quickly. Her voice was guttural now.

"Can't," she grunted. "I—can't!" An instant later she was racing away from the pack and toward the hills. Her heart pounded to keep time with the pounding of her feet. She had been ready to welcome them, and was suddenly filled with great terror. It was perhaps her only chance to escape them now, if they did not decide to track her down and keep her prisoner. She felt their call in her mind—it was as strong as always—but this time it only spurred her flight.

The rest of the pack had rushed forward in that instant that she had bolted, but the alpha held out her arms. She shook her head as the others stepped back.

"But she—" one protested.

"We will always welcome her," the alpha said. "She

can run, but cannot run from the call. Someday she will answer it."

Silence followed while their changes were completed. The pack was in their full four-legged form now. They were still in their circle when they all sat and howled for their prodigal sister.

She stopped her mad flight and pricked her ears to listen. There it was. She had never heard it before, but knew what the howl was for. Her eyes teared, but she shook away the tears and continued the run.

Thirty

She felt their presence at all times, but not as a calling. It was simply a "presence" that could be heeded or ignored, if she wished. She did wish to ignore it, and hunted alone as she always had. Strangely, her appetite was small that night. One small animal satisfied her, and then she spent the rest of the night exploring and basking in the moonlight. The memories of that horrible cage were fading quickly; she was free, thanks to the pack, but she needed to be free of them, as well.

The moon was low in the sky now. She would be forced to sleep again once the sun came. She remembered being in that pale, naked, two-legged form, and shivered at the thought of it. She was bound to be chilled to the bone . . . unless she found the colorful skin that all two-leggers wore. With a grunt she leaped into a run toward the city lights.

She sensed some two-leggers, but far away. They slept during the night; she remembered that. It was such a shame to waste the moon like that. She found a part of the city where one could see right inside the caves. She passed by many of them, until one displayed its colorful skins within. She pushed at the door, which resisted. Shifting into an erect form, she grabbed hold of the handle and pushed harder. It resisted, and then snapped open, sending her rolling across the floor. She ignored the chain lock and deadbolt that had snapped in two from her strength. To her, the door had just seemed to be sticking.

She kept low and sniffed at the ground. The floor reeked of past scents, but nothing was recent. So many skins . . . what would keep her warm? She was growing frustrated, but snatched two skins and raced from the building. She bounded across the street and between some buildings, unaware of the two-leggers who arrived moments later in response to a silent summons.

Bushes, and then some woods provided splendid cover for her. The moon was nearly gone now, and the sun was peeking in between the trees. It was no longer comfortable for her to be on all fours. She shifted to two legs and rubbed her cold, furless arms. She shivered from the chill of the morning air, then bent over and rubbed her body as her beautiful fur disappeared once again. A soft, sad moan escaped her pale lips.

Loraine stayed crouched a few moments longer, wondering why she needed to fight off tears. She was not surprised to find herself naked, but was surprised to find clothing beside her. She picked them up, price tags and all, and smiled.

"It worked," she whispered.

The too-small shirt was tucked into her too-large pants. There was no belt to hold them up, and the shirt left little room to breathe. They were much better than the alternative. Her plan was to find the cheapest motel she could find before working her way out of Los Angeles. She ducked into the shadows or around corners anytime a police car drove by, which was seldom, fortunately.

The city was slowly waking up. Loraine took care to use sidestreets and alleys while seeking some means of finding money, or shoes, whichever came first. The thought of a cardboard sign crossed her mind; it made her laugh in frustration. She had no watch, so she had to use clocks in stores and at car dealerships to tell time. Finally she spied possible salvation: a branch of her bank. Going inside of any public place was probably a terrible idea, but she had no choice. She pulled up her pants and held on while going inside. She was the only customer. None of the employees seemed to notice her bare feet yet. She raced up to a teller.

"Listen," she said, "um . . . my wallet was stolen. This is my bank, and I need money, but . . . well, you know, everything was in the wallet. Could I just give you my name, and I think I even remember my account number. Can I make a withdrawal, please?"

The teller was new, and called over her supervisor, who began preparations for replacing Loraine's ATM card. For verification she was forced to remember her account and social security numbers, not to mention her mother's maiden name. Only after the supervisor brought out Loraine's new card did she notice the bare feet.

"Uh . . . ma'am, you really shouldn't be in here without shoes," she said.

"I know, I'll be buying those, too," Loraine said. "Everything was stolen."

"Oh, dear, do you mean you were robbed?" the supervisor said, running the new card through the verification machine.

"Yeah," Loraine said. She drummed her fingers impatiently while the verifier dialed in to the mainframe. Finally the proper numbers appeared, and the supervisor handed her the card.

"Thanks," Loraine said, and started to leave.

"Oh, wait, ma'am!" the woman called out. "It won't work until you enter your personal code!"

"Oh, shit, that's right," Loraine grumbled. Her mind went blank then. What did they used to be? She couldn't remember. Then the perfect code came to her: 9653. "WOLF." She punched them as quickly as possible, and was out the door as soon as the woman announced her card to be active.

Loraine scanned the streets immediately after leaving. No cops. She raced to the side of the building, jammed the card in, and requested the maximum of three hundred dollars. Her pants almost fell as she stuffed the bills into her pockets. She rushed into the first clothing store she could find and threw down the cash for sandals and a belt. She was only slightly more presentable now. Next stop would be the bus station. Or . . . the cops would be looking at places like that, wouldn't they? There had to be a dragnet going on for her. She was a fugitive from justice, after all.

The original plan to find a cheap motel was put into action. Of course, cheaper meant more dangerous in Los Angeles, if that's where she still was. This was not a familiar city, at least. Perhaps she was somewhere in the next county. That would be to her advantage.

She found a run-down place that "asked no questions."

There was little about her to question, anyway. Her pants were baggier than a trash bag, but stayed up thanks to her new belt. She grabbed the key and took the stairway instead of the elevator. No sense being trapped in a box if she needed a quick getaway. The room was at a middle floor. Closer to the ground was preferable, but she couldn't be choosy. Loraine looked both ways down the hallway, and unlocked the door.

Inside was a tiny bed, tinier bathroom with a dirty sink, a dresser, a twelve-inch television, and somebody on a chair, reading a newspaper. Loraine gasped and stepped back from the threshold.

"Oh!" she said. "I'm sorry! That guy screwed up and gave me your room! I'll just—" The stranger lowered his newspaper. *Her* newspaper. Loraine's jaw dropped and eyes bugged out. After a long silence she forced her mouth and tongue to move again.

"Tamara?" she said. Tamara folded up the newspaper neatly, then tossed it onto the bed. She gestured toward the bed.

"It's your room," she said. "Don't you want to come inside?"

"My—my room?" Loraine said. "You mean—you're not staying here?"

Tamara smiled. "Well, you know, I can see how anyone would kill to stay in a place like this, but . . . I don't know, I usually settle for Marriotts and Hyatts."

"Wha—? Oh! Uh, yeah, of course you'd—Jeez, I better get in." Loraine stepped inside and shut and locked the door behind her. "Wait a minute," she said, wagging her finger at Tamara. "How did—? I mean, you—Shit, you know what I mean, don't you?"

"Yeah, I know what you mean," Tamara said. "Sit. On the bed, or did you want the chair?"

"Maybe I'll just stand. Wait, you know where I am. Does that mean the cops . . . ?"

"I don't think that anyone else on earth knows I'm here but you," Tamara said. "Not even the manager knows."

"You snuck inside? Why?"

"Oh, I don't know. For fun, I suppose. You don't want to sit?"

"How did you know what room I was in?" Loraine asked. "What hotel? Where I was . . . *at all?* What's going on?"

"I followed my nose," Tamara said, tapping it and smiling. She pulled out a file and went to work on her nails. "Guess things got pretty hairy for you last night, huh? I heard about the jail. I think some cops were killed. Were they?"

"I . . . I have no idea," Loraine said.

"Yes, you do," Tamara said, leaning forward. "You could remember everything, if you'd just stop fighting it all the time. You only end up hurting yourself more."

"Wait a minute, you're starting to sound like . . . like . . . I don't remember what like!"

"Like the pack?" Tamara offered.

"The pack . . ." Loraine whispered. "My God . . . Uh—I'll sit down." She fell onto the edge of the bed. After a pause Tamara got up and sat down beside her.

"Yeah, I'm sure they thought they were doing you a big favor, busting you out like that," Tamara said. "But they've just screwed you even more, huh?"

Loraine seemed to have been ignoring her, but then shot up from the bed and backed away slowly.

"You were . . . you were with the pack?" she said. "You followed me because you're with them and—Jesus Christ, you're a *werewolf*? You??"

"Shhhh, it's okay, hon," Tamara said, rising and holding out her hands. "I wasn't with them last night. I'm on my own. I've been on my own for years now. I'm not gonna hurt you."

"But you're a werewolf!"

"Well, so are *you,* dear," Tamara said. "I knew it from the first. The pack knows you're here just as much as I do. They might even know that I'm here, too. They won't come after us, though. Trust me."

"How could—*you* be a werewolf?" Loraine stammered. Her face was flush, and her hands quivered. Tamara took small, slow steps toward her, but Loraine backed away each time. Soon there was no more space to back into.

"Same as you, I suppose," Tamara said, shrugging. "I was bitten while on a camping trip, *long* ago. You know, it's funny, but did you know that being bitten is really the least common way to be brought over?"

"Uh . . . yeah, I, uh . . . read about that," Loraine said.

"While trying to find a cure, you mean," Tamara said. Loraine nodded. "You know, I didn't do that at first. You see, I was brought into a pack almost right away. Not your pack, or not the ones who wanted you. Another one."

"How many packs are there? Are werewolves all over the place something?"

"Nahh, I doubt it," Tamara said, going back to her

chair. "I really don't know, to be honest. Packs do a good job of keeping out of sight, away from people, which isn't very easy these days, you know."

"I can imagine."

"Yeah, well, I wasn't very happy with my life at the time, so I welcomed them," Tamara said. "And you know, it may have just been the time that I was happiest. Running free, living off the land, being with a family. A pack really does have a . . . like a stronger bond than a 'real' family, but in a different way. A pack is so close that it's like a group mind. Does that make sense?"

"I remember . . . talking to someone who said almost exactly what you said," Loraine said distantly.

"The wolf can never be fully suppressed when the moon is out," Tamara said. "You can keep your human form, in time, but the wolf will do all the talking. And you can talk to it, you know. It can talk to you, too."

"So werewolves are all basically schizophrenics?"

"Uh, well, I wouldn't put it that way exactly, but there's a dual personality there," Tamara said, nodding. A silence followed. She stared at Loraine, who seemed baffled. Then Tamara stood up abruptly.

"Don't you get it?" she said. "Do you think I hired you because you're a werewolf like me? No! I hired you because you're a great dancer! You'd tapped into that part of you that made you push yourself to the end, that made you the dancer you are now, and still could be! You found the wolf!"

"But I know that!"

"No, you don't know that," Tamara grumbled.

"What?"

"You're just like how I was!" Tamara said. "I figured

it all out, too. When I tapped into it, I could sing. I could
finally sing! I'd always wanted to, but nothing worked.
Singing lessons, choirs, all that shit. I still sounded like
a cat in a waffle iron. Then I was brought over, and—and
I found the wolf. *Finally* I found that part of me that
could make me sing! But even then I tried to reject it. I
knew why I could sing, but I was convinced that it could
still be just me doing it, without the wolf. But it doesn't
work that way."

"So you're saying that I sucked until I turned into a
werewolf? That's bullshit!"

"You know that's not what I'm saying," Tamara said.
"Maybe it'd help if you thought of it as . . . oh, a focus
for what was there already. You've always had the drive
and the urge, just like I did, but no focus. If the wolf is
what finally did it for you, then embrace it! And as long
as you believe that you don't need that focus, you'll never
be the best," Tamara said. "If you figured out that the
wolf made you the dancer you are, then why are you still
dissing it?"

"Huh?"

"Why are you still trying to smash it down and do it
on your own? To shove it into a corner? To kill it?"

"I don't wanna go out killing people every goddamned
full moon!"

"Have you killed anyone?"

"How the hell should I know, I can't remember anything in the morning! I may have killed my best friend!
Do you think I haven't *tried* to remember what happened?"

"Why don't you ask it what happened, then?"

"Ask it? What are you talking about?"

Tamara sighed. "Guess we've got a long way to go."

"I guess *so,*" Loraine said. "Look, I appreciate what you're trying to do, but it's not worth it to get messed up in this. First I was wanted for murder, and now the next thing I know I'm a fugitive because some mangy hounds busted me out! I'm only here for today, and then I'm getting out of town fast."

"So you're choosing to stay a fugitive?"

"Who's choosing, I don't have a choice!"

"How about staying here and proving your innocence?"

"Yeah, right," Loraine said. "Maybe that'd work in a movie."

"Hmmmm," Tamara said, and was lost in thought a moment. "Do you wanna know why I left the pack?"

"I guess so. I mean, yes, why? You said you were really happy."

"I was," Tamara said. "Like I said, I didn't really feel . . . connected to anyone. My family was never really that close. My parents probably had plenty of love for us, but didn't know how to show it. So . . . when I was first brought over, naturally I was scared shitless. The pack showed me that it didn't have to be a total nightmare every month. It could be a good thing. The wolf doesn't have to kill and destroy; it can create, too."

"Like your singing, you mean."

"And your dancing," Tamara added. "Anyway, to push a cliche, the pack became my family, and it was a real close one. Almost unbreakable bonds."

"And . . . ?"

"I guess it just came down to that I've always liked people," Tamara said. "I've always been pretty gregarious, even if I didn't really know how to get close to people, with family or to have really close friends. Know what I mean?"

"Yeah."

"Sure, I learned how to really, really open up and . . . well, bond, I guess, with the pack, but they really had a bad attitude about people. Like humanity should be blown to little bits so the werewolves can run and hunt all they want. And we all started human. I guess I just never forgot it. I also did miss my real family, in time."

"So you went back to them?" Loraine asked. "You didn't tell them, did you?"

"I did," Tamara said. "Can't say much for their reaction. To this day I don't think they believe me, even though it's obvious that I haven't exactly been aging along with them."

"Not aging?" Loraine said. "You mean that werewolves don't get older?"

"Not to my knowledge. It could be that we age so slowly that it takes centuries for us to get one gray hair. Unless you're already a gray wolf," she added with a smile.

"I have . . . I think I have brown fur," Loraine said. "It's always so hard to—I can't believe I'm talking about this! I'm wanted for murder and a jailbreak! You expect me to stay here and work on my dancing because some dog inside of me wants me to? I gotta get outta here!"

"Then you might as well go back to the pack, because it's safer to run in a group than alone," Tamara said. "And if you're threatened, they'll protect you to the end."

"I don't want to run," Loraine said quietly. "I want to . . . I just what all of this to end. Couldn't I just wake up, and find myself back before I even went to Wisconsin?"

"And then what would you do?"

"Live a normal life, for one thing."

"A 'normal' life," Tamara said wistfully. "I wanted one, too. Kind of boring, though. I don't think that creative people *can* live 'normal' lives, though. It goes against the whole definition of creative, doesn't it?"

"Boring is better than this."

"Is it? Please understand that I'm not belittling the life you had before," Tamara said. "Roxanne's death *was* senseless. It was a cowardly act committed by a coward."

"Gee, thanks."

"You didn't do it, hon," Tamara said, holding her by the shoulders firmly. "I don't know who did, but it was *not* you. The wolf knows your friends and loved ones; it won't hunt them. I know this from experience."

"So do I," Loraine said distantly. "I'm not sure how I know, but I didn't do it."

"It's talking to you," Tamara said. "Don't fight it. Or I should say, don't fight *her*. The wolf is always the same sex as you. Someday you might find out her name."

"They have *names?*"

"And why wouldn't they?" Tamara said with a smile. "Look, I can't lie to you. I really don't know if there's a cure. At this point I wouldn't want to look for one. Accepting Song has been the best thing for me right now.

" 'Song?' "

"That's my wolf's name."

"Makes sense, I guess," Loraine muttered.

"Running away from all this would make Roxanne's death meaningless," Tamara said. "That is, right now it *is* meaningless. Staying here to prove what really happened would *give* it meaning. It would . . . avenge her."

"Find the wolf that actually did it, you mean?"

"Yes, unless you want to join the pack."

"I don't think I'd like that right now."

"Someday you might, but for now . . ."

"What do you mean by that?" Loraine asked.

"I mean that, while they may not be seeking you out anymore, they'll always be waiting for you," Tamara said. "You left on your own; they didn't exile you. You'd always be welcome to join them, if you wanted."

"Is that . . . the same deal you got?" Loraine asked warily.

"I left on my own, so yes, I did get the 'same deal,' " Tamara said. "You can feel it now, can't you? That feeling here?" she added, pointing to her head, "And here?" to her chest. "I've been away for almost ten years, but I can still feel it. The bond with the pack. I'm not ready to go back, either. I may never be. You may never be. But isn't it a wonderful feeling, knowing that you always could?"

"Yeah . . ." Loraine said, feeling her chest. "Yeah, it is." Her head shot up. "They exiled Roxanne's killer. They said he was a coward. I remember that. They cut him off completely, then, didn't they?"

"Let's just say he doesn't have that 'welcome' feeling that we do," Tamara said.

"We can't find him that way, then, can we? Or me, I mean," Loraine said. "I can't get you messed up in this. You're a celebrity, for Godssake. The press would eat you alive!"

"If I don't eat them first," Tamara said, licking her

lips. She slapped Loraine's arm playfully. "Chill out, girl, I'm joking!"

"Oh, thank God."

"Seriously, don't worry about me. I'll find ways to help," Tamara said. "If you've made your decision, that is."

"I'm scared," Loraine said. "I'm scared shitless!"

Tamara held out her hand, which Loraine took. They both were motionless for a moment, until Tamara pulled her into a long, tight embrace. Eventually she rocked Loraine back and forth slightly as she hummed Loraine's favorite ballad. Loraine's fear melted away; she had never felt safer, but the feeling was doomed to end. Why waste the moment, then? She held on as if it would mean her death to let go.

Tamara had to all but pry Loraine's arms from her before they could part. She pushed away some straggling hairs from Loraine's face.

"Ready for a hunt?" she asked.

Loraine looked down briefly, then closed her eyes and nodded.

"When I'm done with the guy that did this," she said, "he'll be sipping his doggie biscuits through a straw."

Tamara smiled.